The Samurai's Inro

P. J. MacLayne

The Samurai's Inro
Copyright © 2020
by P.J. MacLayne

The Samurai's Inro is a work of fiction. All names, characters, events and places found in this book are either from the author's imagination or used fictitiously. Any similarity to persons live or dead, actual events, locations, or organizations is entirely coincidental and not intended by the author.

ISBN-13: 978-1-7349587-0-6

Published in the United States of America.

Acknowledgments

Many thanks go to K.M Guth for her invaluable work on the book cover and other graphics assistance. I'd be lost without her

To Deb Staab, for taking the time to edit this book, despite other commitments. Her keen eye caught many things I'd missed.

Image credit for the inro used on the cover goes to The Walters Art Museum under the Creative Commons License.

Chapter 1

The red Mustang parked behind my Jaguar, Dolores, was the first bad sign. The scowling man propped against the driver's side door, the second. Detective Thomason would have searched me out in the library for a friendly chat. This scenario screamed official police business. At least he wasn't there to arrest me; he would have brought a squad car instead of his personal vehicle for that.

After a long day of squinting at charts in business magazines, I had a headache and no patience to deal with an angry cop, no matter how good-looking. I pushed my glasses higher up on my nose and plastered a smile on my mouth as I closed the distance between us. "Hey, Freddie," I called, my voice light, testing the waters.

He waited until a green motorcycle rumbled by and we were face to face to respond. His scowl never wavered. "Harmony. Where's Hennessey?"

Which Hennessey? Jake, the reformed felon or Eli, the owner of his own company? I feared I knew the answer, but annoyed by his attitude, played innocent. This wasn't a game, but I'd make my own rules.

"Eli has meetings in DC all week." That's as much as I knew. As my boss, he hadn't told me what the meetings were about, and I hadn't asked. As my lover, he'd told me not to expect any calls from him. He still kept secrets, despite our complicated relationship.

The lines around Freddie's mouth deepened and he ran a hand across his short, brown hair. "This is serious, Harmony. I'm not talking about Eli. Where's Jake? His landlord said he moved out and didn't leave a forwarding address, and he's not at Eli's place. Or yours. Where is he?"

I didn't want to push too hard. Freddie and I were friends. Most of the time.

"He's in Cleveland. Working. Not that it's the police department's business. He's not required to report his location to anyone." He'd served his time in prison and wasn't on parole.

"When did he leave?"

I counted backward. "Eight days ago. Two days after he got the job offer." He'd jumped on it, not wanting the opportunity to vanish after waiting for the opening for several months. Although he'd start out as a bouncer and bartender, the bar's owner promised him there'd be a chance for him to move into management. It saddened me to remember how little he had to his name when he packed.

Freddie's shoulders relaxed. He uncrossed his arms, sticking his hands into his pants pockets. "Can you verify that information? I don't want to jump to conclusions, but I can't overlook any possible suspects, either."

The faint scent of spring flowers blooming in the distance wafted our direction. I took a deep sniff while I formulated my answer. "Are you asking if I've gone to Cleveland to meet his boss and check out his new digs? Of course not. I'm not his mother. Do I believe he's telling me the truth? Yes. The big question is why? Why do you care?"

"Do you know who the Cookes are?"

"The sweet old couple who dabbles in buying and selling antiques?" Occasionally, I'd see them in the library, researching their latest find. My headache reached massive proportions in a heartbeat. "I've met them."

"They were out of town for a few days at a collectibles show. When they got back, they found their house had been broken into."

"And you immediately thought of Jake, who has been a model citizen and helped law enforcement several times in the past few years. And was never proven to have anything to do with the jewelry thefts the FBI accused him of, and without a shred of evidence to implicate him." Okay, calling him a model citizen stretched the truth, but he hadn't been involved in anything illegal. At least, not lately. Not that I could prove.

Freddie stared at his shoes. "I'm just doing my job. Has Jake been back to see you?"

I shook my head, letting a tendril of hair escape from my bun. If I wanted to prove Jake innocent,

I needed Freddie on my side. "No. I expect it will take him some time to get settled. Why? What was stolen?"

"The only items the Cookes identified as missing were a Japanese inro and the ice cream cones in the freezer. The culprit trashed the house, so they are still trying to get things cleaned up and figure out what else is gone."

I tilted my head. "A bunch of kids broke into the house to throw a party and ate the ice cream. The what did you call it—inro?—is somewhere in the mess. And you want to blame Jake?"

"Not according to the neighbors. They claim they didn't see anything out of the ordinary."

"Someone wanted to make it look like a random robbery but knew exactly what they wanted?"

He nodded. "That's as good of a theory as any and the one I'm going with until I collect more evidence. We're checking for fingerprints but are coming up empty."

Not Jake's MO at all, if the stories the FBI told held any truth. "What's an inro, anyway?"

"A fancy carved storage box. Japanese. They had it hanging on the wall in their bedroom. It's worth several thousand dollars." He ran his fingers across his short brown hair. "Mr. Cooke promised he'd find a picture. They keep a digital inventory for insurance but were too shaken up to access it when I talked to them."

My fingers itched for a computer keyboard and I debated sprinting back inside the library to start my research. But it was Monday, and I didn't want to skip my weekly self-defense class. My gut told me life was about to get interesting and I needed to be ready for whatever came my way.

My throat hurt from yelling. That had been part of the lesson, screaming as loudly as possible to attract attention. It was a good thing that no stores in the neighborhood where the self-defense class was held stayed open this late. I foresaw a hot cup of tea in my future, along with a long session with my laptop.

Three of us walked to the parking lot together, chatting about the plans for the high school graduation. Thalia and Joan both had kids in the senior class and were on the committee to plan the awards dinner. That made me odd woman out.

Thalia stopped and grabbed my arm, almost knocking me off my feet. "Where's my car? I parked there," she said, pointing with her other hand to the space beside Dolores.

"Are you sure you didn't park somewhere different tonight?" Joan asked.

"I always park next to Harmony's car. That way I protect it from getting scratched."

The warm glow from knowing that people cared about me enough to care about my car warred with worry. Why would someone take Thalia's 1980s rusty old sedan and leave my car untouched?

"Any chance your husband swung by and took it?" I asked.

"He wouldn't do that without calling me." She pulled out her phone. "No missed calls, no texts, no nothing."

"Call him," Joan urged. "Make sure he doesn't have it before we call the cops. We don't want to waste their time."

Most of Oak Grove's force would love the break in their normal routine, but I didn't say that out loud, not wanting to give anyone the wrong idea. Instead, I took the time while Thalia made her call to walk around Dolores, checking for any sign of tampering. She looked fine, but I'd check again tomorrow in the daylight.

"An officer will be here soon." Thalia sniffled, clinging to her phone. "I don't understand. Why steal my car?"

"Teenagers, taking it for a joyride?" Joan looked at me, her eyes begging for my support.

I hated myself, knowing I was going to lie to my friends. "Probably. When it runs out of gas, they'll ditch it. It'll be found in a day or two." More likely, it would end up crashed into a tree and be a total loss.

Thalia sniffed again. "At least it was almost empty. I planned to fill the tank before I came to class but got out of the house late and came right here."

The police sirens I'd been tracking drew closer. I wondered which officer was on duty. There were only a few I didn't get along with, but Sergeant Kinchloe, one of the most experienced officers, came as a surprise. His seniority meant he normally worked days, but his calm presence was reassuring.

He adjusted his duty belt. I wondered if he'd

shrunk an inch since the last time I spoke to him. His age showed and it was past time for him to retire, but he refused, saying he had nothing better to do. At least, that was the story the Oak Grove rumor mill passed around. Most of the time, he worked desk duty and his age didn't matter.

With a nod in my direction, he glanced at Dolores and then introduced himself to Thalia and Joan. He pulled out his notebook and coaxed the needed information out of Thalia without making her upset—make, model, year, color, identifying decals—I would have never thought of that one. Thalia's husband pulled in during the questioning, and there wasn't anything else for me to do. But I couldn't leave, not with everyone standing around Dolores, although they all took care to not lean against her.

I sat on the curb and waited for the excitement to die down. A second police cruiser pulled in and parked behind Dolores. Yep, I'd nailed it. Another slow night in the sleepy little metropolis of Oak Grove. The light wasn't good enough to read the paperback stuffed in my purse, so I just sat back and observed the action. What there was of it.

Kinchloe dismissed the new arrival with a wave, not needing assistance. Joan left next, then Thalia and her husband. I stood, stretched, and headed to Dolores, ready to go home, but Kinchloe had other plans.

"Do you have a moment, Miss Duprie?" he asked as I reached for the door handle.

"What can I do for you, Sergeant?"

"I have a few questions about the stolen vehicle."

He didn't think I had anything to do with it, did he?

"Not that you were involved," he added hastily. "But I'd like to get your perspective."

"You've got more experience than me."

One side of his mouth rose. "No argument there. And you have more experience than the rookies I'm saddled with tonight, even if it's unofficial. Please?"

❊ ❊ ❊

The situation called for coffee and the sludge they made at the police station wouldn't cut it. I made my grand entrance carrying a box of coffee and a bag of condiments. Better than the traditional gift of donuts this late at night.

Once we'd filled our cups, Kinchloe and I settled in one of the unoccupied offices. He gave me the more comfortable office chair and took the old wooden one himself. It felt weird, sitting behind the working side of the desk. I was used to being on the other side.

"What's going on?" I asked after blowing across my coffee and taking a sip. The warmth slid down my throat and eased the soreness.

"What's your take on tonight's incident?"

That was a leading question, and I didn't fall for it. "What do you want to know? I can't tell you anything more than Thalia did."

"Why do you think her car was stolen and not yours?"

Yeah, that had been bugging me, too.

"Two theories. First, whoever did this was an amateur and couldn't get past Dolores' security features." I took another sip of coffee. "But I didn't see any marks on her so, if they tried, they didn't try too hard."

Kinchloe nodded. "And number two?"

"They were local and knew the car and my connection to the police. They also were aware anyone besides me seen driving her would be a big fat target for you guys and weren't willing to take the risk."

"Which ties into another possibility. Whoever stole Mrs. Anagnos' car needed to be anonymous. No one looks twice at an old gray sedan. Your car attracts too much attention."

I mulled over his suggestion. "Someone who wanted to leave town unnoticed?"

"It's not like you can hop on a bus."

He was showing his age. No one rode cross-country buses anymore. It had been at least five years since the Oak Grove depot closed.

"A kid running away from home or someone leaving an abusive relationship?" I rotated the coffee cup in my hands, deep in thought.

"Or making a getaway from the scene of a crime." Kinchloe leaned forward. "Like the thief that burglarized the Cookes' home."

Chapter 2

I set my coffee cup on the old wooden desk, crossed my arms and stared at the cracked ceiling tile, collecting my thoughts. "You're suggesting someone local committed the theft and after a day or two left town? Why?"

Kinchloe shrugged. "Because they couldn't sell the box locally and needed to get rid of it? But there's a flaw in my theory."

At least one. I kept my mouth shut because I wanted to hear his before I told him mine.

"The Cookes' have a sophisticated alarm system. I'm not aware of anyone around here with the knowledge to bypass it." He covered his mouth and coughed. "Except your friend Hennessey, if the rumors are true. And Detective Thomason spread the word that he isn't in town anymore. So how did the culprit get to Oak Grove and not have a way to leave?"

Good question. But why hadn't Freddie told me about the alarm? "You realize you've disqualified the idea that whoever stole Thalia's car is a local? It sounds easy on the surface, but without evidence, we can't tie the two crimes together. Someone able to bypass a good home security system might get around Dolores' security, too."

As good as Jake was with cars, he'd never mentioned being able to hotwire one or bypass their anti-theft devices. Was I jumping to conclusions?

"You're right." Kinchloe blew out a deep breath. "That's why I wanted to talk to you before I called Thomason. Plus, I hate the idea of one of the town's teenagers stealing the car."

"Didn't you ever get in trouble as a kid?"

"I never broke the law—at least, I never got caught." A smile lit his face, and he winked at me.

Thankfully, I'd never been caught either. Not even the time I broke into the high school to finish an assignment. With help. From one of the senior boys. Stan. "Were you the kid who stole candy from the corner store?"

He shook his head. "Nope, not my style. I was a prankster. Graffiti on the water tower, that sort of thing. Back then, punishment would have been a weekend picking up trash. Now, kids go in front of a judge and end up with a record for that kind of trick. Not sure I like the new laws."

I'd read some of those records for Chief Sorenson's monthly report to the City Council. Luckily, the juvenile judge in Oak Grove was more lenient on youthful offenders than judges in other parts of the state. The cleanliness of our city parks was a tribute to his style.

"Where does that leave us?" I asked, getting back to business. I wouldn't have any official involvement. Still, I had the feeling I hadn't heard the end of it.

"Back at the beginning." Kinchloe shrugged. "We'll keep an eye out for the car for a few days, but there's a good chance it'll be dumped out of town somewhere. One of the county deputies will stumble across it while investigating a different incident. As for the burglary, that's up to Thomason."

❊ ❊ ❊

Around noon, I closed the lid of the laptop and prayed Eli would forgive me. It was supposed to be a quick five minutes' worth of research, enough to satisfy my curiosity about the missing inro. It turned into a morning-long dive into the culture of the samurai. I hadn't touched any of the research I owed Eli. And it felt good.

At least I understood the stolen item. In the back of my brain, I pictured inros as early man-purses with a twist, because they were skinny mini-boxes, held together with a cord or a carved outer holder. I'd never say that out loud for fear of offending someone. They held small objects like seals or medicines and sweets.

The ornament used to hold everything together, the only part of the whole contraption I imagined Jake having an interest in, made them intriguing. Called netsuke, they reminded me of fancy big buttons. The expensive ones were made from ivory and other pricey materials. I wanted to see one in person instead of looking at pictures.

My mind wandered. What would Eli look like in traditional garb, the hitatare? He fit both the warrior and the scholar profiles. I'd greet him in my kimono when he returned from his mission. We'd have fun removing each layer with the inro being the first thing to go. I'd find an 'interesting' use for the belt that came with the kimono.

A patron's chair squealed as she pushed it back to stand, and I returned to the present. I justified my research as a way to help Freddie. That's what I'd tell anyone who asked. It had nothing to do with the niggle of worry of Jake returning to old habits. Cleveland was only a couple of hours away by car.

Janine, the town's chief librarian and my friend, slipped into the chair across from me. "You still on for lunch?"

An occasional lunch together had replaced our traditional Girls' Night Out. With Merrilee in Pittsburgh, Night's Out weren't any fun. The last time we tried, Janine was still in mourning for her mother and nothing brought her out of her somber mood. Now, several months later, lunches were pleasant and less stressful. We didn't have to fight off the occasional over-enthusiastic man who figured women out drinking were easy pickings.

"Is Sarah going to make it?" I asked. Last week, she'd been busy with a client, showing houses. The week before, she'd been having one of her social anxiety attacks and we'd bought sandwiches and gone to her house.

We both reached for our phones. Janine was faster.

"She hasn't canceled," she said.

I didn't have any new messages either. "Hopefully, she's waiting for us. Can I stick my laptop in your office?"

"Sure. What are you working on today?" She grinned. "Or is it a business secret?"

I leaned forward and, in a whisper, asked "Promise not to tell?"

Janine tilted one ear closer. "I promise. What is it?"

"I played hooky this morning. Researched feudal Japan to satisfy my curiosity. The boss is out of reach all week, so he'll never know."

"When you talk to him next, tell him those business magazines he donated to the library have been a big hit. College kids love to reference them for their reports."

I'd talked Eli into buying subscriptions to several lesser-known publications the library didn't already have. First bonus was he got to take the cost as a tax deduction. Second bonus was I got the electronic versions for free and I didn't have to wait for the paper copies to come in and compete for them.

"That makes sense. They focus on small businesses rather than the industry giants. Gives the kids information to help them stand out and not look like a clone."

"Or being accused of plagiarism." Janine stood. "Drop your stuff in my office and let's go before someone finds an emergency for me to handle. You're driving, right?"

Janine loved riding in Dolores, so I took the long way to the Dairy Barn. Sarah's car occupied a space in the parking lot and I snagged the empty spot beside her. We laughingly referred to the old GM as her blue bus because the sedan was big enough to hold a small family. And many times it did, when she showed houses to prospective clients.

We placed our orders and got our drinks before joining Sarah at the table she'd saved. In the noisy restaurant, it was hard to hold a conversation, but being together was the important part.

"Only three?" I pushed the remnants of my turkey sandwich around my plate. The constant niggle at the back of my neck had destroyed my appetite. "Only three kids applied for next year? That's terrible!"

"It almost makes me want to give up on the program," Janine admitted. "It doesn't seem worth the expense of maintaining the high school volunteers if no one wants to do it anymore."

"But the library has used senior volunteers since forever," Sarah objected. "Didn't both of you get your start as volunteers?"

"Sure. But it isn't cool anymore." Janine shrugged. "Now the kids want to save the world. The principal says the majority signed up for environmental projects or political groups."

I rubbed the back of my neck. Something beyond Janine's issue bothered me, but I couldn't figure it out. I'd checked several times and didn't spot anyone spying on us. "Can you get an adult volunteer to run the teen program?"

"It's an idea." Janine grinned. "Are you offering, Harmony?"

"You've been trying to rope me into a position for weeks. When are you going to give up?"

Sarah grinned. "You're in for it now. You might as well say yes."

I didn't say yes. But Sarah still had the grin on her face when we walked outside after lunch. She stuck around to keep me company while Janine stopped to chat with Mrs. Mondrick, one of the library's biggest donors. But her smirk wasn't responsible for the itch at the base of my neck. I looked around, trying to identify someone who didn't belong, then glanced at cars in the parking lot. Dolores was right where I left her, and the spaces on either side of her were empty.

Sarah hadn't left the table during lunch.

"Does anyone else have a copy of your car keys?" I asked, hiding the fear crawling up my spine.

"Freddie does, in case I lock the keys in the car." She'd done that several times, to the best of my memory. "Why?"

I raised a hand and pointed. "I parked Dolores beside your car when we got here."

Freddie pulled in, siren screaming and lights flashing, before I even hung up from the 911 call. His hurry wasn't for me, but for Sarah. They practically lived together. He'd asked, but Sarah wasn't ready to say yes yet. On the live together part. As far as I knew, marriage hadn't been discussed.

What followed was the most unprofessional professional questioning I'd ever seen. With his arms wrapped around her, Freddie asked her all the needed questions, wiping away her tears as they talked. He knew most of the answers—make, model, year, even the plate.

Janine called a taxi to get back to the library because I wanted to stay to provide moral support. Mostly I sat on one of the outdoor benches and reviewed crime statistics in my head while watching the police do their job. I couldn't come up with any time in the past few years when autos got stolen two days in a row. Except for that one time when the Hager twins 'borrowed' their divorced parents' cars in a scheme to get them back together. It hadn't worked.

Freddie guided a still-sobbing Sarah to his vehicle and fastened her in. He held a quick conference with the officers assigned to the case, then walked towards me. I stood and brushed imaginary dust off my pants.

"Is there anything I can do to help?" I asked.

He shook his head. "No, I'll take her home, get her meds into her. The Chief cleared me to take off the rest of the afternoon. Ortez will cover the senior field trip for kids thinking about getting into law enforcement." He paused. "You didn't see anything out of the ordinary, did you?"

Freddie loved and hated those field trips. Hated because it was a pain to clean the station and put paperwork where prying eyes couldn't see it. Loved because he could share his passion for police work. "Not a thing. No shady characters hanging around the parking lot, no weird vehicles, just a normal day."

"Sarah said she wasn't able to see the parking lot from the table."

"No. the half-wall in the middle of the restaurant blocked our view."

He grimaced. "That's what she said."

"This wasn't a teenager out for a joyride." Sarah always locked her car, and the absence of glass in the parking lot suggested her window hadn't been broken to gain entry.

"We have to consider all the possibilities, but you know her car. It isn't one a teenager would want to be seen in." Even he joined in when we teased Sarah about her old-lady vehicle. "Your car, on the other hand…"

"And Dolores wasn't touched." I shivered as if a cold wind had blown around me. "That's two cars stolen when mine should have been the target."

"Right." Freddie rubbed his neck. "Speaking as both a friend and as a cop, I suggest you take your car home. Put her in the garage, lock her up, lock the garage, and get a rental car for a week or two. Give us a chance to figure out who is behind this."

It was good advice.

Before going home, I stopped at the library to retrieve my laptop. Which meant I had to spend a few minutes filling Janine in on what happened. And then, since it was such a nice day, and I wasn't in the mood to work, I went for a long drive in the country. With the top down. Dolores wasn't built for dirt roads so, I stuck to the paved ones.

It was late when I got home, and I considered parking on the street because I didn't want to mess with the heavy garage doors. But Freddie's words chewed at my brain. I pulled into the garage, put up the top and locked Dolores. I yanked the old-fashioned garage doors closed, slipped the rarely used padlock through the metal hoops and clicked it shut. She was as safe as I could make her.

I didn't pay attention to anything but my phone as I tromped up the stairs to my apartment, hoping for a message about Sarah's car, but not expecting one. I didn't even count the steps on the way up. I wondered for a mere second why Piper, the landlords' dog, hadn't greeted me at the gate, but remembered Luke talking about a visit to the vet. Piper was showing his age as badly as Joe and Luke, my landlords. When I got to the landing and pushed my key into the lock, I reveled in the return to normal.

I should have known better.

Chapter 3

The supper dishes were drying in the drainer and soft rock music played on my stereo. I sipped a glass of wine while finishing up the kitchen cleanup. The prospect of spending the evening digging into crime statistics enticed me, but first things first. I wouldn't be able to concentrate if everything wasn't in its place.

It sunk in as I put away the spices in alphabetical order. Somewhere in the house, Piper was barking like crazy. My first thought was that something had happened to Luke or Joe.

Instinct compelled me to stick Betsy, my Beretta, in my waistband before heading downstairs. I wouldn't take any chances.

Like James Bond, I glided down the outside stairs with my back to the wall. The lights cast long streams of brightness in the side yard. Catching movement in one of them, I reached for Betsy.

My phone rang. So much for being a shadow in the night. After a quick glance at the screen, I answered in a whisper.

"Luke! Are you and Joe all right?"

"We're fine. Are you okay? Where are you?"

"On my way to check on you. What's up with Piper?"

"We aren't sure. Joe will meet you at the bottom of the steps. I'll try to get Piper to settle down."

"Sounds like a plan."

I hung up, waited for the squeak of the back door, and restarted my descent. Light reflected from the pistol in Joe's hand when I reached the last stair.

"I thought I saw something in the yard," I said, still in a whisper.

Joe nodded. "Stay behind me."

It made more sense to split up and go around the house in opposite directions, but it wasn't the right time to argue. He opened the gate, and I followed him.

He stopped for a moment. Even when I held my breath, I didn't catch anything out of place. No footsteps, no one attempting to open a door or break a window. Without explaining, Joe moved on, with me close behind.

We turned the corner of the house. The light illuminating the front porch revealed nothing out of place. Every chair and table was in its proper position. No spots of darkness existed where they didn't belong. Inside, Piper's barking quieted to a soft growl.

Another turn led to the most dangerous part of the search. A narrow strip of grass separated the house from the hedges lining the sidewalk on the side street. If someone hid in the bushes, they'd be hard to spot in the dim light cast by the streetlights. Our forward movement slowed to a virtual crawl.

Joe raised one hand and came to a complete stop. I halted a mere foot behind him. A faint scratching reached my ears. It came from the garages. I flicked off Betsy's safety. If someone was trying to get to Dolores, they'd have a surprise coming their way.

Joe inched forward until he reached the back of the house. The sound stopped. I peered over his shoulder. In unison, we chuckled.

The intruder stood on his hind legs and stared at us. The overhead light between the two garage doors highlighted the black mask across his eyes. Joe relaxed and lowered his gun.

"Shoo," he yelled, waving his free hand. "Get out of here. Vamoose!"

The critter lowered itself, so it stood on four paws and continued to stare. It was the biggest raccoon I'd ever seen. Joe took two noisy steps forward, stomping his feet. "Skedaddle!"

It turned and lumbered off, heading for the relative darkness of the backyard next door. Its musky odor drifted back to us. "It must be the one that's been raiding the garbage cans," Joe said. "The neighbors have been complaining about the messes it leaves behind. Sure is fat for this time of year. No babies in sight, so likely a male."

I clicked on the safety and slid Betsy back into my waistband. "Your cinder blocks did their job." A cement block sat on the lid of each garbage can, holding them closed.

"As big as that feller was, he might be able to tip

them over. I'll call animal control in the morning and check on setting a trap for him. In the meantime, we'll need to keep a close eye on Piper. Wouldn't want the two of them to tangle."

I nodded as we walked back to where we'd started. "I'll be up late tonight," I said as we reached the bottom of the stairs, thinking of the research I wanted to tackle. "So, don't worry if you hear me moving around."

Joe grinned. "Shoot, you're one of the most light-footed people I know. You've got nothing to worry about. 'Night, Harmony."

I had plenty to worry about. But I wouldn't share any of it with him.

While I didn't have access to the police departments of the towns surrounding Oak Grove, I had another way to gather the information. It was slower and less efficient, but worked. Each town published a police blotter, either daily or weekly, in a local publication, and most of those publications had on-line access. Since I'd saved the web pages in my favorites, half the work was done.

With a cup of coffee close by, I dug into my project. With a spreadsheet open, I gathered the statistics for recent crimes, avoiding minor things like noise complaints. Every town had a curmudgeon or two who reported every backfire or kids playing basketball late at night. I didn't care about those.

I avoided the domestic quarrels category. Those reports did nothing but depress me. I hadn't learned how to detach myself from the tragedies they represented.

I was hunting for stolen car reports and not finding anything out of the ordinary. Sure, the towns closest to Pittsburgh and Cleveland reported more, but that was typical. Even a cursory look through the Pittsburgh papers didn't show an upsurge in stolen vehicles. The knowledge didn't make me feel any better.

Without more data, I couldn't establish a pattern. At the same time, the last thing I wanted was more data. Because that meant one of my friends would fall victim to the crime spree.

Before going to bed, I wrote myself a note to call the car rental agency in the morning. With Dolores tucked away somewhere, at least I could make me and my friends less of a target.

❋ ❋ ❋

Huh. That raccoon was big, but I didn't realize he was tall enough to reach the lock on the garage door. Or that his claws were sharp enough to leave scratches on the lock itself. The only thing I could figure out was he was drawn to the light reflected from the shiny surface. Which wasn't so shiny anymore. But there was nothing in the garage a raccoon would want.

At least the lock still worked. It unsnapped with a healthy click when I turned the key. I pushed the door up and hung the lock on a hook inside the door. I patted Dolores' trunk, my normal morning greeting to her.

The back door of the house squealed, and Piper barked. I turned to see Luke with Piper on a leash. That wasn't normal, but it seemed to be a sensible precaution.

"Good morning," I said cheerily. "Too bad you missed our visitor last night."

Piper sniffed the ground in front of the garage, making zigzag circles as he explored.

Luke grinned. "Joe told me it was a big one."

"And strong. He scratched the lock."

"Let me see." Luke grabbed the lock from its hook and carried it to a spot in the sun. "No raccoon did this, Harmony. Someone took a screwdriver or something metal to this lock."

It took a moment to process. "They tried to break in?" I squeaked.

"Sure looks like it." He juggled Piper's leash and his cell phone. "I'm calling the cops."

"They filed a report, but there wasn't much they could do," I explained to Janine as I set up for my day's work at the library. "Any fingerprints got smeared when Luke and I handled the lock."

"Is there someplace more secure for your car?" she asked. "I'm not sure she's safe behind the library."

I didn't either. But I hadn't figured out where to put her yet. "I'll call around to the storage places and see if they have any open spots. That way she'll be behind both a fence and a lock. I'm hoping one of them offers twenty-four-hour security. I can rent a car for a while."

"I was afraid of something like this when you bought her. As much as we pretend big city problems don't happen here in Oak Grove, you and I both know it's not true."

Dolores stuck out like a sore thumb. I'd noticed a few new sporty cars in town, but she remained my favorite. But no one had bothered her in the last two years, so why now?

"I have a meeting in the conference room this morning. You can use my office to make the calls and that way no one can listen in." She cocked her head towards Mrs. Donnelly two tables over, one of Oak Grove's favorite gossips. "I'll tell the ladies at the front desk."

"I'll take you up on that. Thanks. Have you heard from Sarah?"

She shook her head. "Nothing. I was hoping for an update."

I tapped my phone. "Me neither. Not even a text. Not that I blame her. I'm not safe to be around right now."

"Don't blame yourself for something you can't control. It's coincidental."

Except I didn't believe in coincidence.

Secure Storage. As I punched in the code to open the gate to leave the facility, I hoped it lived up to its name. An eight-foot fence surrounded the grounds. Dolores was tucked into one of the innermost storage containers, with a shiny new lock safeguarding the door.

The guard in the office nodded my direction, and I returned the gesture. A taxi sat on the street out front, waiting to take me to the car rental agency. There wasn't a way to erase my tracks, but I was trying to hide them as much as possible. Unless the taxi driver gossiped about my trip, no one besides the guard would know I'd been there. And the only people who had access to the computer records about which unit held Dolores were the storage company's employees.

As we drove away, I worried I was abandoning a friend.

Chapter 4

I sat on the bottom step, clutching a damp tissue. "I locked my door when I left this morning," I insisted. "This isn't my first go-round."

Officer Bo Holt, the newest member of the Oak Grove Police force, nodded, but he didn't seem convinced. He was the first officer to respond after I placed the call to 911. Now, two other policemen searched my ransacked apartment, hunting for clues.

It had been deja vu when the door swung open, revealing the disaster. Overturned furniture, books scattered everywhere, coats and sweaters from the hallway closet tossed on the floor. And that's just what I saw from the doorway. I'd fought back the urge to pull Betsy from my purse and see if the intruder remained inside. Instead, I'd taken the safer course of action.

"This happened before?"

He wouldn't know. It had been a couple of years ago. I didn't want to explain it. "Yes. Check the files or ask Sergeant Kinchloe. He'll fill you in."

He scribbled in his notepad. "Any idea what they were looking for?"

I didn't keep anything of value in my apartment except for a few first edition books. Someone wanting to steal them wouldn't need to destroy the place searching for them. They were in plain sight on a bookshelf in the front room. Even my jewelry was flea market and pawnshop finds. I'd put my good stuff in a safe deposit box after the last incident. I shrugged. "Not a clue."

"Do you have any enemies who might have done this?"

There was a long list but as far as I knew they were all in jail. Still, they could have friends capable of the destruction. "More than I like to think about." I wiped away the stray tear trickling down my cheek. "All earned honestly."

Holt arched an eyebrow. "You think those kids who set the fires this winter had something to do with it?"

I snorted. "Them? Not a chance. They wouldn't have the nerve. No, I've had run-ins with too many bad guys." How my life had changed in the past couple of years. "Talk to Freddie—Detective Thomason."

"I'm surprised he hasn't shown up yet."

I figured he was still with Sarah. That was why I'd called the emergency line and not him directly.

Frowning, Officer Sloan came down the stairs. "Is there somewhere else you can spend the night?" he asked.

The knot in my stomach tightened. "That bad?"

"Whoever did this gained entrance through your bedroom window. There's broken glass everywhere. We found a ladder leaning against the house. As late as it is, you won't be able to get it repaired and cleaned up tonight."

Joe and Luke had been fixing the gutters. When they left to go shopping, they must have left the ladder where the perpetrators could get to it.

"Then it was a random break-in? Someone destroyed my place on a lark?"

"That was my first reaction. A druggie looking for something to steal and sell to get their next fix." Sloan's frown deepened. "It happens, even in Oak Grove. But this is you we're dealing with, Miss Duprie."

I shivered in the cool evening air.

He continued. "This is a message. I don't understand it, but maybe you can give us some insight." He pulled out his phone and flipped through the display. "Does this look familiar?"

It was a picture of my bedroom, with the mattress pushed off the bed, my knickknacks scattered everywhere, and clothes tossed haphazardly. It brought back memories of the previous break-in. At least my underwear wasn't prominently displayed. The one thing that stood out in the debris was the one thing that didn't belong.

On the wall where a picture of my parents hung, or used to hang, was a box. More precisely, a series of small boxes. Grouped together in a wooden case. A Japanese inro.

❋ ❋ ❋

"It isn't the Cookes'," Freddie confirmed. "They say it's a tourist shop generic take-off."

We sat in the overstuffed brown leather chairs in the front room of Eli's house, the sky-blue Victorian I'd remodeled. I'd taken up residence there. The logical move, as it was stocked with the essentials, including several changes of clothes. Plus, it was guarded by a state-of-the-art alarm system designed by Eli himself. If anyone breached the perimeter, an angry horde of computer geeks would descend on the premises in no time flat. At least, that's what Lando and Scotty, two of Eli's employees, assured me.

"Officer Sloan suggested it was a message," I said. "But I don't get it. What did the theft of the inro have to do with me?"

"That's what I need to figure out. And you need to stay out of it. If you have a secret admirer, I don't like the way they're doing business. The last thing I want is for you to get kidnapped again."

I snorted. "Me? A secret admirer? That's a stretch."

"Really? Think about it. This is the first time in how long Jake has been out of the picture. Eli's not here either. And if we assume that the theft of the inro is a coincidence, there's one common factor. You."

There was that word again. Coincidence. "I'm not getting any mysterious calls or hang-ups. No unexpected flower deliveries and no one is following me." At least not that I'd noticed, but I hadn't been watching carefully. "And it's too weird to think someone is trying to woo me by stealing my friends' cars."

"If anyone has been stalking you for any length of time, they would know it will take more than hearts and flowers to win your attention."

He had me pegged. Fast cars and fancy driving were more my speed, thanks to Jake. "What's my next move?"

"You know the drill. Switch up your schedule. Go to the library at a different time or don't go at all. You have a rental car, but swap it out every few days. I'd suggest staying with Sarah, but she'll be with me for a few more days. Bunk with Janine or have Janine stay here. Once Joe and Luke get your window repaired, you can hire someone to help you clean. Don't go anywhere alone, if possible."

Good advice, but the chances of me following it for more than a day were slim. "Or you could wire me and use me as bait."

Freddie nearly spit out the soda he was drinking. "This isn't a game."

It had sounded like a good idea to me. "I was teasing you," I said, covering my gaffe. "You need a laugh."

"Your 'joke' almost gave me a heart attack."

"Sorry."

He swirled the liquid in his glass. "I'm worried, Harmony. Nothing about this feels right."

"It's late, you're tired and worried about Sarah. Go home and give her a hug from me. Nothing else will happen tonight."

"I hope you're right." With a yawn, he set his glass on its coaster. "Make sure you lock up behind me."

If I didn't, I'd get calls from two or three concerned guys. And I wasn't ready to explain what was happening.

❊ ❊ ❊

I called Janine in the morning to tell her not to worry when I didn't show up at the library. Then I settled in with my coffee and business reports on the big screen TV. If I lost myself in charts and numbers, I wouldn't think about other problems. That was the plan.

At least, until mid-morning, when I craved a donut. Then it only made sense to hit up the grocery store for fresh fruit and necessary supplies. I even checked online for coupons for the 'other' grocery store, the big box one where I hated to shop.

After surviving the crowded aisles and inconsiderate shoppers, I decided to swing by my place to check in with Joe and Luke. And to see how bad the rest of my place was. Even though I loved Eli's house, I loved my cozy apartment more. This would be my chance to repaint my bedroom and deep clean everything else.

But a few blocks from home, a tingle started at the base of my neck. I glanced in the rear-view mirror. None of the cars seemed out-of-place. I made a last-minute right-hand turn without signaling. It took me off my normal route, but not out of my way. No one followed. The tingle persisted.

A loop around the block put me back on my original path. Again, all the cars belonged. Even the silver-colored economy car that pulled into traffic after I passed it.

On edge, I made the next left-hand turn. Legally. Blinker on and everything. The silver car followed. That was dumb. If they were following me, they should have pulled into the street in front of me to throw me off.

For one final test, I exited into the parking lot of Dell's Appliance store. I parked in a spot that allowed me to either pull forward or back out if I needed to make a getaway. The silver car rolled by on the street, braking before the second entrance, then continued on its path.

With the rental still in gear, I waited, one foot on the brake, the other hovering above the gas pedal. As I waited, I took my cellphone out of my purse and put it in my lap. Betsy got placed on the passenger seat for easy access. It wasn't time to call in reinforcements—yet.

Seconds, then minutes, passed without another sighting of the car. The tingling eased. Watching the traffic closely, I pulled out of the parking lot and headed for the rental agency. I could always claim I thought I heard a misfire in the engine when I swapped out vehicles. I'd check in with Joe and Luke later.

The replacement was a soccer mom's dream and my nightmare. A bright blue SUV with seats for six and space for a zillion suitcases. It handled okay, but for stealth missions, it was a disaster. Granted, Dolores didn't hide well either, so I shouldn't have been too disappointed.

The long, circular path I took to Eli's provided ample opportunity for spotting any followers. None showed themselves and the warning tingle didn't return. I parked behind the house where the SUV couldn't be seen from the street. I hoped the tracks in the grass would spring back quickly and not give the location away.

At least I got my donuts. And enough supplies for meals for several days. I set the alarm, secure in my fortress of solitude. Anyway, that's what I told myself.

Chapter 5

The peace and quiet didn't last long. Around four, Joe called to tell me the window was repaired, now with double-pane glass and a more robust frame. It made me unhappy that part of the original architecture of the house had been replaced, but Luke and Joe did it to protect me.

Nothing could protect me from the sadness that overwhelmed me when I walked in my door. I mean, I knew it was bad, but not *how* bad. They hadn't just thrown everything around, they'd dumped flour and sugar and other seasonings throughout the apartment. Who would do that?

That wasn't the worst of it.

I cradled the pot with what remained of my mother's African violet in my lap. They plucked every flower and bud and pulled off half the leaves. The plant would live—I'd make sure of it—but it would take a lot of effort.

Pages from my books lay scattered around. All my first editions survived, they'd only destroyed the more current ones. The latest Jack Reacher book. A biography of Queen Elizabeth. The popular-for-the-moment romance, The Pirate's Nanny. At least I'd finished reading them.

They used a permanent marker to draw mustaches and beards on the framed picture of me and Eli kept on the end table, a middle school type of prank. Thank heavens the original was digital.

I sat in a kitchen chair and rocked, plotting my revenge. A stream of religious missionaries sent to their door. Dead fish mailed regularly. Confetti bombs. Putting a potato in their exhaust. Nothing legal seemed adequate.

It wasn't a case of a mysterious suitor, of that I was convinced. It felt darker, bordering on evil. Like the culprit was taunting me. Someone who knew me. Someone I thought was a friend. How else would they understand where to draw the line in the damage they'd done?

But I couldn't explain this to Freddie without sounding crazy. Either Joe or Luke had called him. The three of them were working on straightening out the furniture in the front room while pretending not to keep an eye on me. They had a right to be concerned. That didn't make it any less irritating.

What I needed to do was jump in and start cleaning. What I wanted to do was grab my laptop and create a spreadsheet of potential suspects. The police were still questioning neighbors and so far, no one had any helpful information. Freddie, although he hadn't been assigned to the investigation, was following it and keeping me updated.

The short mental list taking form made me hurt as I added each entry. Gary from the pawnshop. Luke or Joe. Big Daddy Al from the Pink Flamingo. That was, assuming they could hotwire cars, something we'd never talked about. And I bet every one of them had an unshakeable alibi.

Jake.

Eli.

Soft tears rolling down my face, I plotted a spreadsheet with columns for ability, opportunity, knowledge, and the biggie—motivation. I checkmarked a few things here and there, but one column remained empty. Motivation. Why would anyone do this to me?

Two wrinkled but still strong hands wrapped around my shaking ones. I looked up into Joe's concerned eyes.

"Let me take the plant, Harmony," he said. "I'll put it with mine. That way, you won't have to worry about it getting damaged more while we clean."

"Why?" I asked as he pried the pot from my grasp.

"We're hiring a janitorial company to come in to do the heavy work. We don't want anything else to get ruined."

I frowned. "No, not that." I wouldn't let them pay for the cleaners, but it wasn't time to argue. "Why would anyone do this?" With a broad swipe of my hand, I indicated the disaster.

Freddie stopped picking up torn book pages and knelt in front of me. I hated dragging him away from Sarah. Her car still hadn't been found. "We can't answer that. Based on your observations, I agree my original theory is wrong. A jealous suitor would have ripped Eli out of the picture, not just drawn on the both of you. Every on-duty officer is working on this in their spare time—making sure everyone you've helped bust is in jail, chasing down their associates, talking to their contacts. There are a lot of theories being discussed. But we're stretched thin with another big case."

I cocked my head and waited.

Freddie sighed. "I'm not free to share, even with you. Give us time, we'll nail this guy."

I wondered how many of the theories featured Jake. "I want to be involved. Analyze the reports, build spreadsheets of the suspects, something."

"You need to get out of town for a few days," Luke said. Deep lines etched his forehead—more than the ones he'd earned working in the sun years ago. "When was the last time you took a vacation?"

Too long. I visited Eli, what was it, ten months ago? For fun, not for work.

"The thing is," Luke said, "We didn't tell you, but Joe is scheduled for minor surgery in Pittsburgh. He's getting his knee replaced. We won't be around for a week or so and hate leaving you alone. We plan on taking Piper with us."

"I agree." Freddie stood. "Even with the security Eli designed at his house. It's an untested system and I don't trust it."

I did.

"What if I promise to only be here when the cleaning company is here? Will that make you guys feel any better?" Not that I would allow any cleaners in my place without me.

Joe shook his head. "That only covers a few hours."

"Sarah still isn't up to visitors. Can't you stay with Janine?" Freddie asked.

I didn't want to impose on her. Or put her at risk. There had to be a way to satisfy both me and them. I couldn't ask Jake to act as an escort, not with his new job.

But experience provided me with another option. The Towers, Oak Grove's best hotel, maintained its own minimal security. "I'll get a room at The Towers. Request a room on an upper floor with no balcony. Switch between staying there and Eli's. If I rent it for a week or two, there'll be no way for anyone to predict where I'll be. By varying my schedule, I'll be harder to track."

It wasn't a perfect solution, but the best one on the table. I wouldn't need to take a suitcase back and forth because I kept enough clothes at Eli's for a few days.

Freddie rubbed his temple. "It might work. I'll talk to the chief and see if he has any other ideas. He's at a conference, so I don't think I'll get an answer right away."

Chief Sorenson had a fierce protective streak. He'd come up with something. Probably something I wouldn't like.

"Or you could hire yourself a bodyguard," Joe said.

That's the last thing I wanted. Someone looking over my shoulder and getting in my way. If I was going to do any undercover reconnaissance, I'd want to do it on my own terms.

❋ ❋ ❋

With one eye on the rear-view mirror, I navigated through the unusually heavy traffic. For an Oak Grove night, anyway. It would have been normal in even the small neighborhoods of Pittsburgh. There must have been a big school activity or something.

I was on my way to The Towers, with Eli's favorite suite reserved. A suitcase with a couple of changes of clothes bumped around in the trunk. A reusable grocery bag stuffed with undamaged books occupied the floor of the passenger side. I'd hit up Gary's pawnshop to replace books I hadn't been able to repair.

The difference in headlights was subtle, but something about a set three cars back bothered me. They didn't maintain the same spot consistently, and I couldn't get a good look at the car. Maybe it was just a popular model. When I made a left-hand loop around the block, they didn't follow. But a few stoplights later, they ended up behind me.

So much for switching out the rental car. I was torn between shaking them or playing cat and mouse. Me being the cat pretending I was the mouse. Just the distraction I needed.

A quick lane change became my opening card. They called the bid by matching the move and nothing more. It was early in the game, but to test their resolve, I threw in a wild card. I turned on my blinker to indicate a left-hand turn and then went straight. They called my bluff and stayed with me.

At least they were serious. They knew I was on to them. That made the game more interesting.

A good girl would call 911 or at least call Freddie and tell him what was happening. But I hadn't synced my cell phone with the rental, so that was out. Darn.

I played my next card, a quick application of the brakes. Not hard enough for a full stop, but enough to wake up everyone behind me. The move might get someone to call the police to complain, and I was good with that.

Without waiting to see the reaction of my shadow, I tossed in the second card of my pair. I stepped on the gas and flew through a yellow light. The space gave me time to plan my next action.

A parking spot near a cross street gave me an idea. I pulled in, turned off the lights, took my foot off the brake and waited. Hopefully, it would seem as if I'd disappeared.

The headlights cruised down the street. By the time they spotted me, it was too late. For them. I tucked in behind the car, a pale blue compact and flashed my brights, wanting them to know I was there. I tried to get close enough to see the plate and memorize the number. But a clouded cover obscured the letters. I'd heard of them defeating cameras on toll roads but hadn't thought about the technology being used to avoid identification in a police chase situation. I added the topic to my research wish list.

But the driver wasn't as anonymous as he'd hoped. In the lower left-hand corner of the back window was a sticker I recognized. A quiet little circle with a sad star in the middle. The symbol of the rental agency. The rental SUV had a matching one.

When the car sped up and pulled away, I folded. For the moment. I was saving my best card for the next game.

Chapter 6

In my darkened top floor suite at the Towers, I stood and gazed over the lights of Oak Grove and plotted my next move. Either an employee at the car rental agency used their GPS system to track my movements, or gave the information to someone else. I couldn't be convinced that I just happened to be spotted twice.

There was only one place to rent cars in all of Oak Grove. Except for Jack's Junkers, and I wouldn't drive one of them. In both Pittsburgh and Cleveland, I'd have my choice of companies to rent from.

In Pittsburgh, I knew the right place to buy theater makeup and costumes, and all the best places to buy used clothes. A call to a friendly customer representative in a faraway location and the arrangements were made. I'd return the car to the Pittsburgh airport and catch a flight to visit a dying friend. And the people here in town would be none the wiser.

I wouldn't really be flying out. I'd kill some time in the airport before going to a competitor's booth and picking up a vehicle. Before coming home, I'd visit the shops and get the supplies I needed. By the time I got back, I'd be a different person.

Next, I had to plan out who I'd be. I closed the curtains, fired up my laptop, and hit up the makeup tutorials. I had several ideas in mind but had to make sure my limited skills were up to the challenge.

❄ ❄ ❄

The gray Charger was subtle enough to drive without garnering too much attention while having plenty of power under the hood. It may have had too much power for Auntie Hilda but was the perfect car for my second cousin Taylor.

Auntie Hilda had shoulder-length gray hair and preferred wearing floral dresses that reached to just below the knees. Taylor had multi-colored hair in blues, purples, and reds accompanied by torn jeans, plaid shirts, and a knit hat. I'd have to wear contacts as Taylor, but for Auntie Hilda, I'd dig out a pair of glasses I hadn't worn forever.

Hilda drove home because I needed more practice with Taylor's makeup before I took her out in public. I planned to use Hilda for everyday errands and Taylor for undercover jobs. The deception would work better with two cars, but I couldn't make those arrangements without revealing my plan. I thought about sending myself out of town for a week, but couldn't get my apartment cleaned if I did. It would be a headache keeping track of myself.

❋ ❋ ❋

Doris from the cleaning company met me at the bottom of my stairs, armed with the tools of her trade. "I hear you have a mess." Like me, she wore old jeans and a t-shirt, except hers bore the logo of the cleaning company.

I'd called Joe ahead of time to let him know I'd be there with help. Piper had greeted me from the fenced-in yard and hadn't even barked at Doris.

"It's bad. I don't expect to get it all cleaned today, but I hope we can finish the front room and the kitchen."

She shifted the vacuum hose to rest on her shoulder. I picked up the bucket and mop. I had my own, but this was a two-mop mess. We'd probably need the entire bottle of cleaner I spotted in the bag on her other shoulder.

"I almost turned down the job," she said as we plodded up the stairs, "when the boss asked me to sign the confidentiality paperwork. I never clean and tell. But it's for you and I needed the money, so here I am."

I stopped so suddenly that she banged into me with the vacuum cleaner. Luckily, we both kept our balance.

"What paperwork? I didn't ask for anything like that!" I said.

"Dunno. It said I agreed to not reveal what I saw or even tell anyone I was here."

Who had made the request? Making a mental note to tip well, I resumed the trudge upwards. "You may change your mind when you see what we're dealing with, but I'm glad you came."

"No worries. I've seen bad and worse."

She was in for a shock. When I opened the door and stepped aside to let her go first, she stopped just inside the door, set down the vacuum, then the bag with cleaning supplies and put her hands on her hips and shook her head.

"My, oh, my. This is bad. Honey, they did a number on this place," she said. "Well, let's get to work."

And work we did, barely pausing to eat the pizza I ordered for lunch. Thanks to Doris, we got the front room, the dining area, the kitchen and most of the bathroom cleaned. We turned up the music and sang along with classic rock. The garbage can got filled with bag loads of items from the kitchen that should have been tossed before, like some of my mother's old plastic storage containers.

We boxed up my more valuable books so I could take them to my safe deposit box later. Doris tutted over my old blue-cover Nancy Drew books, but between a low-power cleaning from her vacuum and a lot of work, we were able to get all the flour out from between the pages. My makeup, what little I kept in the bathroom, didn't fare so well, and it all ended in the garbage. Most of it decorated the walls and floors, anyway.

Between the music and Doris's cheerful presence, I made it through the hours without shedding a tear.

Well, only when Doris would notice. A few may have fallen into the bucket of water as I cleaned the floorboards.

As hard as we worked, there wasn't enough time to tackle my bedroom. I was okay with that because I wanted to do it by myself. It made me queasy when another person handled my underwear. The last time my place was broken into, I ended up throwing almost all of it away.

Doris and I were scrubbing the walls in the bathroom—getting in each other's way and having fun with it—when the music stopped.

"Quitting time, ladies," Joe said. "You've been at it for hours. It's looking a lot better."

The carpets still needed to be cleaned. I'd hold off on doing it until Joe and Luke were in Pittsburgh. I didn't want them to have to help.

Doris rolled her shoulders. "I haven't worked this hard since I tackled the hoarder house over on Willow Street after the old lady died." She put a hand on my arm. "Not that I'm comparing you to her. I had to fight my way through stacks of newspapers and old magazines at that house. Never did feel like it was actually clean. I can tell this place has been taken care of and I'm glad I could help you make it livable again."

The amount of her tip rose, and I gave her a hug. "I appreciate all your help. I know this job is above and beyond what you normally do."

Her smile stretched from cheek to cheek. "But you made it fun. It wasn't like cleaning for some snotty rich lady who complains about the smallest speck of dust. Anytime you need help, ask for me."

I hoped I'd never need to do this again. "I will."

Joe helped Doris carry her vacuum and what remained of her cleaning supplies to her car. "You aren't planning to stay here, are you?" he asked as we watched her drive away.

"Not tonight. We didn't get the bedroom cleaned. I'm considering painting it, anyway. I'm tired of the blue."

"What color are you thinking of?"

"I've eliminated yellow and green. How about a light dusky rose?"

He rubbed his chin. "It would go good with the scavenged crown molding we bought. Didn't know for sure what we were going to do with it, but it was too good of a bargain to pass up. Can you wait until we're back from Pittsburgh to get started? We're leaving tomorrow. The police will run extra patrols in the neighborhood, but you shouldn't be here alone."

The longing to sleep in my bed warred with the need to save Joe and Luke from anything more to worry about. "I'll mostly be staying at Eli's. But I'll swing by here to check things out and water the flowers." If I did a little cleaning while I was here, it wasn't something they needed to know.

He nodded. "Did you find any clues today? Something the cops missed?"

They'd done a thorough job, even without Freddie breathing down their necks. Part of the work

Doris and I had done was removing the traces of the investigation. "I wish, but no."

"I was afraid of that. This whole affair is making me antsy. It's like someone is playing a game and you're the target."

The truth behind his words sent a shiver snaking down my spine.

I contemplated the idea as I loaded the washer at Eli's house with a bag of clothes I'd brought from my apartment. Joe had given me a ride, although I'd offered to call a taxi. The Charger was parked behind the house and I wasn't ready to appear in it yet.

Which reminded me of Jake. I wondered which of us would win in a race. Charger against Charger. And why he hadn't called to tell me how he was doing. Since it was Saturday evening, I didn't want to call him and interrupt him at work.

But I could call Eli. His conference should be over. And I missed him. I didn't want to think about why he hadn't called me.

I considered putting on my Taylor costume, hitting up a bar or two, and catching up on gossip. Maybe the rumor mill had some theories. But, exhausted after the long day, I wasn't up to the effort.

Besides, I was plotting out some research. I wanted to track down the fake inro and see if it had been bought nearby by checking out the museums in Pittsburgh and Cleveland. Oak Grove's museum was a sad little place only open on Fridays and Saturdays, dedicated to the history of the early settlers of the area.

So, supper first, finish laundry, do research, call Eli, do more research. The plan seemed solid. Except I caught myself yawning way too much as I divided up the clean clothes into two piles, one to stay and one to go to the hotel. And I fell asleep while the image search crawled the internet and didn't wake up until after midnight when it was too late to reach out to Eli. At least I remembered to turn off my laptop and lock the house down before crawling into Eli's otherwise-empty bed.

My phone buzzed after I'd fallen back asleep. The only reason for someone to call at that time of the night was bad news. I put on my glasses and grabbed the phone, blinking to adjust my vision. The number was Eli's. By the time I swiped the screen to accept the call, all I got was the muffled end of a distant conversation and a hangup. When I dialed him back, it went straight to voice mail.

I meant to leave him a message—really, I did—but I never even heard the two beeps before my eyes closed again.

Chapter 7

The forecast promised an unseasonably warm day, so I canceled the plans for Auntie Hilda to mingle with the after-church crowd. Instead, plain old me worked on the rose garden at Eli's. It had a long way to go to match its glory years, but I had a vision. Working with the gardening club, we'd mingled heritage roses in with modern stock to achieve a display both colorful and fragrant.

I was on my knees yanking out weeds when the sound of a car's ragged engine caught my attention. I pulled off my work gloves, ready to reach for my phone and call 911. It was Sarah's car, and with the sun in my eyes, I couldn't see the driver until he pulled into the driveway. Freddie.

I walked over to greet him and asked, "Where did they find it?"

"You know that store on the way to Pittsburgh that sold pecan logs?"

I remembered. "Isn't it closed?"

"Someone bought the property, and it's being

remodeled. The crew noticed the car in the parking lot but thought it belonged to one of them. It took them a few days to figure out it was abandoned."

"What's wrong with it?"

Freddie grimaced. "That's beyond my limited mechanical skills. I told Sarah we have her car but need to hold on to it to check for evidence. That will give the garage a few days to get it running right before she gets it back."

"Have they found Thalia's car?"

"Not yet. Everyone's still keeping an eye out."

"You want to come in for coffee?" I jerked my head towards the front door. I wanted to grill him about Sarah and the investigations and didn't want to stand outside in the sun to do it.

"No, I have to run. Sarah is waiting for me."

"Give her my love and tell her I apologize for dragging her into this mess."

"It isn't your fault, Harmony."

People kept telling me that. I didn't believe it.

❋ ❋ ❋

Auntie Hilda limped into the lobby of The Towers and stood at the front desk. The quarter-inch I'd removed from one of her heels insured the limp would remain consistent. I juggled three bags of groceries and placed them on the counter.

"Did Harmony leave a keycard for me?" My voice quavered.

The front desk clerk—Rich, according to his nametag—raised an eyebrow. "You are?"

"Hilda Henderson. She said she left a room key for me. I brought her supplies."

"Ah, yes, Mrs. Henderson." He rifled through the paperwork on the desk until he found the correct envelope. "Here you are. But I believe Miss Duprie is out right now."

"I knew that. Or I wouldn't have needed the key."

"Of course." His practiced customer service smile slipped. "You know her room number?"

I snorted, picked up the bags and the envelope. "The elevators are where?"

"Just around the corner."

"You could have offered to help me carry these," I grumbled as I walked away, loud enough for him to hear. I wanted to make him and his coworkers avoid talking to me as much as possible. I wasn't good enough of a voice actor to hold long conversations in my Hilda role.

Upstairs, I put away the assorted goodies and snack foods. I wanted the suite to have that lived-in look. So, I put some wrappers in the garbage and put a towel on the hook in the bathroom, as if it had been used. I even tore off the nicely folded end on the toilet paper roll.

The idea was to make the housekeepers think I'd spent the night. I pulled down the covers and sat on the uncovered bedsheets while re-arranging the pillows. If they were tracking my presence to share with an unknown party, I'd throw them off course.

Mission accomplished, I called a taxi and went downstairs the back way. I was hungry, and it was suppertime. On Sunday nights, The Dairy Barn attracted a variety of people. It was the right place to find out if the gossip mill had any leads into my case.

❋ ❋ ❋

No one paid attention to the old lady stuck in the little booth meant for two people. Which was good, because it showed my disguise worked. But bad too, because no one within listening distance talked about anything I cared about. It was all discussions about national politics, which didn't help me at all.

City buses don't run on Sundays, so I took a taxi to the convenience store a few blocks from Eli's and walked the rest of the way. Which is where I sat, watching cat videos on the big screen and debating if I should call him. It was Sunday, and surely he wasn't still tied up with his super-secret meetings. I decided to risk it.

After making sure that all traces of Hilda were washed away, I pinged his contact. And held my breath until the second ring. And released it when he answered after the third ring.

"You must have heard me thinking about you!" he said cheerfully, but the image on the screen told a different story. He had dark circles under his eyes, hadn't shaved, and his shirt was as wrinkled looking as something pulled out of an overstuffed drawer without being ironed. "And while you're a sight for sore eyes, I need to switch this to an audio call. Some of the people I'm with would prefer not to be identified."

"Keeping secrets from me, Eli?"

"For now. If this works out, you'll be in the thick of things. Call you right back."

His image disappeared. I stared at a picture of myself in its place for a moment before the program closed. Then my phone chimed with the opening notes for "Dream A Little Dream of Me," Eli's ringtone.

"Hey, Sweetie," I said.

"Hey, Gorgeous, I'm so glad you called."

Hmm. He'd never called me gorgeous before. I laughed. "Okay, laying it on a bit thick, aren't you? What do you want?"

"I can't tell you what I really want with people around. I'll just say I wish you were here instead."

"You can call me later when you're by yourself and tell me."

"It sounds wonderful, but we've been ending our meetings late—like two in the morning. I don't want to wake you up."

I couldn't resist. "Like last night?"

He groaned. "Sorry about that. I didn't realize what I'd done until this morning. I hoped I didn't wake you, but then I saw you tried to call me back."

"What *are* you working on?"

"I want to tell you." His excitement was clear. "But it's big, and if everything works out, you'll be in the middle of the action. We just need to tighten up some details. Once it goes to the lawyers, I'll be able to talk about it."

There he was, the man I loved so much. When he dug into a project, he gave it his total attention.

"I want you to come to Florida when I'm done

here so we can discuss it," he continued. "Or I'll come to you. We'll see how things work out."

I should have told him right then about what was going on. I didn't.

"How much longer are your meetings going to take? You scheduled one week."

"Those meetings are finished. This is different. I ran into some interesting people and made an offhand remark that sparked this idea." He paused. "If I keep talking, I'll let it slip, so I'm going to shut up for now. Tell me what you've been up to."

"I weeded the rose bed today. The buds are ready to bloom. If you come in a few days, you'll be able to see for yourself."

"That's why you're at the house instead of your place."

I'd let him believe that excuse instead of telling him the truth. I didn't want him to worry about me when he was in the middle of whatever he was in the middle of.

"Yeah, I took a break and fell asleep on the couch. I figured I might as well stay. That way I can get an early start on your Monday morning debriefing." I did a weekly roundup of updates in the security world for him.

From the muffled voices in the background, I guessed someone else was talking to him and he'd covered the mic on his phone. I waited.

"I have to run," he said. "But I'm glad you called. Wish you were here."

In a way, I was glad I wasn't there, with my troubles ruining his meetings. "Call when you have a chance, even if it is late. Or way too early." I grinned, knowing he couldn't see my face.

He groaned. "You won't let me live that down, will you?"

"I can think of ways to make it up to me. But you have to be here to do them."

"I bet I can think of a few things too, Buttercup. I'd tell you about them, but I really have to go. Love you."

"Love you, too."

The absence of background noise was my clue he had hung up.

I stared at my face in the mirror. Except it wasn't my face, it was Taylor. I finally had the makeup and wig just right. Maybe I'd risk going for a ride and introducing Taylor and the Charger to Oak Grove. Taxis were expensive.

I added a smidgen more rouge to my cheeks. Colored contacts would have been a bonus, but I'd live with what I had. Taylor's clothes hid in a closet on the third floor, and that was my next stop.

As I headed up the stairs, my phone went off. Not a ringtone or message notification, but a full-on blaring alarm. I'd only heard it do that once before— when I tested the house's security system. Someone was breaking in.

Or trying to. I stopped in the master bedroom long enough to grab Betsy before heading downstairs to the kitchen. Eli's program showed that's where the intrusion alert was from. When I reached the base of the stairs, I turned on the strobe lights on the back porch. I waited for the maneuver to confuse the intruder before turning them off. He would need to adjust his eyesight and I wouldn't. It gave me a momentary edge.

Except for the lights on the various pieces of computer equipment, the downstairs was dark. On my way to the rear door, I kept my back to the walls as much as possible. When I reached a spot where I could peer through a crack in the curtains, I switched the view on the app to an outside camera. Then I flicked on the outside spotlights.

The coverage wasn't perfect, but I scrolled through the video feeds to see most of the porches and windows. No one was in sight, but there were enough shadows to hide an experienced prowler. I'd seen Jake do it. The idea sent a shiver down my spine. Not Jake this time.

My phone rang. I answered quickly. "Hello?"

"Everything okay?" Lando hissed at the other end.

Lando was one of Eli's long-term employees and helped to program the security system as well as install it. It shouldn't have surprised me that he monitored it.

"As far as I can tell, everything is fine. If anyone was outside, the alarms and lights scared them off."

"Let me check. I don't see anything now, but I can make out a figure at the back door a few minutes ago." He chuckled. "Then the alarm sounded, and the strobes came on. Perfect. It looks like he headed out of there as fast as he could. We need to install cameras to catch more of the yard. Hey, what's that?" There was no excitement in his voice, only curiosity.

"What's what?"

"The car out back. That isn't yours."

I had to lie to him. If I didn't, a horde of angry computer geeks would invade Oak Grove. "It belongs to Taylor, my second cousin. She's in town for a few days. I offered to let her stay here since there's an extra bedroom. There have been a couple of car thefts lately, so we parked her car out back to hide it."

"You'll need to change your strategy after tonight. In the meantime, call the cops and ask them to do a quick search around the house and make sure whoever it was is gone."

Or I could do it myself.

He read my mind, even from a thousand miles away. "Don't do it yourself, Harmony. Just because we caught only one person on camera doesn't mean there aren't more."

If he was here, he'd be the first one out the door. Well, maybe second, behind Eli.

"I'll call the non-emergency line, right after we hang up," I promised. And after I transformed back into Harmony.

"Just in case, I'll keep my eyes on the cameras for a while longer."

"Thanks for checking up on things. Talk to you later."

I called the main police number as I headed to the bathroom. By the time a patrol got here, I'd have all traces of Taylor washed away.

Chapter 8

I stood on the porch and watched Officer Sloan drive away. He hadn't found anyone, of course. I caught him admiring the Charger, so that secret was out. Partially, at least. It might take time to make it to the gossip mill, but the information was sure to be shared with the rest of the cops in town.

But my plan could still work. The bars I wanted to visit as Taylor were outside city limits and not businesses the Oak Grove police patrolled. Still, I'd had enough excitement for one night, so they would have to wait.

I was too keyed up to go to bed despite the late hour. Joe's words rattled around at the back of my skull. He'd called it a game, but this was serious business. It reminded me of the news reports about people hundreds of miles away getting the cops to send a SWAT team to someone's house as a prank. Some prank.

It wouldn't work on me, because the police knew me. And Oak Grove didn't have a SWAT team.

They'd have to call the Sheriff's Department, who would check in with the police. Nope, that was one thing I didn't have to worry about.

But what if I'd become the target of a twisted internet game? There were too many strange occurrences with me being the common factor. There was one way to find out, and it would require me to do what I did best. Research.

I didn't remember the last time I'd searched for myself. Probably back in my college days. As I stared at the empty search field, I tried to figure out keywords eliminating any news reports on my recent adventures and came up blank. It might be easier to put in my name and skip the first ten pages of results.

But my logical habits wouldn't let me do that. Instead, I scanned the highlights of each listing, eliminating the obvious. On page three, I discovered a woman who shared my name. Or did I share hers? She was ten years older than me and a kindergarten teacher.

Driven by curiosity, I tried to find out as much as possible about her. Had my parents known her? Were we related? According to those shady internet address sites, she'd always lived in the Pacific Northwest. Sure, I had access to an official law enforcement database that might give me more information, but ethics didn't allow me to use it for personal reasons.

It made me wonder if she was having problems, too. I didn't have rights to the local databases for her current residence, but newspapers are a treasure trove of information. I checked every police blotter I could find for her city going back several months for her name and came up empty. That was a good thing. I wasn't responsible for ruining someone else's life.

The two genealogy sites I checked didn't tie our families together. The name thing seemed only to be a coincidence. There was that word again.

The alarm on my laptop dinged to remind me of the time. I hated giving up. Shoot, I'd barely scratched the surface. But I couldn't stop yawning. The sooner I went to sleep, the quicker the morning would come. I feared what tomorrow might bring.

❄ ❄ ❄

Monday arrived full of promise. Warm sunshine, brilliant blue skies, a few wispy clouds drifting along the horizon. From the distance came the laughter of children as they headed off to school. The perfect time for me to survey the outside of the house for damage and clues.

The recycling bin lay on the ground, tipped over, but it had been empty. If it hadn't been for Lando seeing someone in the recording, I would have suspected another raccoon. Trails of footprints led away from the flower garden by the front porch, but all the plants survived.

None of it mattered. I was a ship blown off course with my anchor ripped away.

A police car slowed as it drove past the house. I

didn't know whether to be comforted or worried. The sun's glare on the car's windows kept me from identifying the driver, but I waved to acknowledge their presence.

The research for Eli's weekly report waited for me. I wasn't in a rush to get to it. How much had changed in a mere seven days? I almost choked on my last sip of coffee. Everything had changed for me.

I tried a different tactic to find out what was going on in the security world. The internet hosts numerous sites where people discuss current rumors and news. Fresh security breaches, the latest companies to get hacked, the newest scams. The alternate would give Eli a fresh view of what was happening and give me a chance to check out the scuttlebutt surrounding happenings in DC.

By the time I hit the fourth forum, it became clear I'd picked the wrong week for creativity, with nothing exciting going on. Which was good for the computer world and bad for my attention span. It wouldn't hurt, I decided, to go back to my place for an hour or two and work on the bedroom. That also gave me a chance to park the Charger out front when I got back. I was tired of taxis.

I started with a quick stop by the store to pick up cleaning supplies. And stopped again at one convenience store for a doughnut and another to top off the gas tank. Although I traveled in a zigzag, there was a method to my madness.

Anyone following me would stick out among the light traffic. The only car that did was a rundown green pickup. It belonged to old Mr. Wesley. I'd run into his wife a time or two and imagined her calling him with a new errand after each stop.

I parked the Charger in the garage to hide it. Out of force of habit, I tucked a doggie treat from the container on the shelf into my pocket. That was foolish, because Piper was still with Joe and Luke in Pittsburgh. I missed giving him his morning loving. It didn't feel like coming home without it.

Which reminded me I needed to call later to give them my best thoughts before the procedure. Which, in turn, reminded me to water their plants and check on the African violet. Right after I carried my bags of supplies up the stairs, counting as I went. The number never changed, but it was part of my ritual.

Before unlocking the door, I checked for the piece of transparent tape I'd placed near the top. It was still there. Just an added way to help my peace of mind. Still, I nestled Betsy in my palm before opening the door as a precaution.

A quick glance assured me that everything was in place, except for the afghan on the easy chair. It had slipped off and ended up puddled on the floor. I must have bumped it on my way out the other day.

A hurried tour of the apartment assured me everything else remained in its place. Except for the bedroom. And it wasn't in as bad of shape as I remembered. Had Doris snuck in and started cleaning it while I tidied up elsewhere?

After locking the front door, I used the inside stairs to get to Joe and Luke's part of the house. A quick sweep assured everything of theirs remained untouched. I'd been worried the vandal would mess with them since he couldn't get to me, but my fear seemed unfounded.

Joe had left a jug of water near the plants, so watering them was a breeze. The African violet showed signs of new growth, and I breathed a sigh of relief that it would survive. Maybe things were finally turning around for me.

Hidden behind the curtain covering the picture window in their front room, I tracked a police car roll past the house. If I turned off my phone, there'd be no way to track me. If I added minutes to my stashed burner cell, I could hide for a week or more. Or longer, depending upon my current supply of cash. The vandal hadn't found it, tucked in a crevice of my closet.

I wondered how to plant a false trail. Reserve a hotel room halfway between here and Eli's home in Florida, then head north instead. Buy a cheap car with cash, then run it on the temporary tags for as long as it was legal. Would Jake help?

As I climbed the interior stairs to my apartment, I pondered the possibilities. It could be done, but not easily. But what would it accomplish? Would the vandal get right back to business when I returned?

A month wandering and sightseeing sounded like fun, but it wouldn't be fair to my friends. They'd worry about me. At least, I hoped they would.

My phone buzzed, shaking me from my reverie. To my disappointment, Freddie's name showed up on the screen, not Eli's.

"Hey, Freddie."

His voice was taut. "Where are you?"

"My place. Cleaning. Why?"

"A neighbor reported they spotted someone moving around downstairs. Stay where you are. I'm on the way."

"That would be me. I was watering the plants." My sneaking skills needed work.

"You shouldn't be there alone."

"I can't hide forever, Freddie."

He swore softly. "I'm on my way. No arguments."

The coffee was ready by the time he arrived. I put a stack of napkins on the table to protect its surface because I hadn't found my coasters yet. As normal, he drank his black.

"You've done a lot of work," he said after a few swallows, breaking the uncomfortable silence. "What was so urgent you had to be here today?"

"The bedroom isn't clean, yet. I saved it for last." I'd made a small dent in the cleaning needed while waiting for him. "But I can handle it. That's not why I agreed to have you come. I want to hear about the progress in the investigations."

He set his cup on top of a napkin. "You are aware of the limits of the department's resources."

That was all I needed to hear. "You've got nothing."

His eyes met mine, and he shook his head. "We've got nothing. All we have are dead ends."

"Not even any ideas?"

"We've got lots of ideas, but none of them are panning out. Hell, we have guys tracking down everyone busted because of you to make sure they're still in prison. And they are, so far."

"That doesn't eliminate their associates." How many of them had friends of friends? But that didn't feel right either. A criminal wouldn't be toying with me. "Joe suggested this was a twisted game but I've been unable to find any evidence to back that theory."

"The Chief assigned Hunt to track that down. Turns out he's got some sharp computer skills. Not as good as yours, but he doesn't have as much experience either."

"And?"

"And nothing. Just another dead end."

This was a direct challenge to my reputation. I had to show up the newbie. "I'm still searching. Haven't given up yet. The problem is how scattered the incidents are. I can't concentrate on just one thing. You know the inro they found here? I don't even have a picture of it to trace where it came from."

"I'll check if Hunt worked that angle."

"That's my point." I twisted a napkin until it tore into pieces.

Freddie picked up his coffee but didn't take a drink. "The department doesn't have the resources to do any more than we are. The consensus is we're letting you down."

I suspected not everyone felt that way. A few people on the force still had their doubts about me, figuring I'd sidestepped the charges brought against me back when I was accused of drug trafficking. No matter how much the Chief and Freddie trusted me, I'd never sway the holdouts.

"Is there any chance of getting the State Police and their resources involved?"

"With the state-wide budget cuts, their assistance is limited. The incidents don't rise to a level that's considered important."

As much as I hated it, I had to agree. Which left me where I'd started. Nowhere.

Chapter 9

"How?" I wailed, kneeling next to a rosebush, cradling a broken stem in my ungloved hand. Its leaves were brown and curling, like many of the leaves still on the plant. So much for having a good day.

M.J., one of the town's master gardeners, crouched by another bush. The fading daylight didn't camouflage the damage. "Have you put down any weed and feed on the lawn in the past few days?"

Eli and I had discussed it, but I hadn't gotten around to hiring someone to do the work. "No. Why?"

He didn't answer. Instead, he got up, walked to the edge of the garden, placed his hands on his hips and crunched up his mouth. As short as he was, and with his long silver beard, he resembled a gnome. "You know what this looks like?" he asked.

If I did, I wouldn't have called him. "What?"

"There's an old weed killer—not on the market anymore—that kills foliage like this. Come here."

I thought I'd seen enough damage, but I joined him. He pointed towards the center row and waved his finger back and forth.

"See the pattern of the dead leaves? That's not natural. If this was a fungus, it would be scattered throughout the garden. This looks more like someone deliberately sprayed the plants. But they didn't have time to do a thorough job, just a quick dash down the one row."

It seemed obvious once he pointed it out.

"But why would anyone do this?" he asked.

I knew the answer. Another way to hurt me. But I didn't share the information. "Will the roses survive?"

He took a thoughtful breath. "Depends upon what chemical they used. We can keep an eye on them for a few days, but there's a couple that have me worried. It might be easier to replace them right away. Luckily, none of the heirloom plants got damaged."

He'd helped design the layout of the garden and knew it better than me. That's why I'd called him. "You're the expert."

"Who's got something against you, Harmony?" he asked abruptly.

If I had the answer, my life would be so much easier.

There was still time to make the weekly self-defense class. I decided the hell with it and took the Charger. I parked in front of the storefront that hosted the course under the brightest streetlight possible. If someone wanted to mess with me, at least the other women in the class wouldn't be hurt. Thalia hadn't shown up, and the buzz said her car was still missing.

The night's lesson appeared to have been created with me in mind. More street fighting than style, we flailed away at various dummies, trying to knock off the loosely attached targets on their arms and legs. The perfect excuse for me to take out my anger on a non-human target.

The more I released my aggression, the angrier I got. It wasn't the way I wanted to live my life, in fear and always looking over my shoulder. The time had come to take my life back. I was angry but not broken.

"Anyone hear about a big event tonight?" Joan called from the rear door, which she'd opened to allow some cooler air to creep into the workout room. "Traffic is crazy."

A big event on a Monday? Not likely. It didn't matter to me, anyway. Sweat rolled down my forehead as I landed another punch on the manikin, but didn't knock off the small ball attached by velcro.

A wadded-up towel hit me on the arm. "Take a break, get a drink of water." Tim, our instructor, ordered. "You're tired and sloppy."

I didn't argue. After getting a cup of water from the cooler, I stood and stared out the front window. The mirror-like coating assured that no one could see in. Traffic was heavier than normal, especially for as late as it was. I recognized a few of the vehicles as belonging to local college kids. Which seemed odd. It wasn't Spring Break, and they should have been home working on their papers or other classwork. Still, everyone seemed to be following the traffic laws and driving safely. The only annoying part, beyond the sheer amount of traffic, came from the volume of the music coming from their speakers. It was loud enough to rattle the front window as an especially noisy car rolled by.

Two other ladies, sisters, joined me at the window. Both were widowed and on the crotchety side. "Looks more like a Saturday than a Monday," the older sister pointed out.

"Was there some kind of game tonight?" the younger one asked. "I hate traffic after high school games."

"Not on a Monday. And not this time of year," I said. A car I'd seen earlier rolled by, distinguished by the dragon decal on its side window.

"Kids," snorted the older lady. "They have nothing better to do than drive around town making themselves a nuisance."

Instinct told me this wasn't a random happening. The roads out front and back weren't the normal route for kids to drag. Had there been an accident that forced a change in the traffic flow? But that didn't explain the number of cars out on a Monday. I didn't like it. It felt like trouble.

Only a few of the ladies still tackled the assigned exercises. I caught Tim shaking his head at the number of cell phones being dug out of purses.

"Got it!" Joan half-shouted, staring at her cell

phone's screen. "My son said there's a block party going on down at Main Street and Central. People are coming from all over. He says he's even seen posts by kids from Pittsburgh. The cops are rerouting traffic."

Which explained why I hadn't seen a single cop car cruise by. Everyone on duty was probably assigned to crowd control. It was also the perfect opportunity for me to mingle with and eavesdrop on unsuspecting partygoers. Not as me, of course.

I made do with bits and pieces of my wardrobe and old Halloween costumes stored in Joe and Luke's basement. A black t-shirt and jeans, black short boots, and a long black wig to complete the ensemble. I topped it off with a blue jean jacket that didn't match but had an interior pocket to stash Betsy in.

My makeup was as simple as I could get away with. I knew how to make myself look older, looking younger was a challenge I hadn't conquered. But in the dim light cast by streetlights, my disguise didn't need to be perfect.

By making a right-hand turn on a green light, I slipped the Charger into the traffic flow at the west end of town. I planned to make three or four circuits, so people became used to seeing the car. It would take at least that long to get lucky enough to find a parking spot, anyway.

It also gave me time to get a feel for the crowd. Sure, some people were drinking, and I spotted one or two smoking something other than tobacco, but everyone was having fun. No one seemed to care about the heavy, slow-moving traffic. The guys were too busy flirting with the girls to complain, and the girls flirted right back. I even earned a few hollers, 'Hey, girl!' and reciprocated with the appropriate waves and smiles.

This wasn't a crowd I'd expect to know about the bad things happening to me. But down in the barricaded section of town were a few bars that attracted a less-gentile crew for normal business. They became my destination.

I found a parking spot six blocks from the center of the party. Even this far out, I picked up the faint beat of loud music. I shared the sidewalk with other people headed in and out of the area.

The music and other noise got louder the closer I made it to the closed-off street. I trailed behind a group of three guys and two girls. From their conversation, I figured out they'd seen a post about the party on a social website and made the trip up from Pittsburgh to check it out. It seemed a long way to come based on a rumor.

But that told me they weren't the people I needed to follow. I stopped to buy a can of soda from a stand a couple of kids set up in front of their house. A little farther down the street, other kids sold popcorn. I gave them five dollars but didn't take a bag.

The house band from Terry's Bar and Grill had set up in the street. They weren't really a band, just a bunch of guys who hung out together and played covers. Anyone who wanted to was free to jam with them, but nobody ever wanted to. Which was too bad, because they were decent musicians for amateurs. I hung around and listened to them awhile, but the music was loud enough that people weren't trying to hold conversations over it. That defeated my purpose in being there.

I pushed my way through the crowd to get into Terry's. Some noise would be blocked, and I'd have a better chance of eavesdropping. The bar was packed solid, and the lone bartender couldn't keep up. I hoped he'd get the tips he deserved for putting out drinks faster than I thought possible.

Terry's held the honor of being the 'edgy' bar in town. The one people went to when they wanted to believe they were living on the wild side, but fooling no one but themselves. Sure, the place garnered its share of police reports for drug sales and scuffles, but most nights it ran to the quiet side. The brightly colored streamers and 'Happy Birthday' sign dangling from the wall didn't appear out of place and explained a lot. Someone had planned a party and lost control.

It took only a few minutes to figure out this wasn't the crowd I needed either. They were discussing the baseball game on the big screen on the back wall and the prospects for the Pirates. I hung out for a few minutes to make myself inconspicuous, then left.

And almost ran into Bo Hunt, the rookie, as he talked to a group of smiling local college kids. I recognized them from the days they spent in the library. But I didn't want them to see me and blow my cover, so I crossed the street to avoid them. He didn't need me to back him up.

Across the street was The Red Door. Local legend told of how it got its start in the days of Prohibition. Now it drew a rough crowd, and I'd only been in it once, on a first and only date before I met Jake. Even though I'd been with someone, it hadn't stopped a few of the regulars from hassling me.

But with all the extra people, I wasn't sure what to expect. Would the regulars slink away to a different bar to avoid the tourists or cluster together?

I followed two college-aged guys inside. They paused, looked around, and headed back outside. I took the lone empty stool at the bar next to a middle-aged biker type and planted the soda can in front of me.

"You can't bring outside drinks in here," the bartender growled.

"It's empty. How about giving me a beer to replace it?"

"Light?"

I arched an eyebrow. "Did I ask for swamp water?"

That earned me the shadow of a grin. The guy beside me chuckled into his own mug of beer.

The pour was short and the head too tall when the mug was put in front of me, but I didn't complain. I took a swallow and wiped the foam off my lips with the back of my hand. The biker seemed to approve.

"What brings you here, honey?"

Not bad for an opening line. "Kid sister wanted to check out the party. 'Course, she ditched me as soon as we got here."

He nodded and returned his attention to his beer, a lager. I did the same. I'd passed the test but failed to attract his interest. That worked well for my plan. I wanted to be free to listen to other conversations instead of focusing on one person.

But the gossip centered on the strangers that popped into the bar only to quickly leave. Oddly, the biker didn't take part in the gossiping, though he appeared to be paying attention to it. He didn't fit in with the regulars but didn't look like he belonged with the crowd outside either. I wondered if he picked the wrong night to visit Oak Grove. He was a puzzle I couldn't solve, so I kept my head down and focused on my beer. The first and the second. The flavor got better the more of it I drank, a signal that I'd had enough and it was time to go.

Something about the biker bothered me. The way he'd glance at me and then fiddle with his phone. The more I studied him, the more I decided something was off. What biker dyes his hair and his beard? Although the beard didn't quite look real. The tattoo on his bicep was either a bad job or fake and fading. I left a too-large tip and returned to the party outside, still going strong. A bunch of locals strolled by and I slipped in ahead of them, using them as cover.

But only as far as the end of the block. I peeled away from them and mingled with a group standing on the corner. It gave me a chance to check my trail. Sure enough, the biker stood by The Red Door, looking up and down the street.

I stuck to the alleys to return to the Charger. No one followed.

Chapter 10

The next morning, I checked out of my room at The Towers. It didn't make any sense to stay. I didn't feel any safer there than anywhere else.

On the way back to my place, I stopped for a cinnamon roll. I needed to restock my cupboards and indulge in an entire day of cooking to refill my freezer. But first I had to make my bedroom livable again.

I unlocked the door after double-checking the tape remained in place. I set the roll on the kitchen table and started a pot of coffee, then picked the afghan up from the floor. It was becoming a habit.

From the doorway, I studied the bedroom. I'd gotten more done than I thought. A couple of hours' worth of work for the finishing touches and I'd be able to move back in. At least until I tackled the painting. I pulled up the classic rock playlist on my music player and started to work.

Mid-morning, I stopped to eat the roll and check email. And messages, to see if Eli had tried to reach me. He hadn't.

I considered my options. Hang here and do nothing. Normally the safe option. Normally. Hop into the Charger and make a quick trip to D.C. to check up on Eli. Make sure he hadn't been kidnapped by some organization that wanted to use his skills for their own nefarious purposes. But I didn't even know where he was staying. Call his secretary, Darla, and see if she would tell me his location. But she wouldn't. Tell me, that is. I didn't know where to even start looking for him in D.C. Or if he was in D.C. at all. He could be anywhere.

I settled for sending him a message. *"Missing you."* That would be enough.

❊ ❊ ❊

I cringed as the total on the checkout screen kept rising. Replacing all the seasonings at once turned out to be more expensive than I'd budgeted for. Another reminder of the damage done.

At least I'd sleep in my bed tonight. I also bought rubber doorstops. They were low-level security but effective. Even if someone picked the lock, they'd supply an additional obstacle for anyone trying to break in.

When I pushed my full cart out to the parking lot, I had a moment of panic when I didn't spot Dolores. Then laughed at myself, because I'd driven the Charger. It had more room for all the bags than Dolores did, and I was glad for a moment. Then sad, because I was cheating on my dear friend.

The roar of a motorcycle barely scratched the

surface of my thoughts, only background noise. I glanced its way when the bike rolled by as I pushed my cart into the corral. I paid a little more attention when the biker parked in the empty spot beside the Charger. And I paid a lot of attention when the rider pulled off his helmet and revealed himself to be the same guy from the bar.

Head down, and angled away from him, I pretended to be busy with my phone. In reality, I kept my eyes on him. He glanced at the Charger before heading into the store. It all seemed coincidental.

As I drove away, I reminded myself I don't believe in coincidence.

After hauling the groceries upstairs, I dug my magic wand—the device I used to check for 'bugs' in my apartment—out of the closet. I wasn't sure the technology would work on cars, but it was worth a shot.

To avoid prying eyes, I moved the Charger into the garage. The tight space made things harder, but I knelt on the floor and waved the device across the undercarriage, listening for an out-of-place beep. I'd seen a tracker only once, but at least I had an idea of what to look for.

After a lot of getting up and down and crawling on the floor, I decided the wand didn't work anymore. Either that or there wasn't a GPS unit on the car, other than the one that came installed from the manufacturer. If someone had access to the rental company's computer system, they didn't need their own. Jake had taught me how to disable that if I wanted to. But that didn't explain the random beeps my detection wand put out during the examination.

I leaned against the garage door frame and blew out a deep breath of frustration, wishing for Eli to show up and show me what I'd missed. With the wand in my hand, absentmindedly clicking the on-off switch, I studied the car. If I only had a few seconds, where would I put a magnetic device?

The obvious choice, the bumpers, wouldn't work because they were plastic. A tracker wouldn't stay attached to roof for long and could be easily spotted. Without the key, under the hood was inaccessible. That left the fenders.

It didn't matter which of the four I started with, I'd be wrong. So, I started with the one closest to me, the rear right. I didn't get a reaction from my tester, but I leaned over to eyeball underneath to double-check. Nothing. I moved up to the front right side. It was cramped and dark, and the wand didn't go off. I called it good and returned to the back.

The mental coin I flipped landed on tails. That meant the back. Halfway around the fender, the wand beeped—softly, but not my imagination. I ran the wand around again and got another beep, louder this time.

On my knees again, I ran my hands under the fender until they bumped into an obstacle—a clod of dirt. I tossed it outside, tried again and came up with the prize—a small black box attached to the car with a magnet. It wasn't labeled and had no telltale sign of an owner.

Now I'd found the device, I didn't know what to do with it. Attach it to some random car to throw off whoever was tracking me? What would happen if an innocent person got hurt? Toss it in the garbage? The weekly pickup was in the morning. That might be good for a few laughs. In the end, I left it in the garage. It would continue to send out its signals, and I didn't have to worry about it. At some point, they'd figure out I'd found it, but hopefully, it would confuse them for a few days.

I'd accomplished something. After patting the Charger's trunk, I closed and locked the garage door.

❀ ❀ ❀

The big screen at Eli's house had spoiled me. Either that or I needed new glasses. Snug in my little apartment, I felt safe again. Safe enough to put on my headphones while I worked on the weekly report for Eli. I needed to finish it before he got back from his meeting.

Truthfully, it bothered me that he hadn't contacted me. No matter how I tried to justify his silence, I couldn't convince myself everything was all right. I wondered if everyone else in his life worried as much as me, or was I overreacting?

With the push of a button, I sent the report off to his email. He'd get it when he got it. Now, I could work on my research again without guilt.

I didn't want a repeat of my earlier work, so I added in a new search term-game. I might find a lot of nonsense, or I might find nothing. If I started with low expectations, I wouldn't be crushed if I didn't find anything.

Garbage. I ended up with pure garbage. Ads for every game ever popped up on my screen. I waded through a few of the pages of results, then gave up.

But only temporarily. Long enough to use the interior staircase and verify that Joe and Luke's part of the house was locked. I turned on two lights to create the appearance they were home. The illusion of their presence made me feel safer. My door was securely locked with the rubber bumpers slid under it as far as they would go, the curtains closed, and my lights dimmed to make it seem I'd gone to bed.

I was about to break a rule, and I wanted no interruptions. Or witnesses. The plot was unethical at best and illegal at its worst. I planned to use my access to the Oak Grove Police Department's records for personal gain.

Over a year ago, I'd accidentally discovered my login to the records gave me more access than it should. I was only supposed to get to aggregate statistics. Instead, I had the rights to pull up every record. I'd mentioned it to the Chief once. As far as I knew, he'd never requested a change. Frankly, I'd forgotten about it. Until the other day, when I mentioned to Freddie about needing a picture of the inro. He hadn't remembered to send me a copy of the picture, but I didn't need him. I'd get it myself.

I was entitled to a copy of the report about the break-in, anyway. If I went through official channels, it would take several days. My plan didn't include waiting that long.

After closing all my browser tabs, I opened a new one and switched into incognito mode. From there, I opened one of my favorite proxy sites. It would take an expert to track my on-line maneuvers. I'd have to log into the database as myself, but that couldn't be helped. It wouldn't be questioned by anyone but the Chief. *If* he happened to hear about it. He was already mad at me, at least that's what it felt like since he hadn't reached out to me.

I pulled up my case first. It took only seconds to locate and download the picture I needed. I avoided looking at all the other images; the ones showing all the damage and destruction. I didn't want those memories flooding my brain.

Next, I pulled up the report on the Cookes' burglary. I got the picture of their inro, too. Somehow, the incidents tied together, and I needed to find out how. Maybe I could solve both in one shot since the police hadn't been able to.

Out of curiosity, I pulled up Thalia's report and was surprised to read that her car had finally been located and retrieved, still in running condition. All it needed was gas. But the good feeling was short-lived as I wondered why I hadn't been told.

No one pounded on my door demanding I open up and turn off the computer, so I kept going. I searched for anything that seemed out of the ordinary for our quiet little town. I remembered Freddie's statement about someone else needing attention, but couldn't find any trace of those reports.

Last night's party seemed to be the only extraordinary event. My guess was correct. A post on social media about the birthday party for a local guy turning twenty-one had gone viral and people flooded into town. The police, realizing there was no way to stop it, had set up the roadblocks to contain and control it. There'd been some underage drinking, a few reports of drug use, but overall, the plan had worked and no one got hurt.

On paper, the explanation seemed logical. I didn't believe it. But there wasn't a way for me to prove it bogus. It took extra time, but I re-read the report, looking for any additional hints about what really went down, expecting to find nothing.

I even read the scanned raw notes from the officers who worked the event. That's where I found gold. Or bronze, at least. One line, that I didn't understand, stood out in Hunt's handwritten report. "Made contact with Dawson."

I sat back in my chair and stared at the ceiling. Who the hell was Dawson? No one by that name was on the force. Possibly he was an informant, but was Dawson a first or last name? And why did it seem familiar?

I'd puzzle over it later. I had what I needed and was pushing my luck. Time to turn my attention to tracking down the fake inro.

Chapter 11

It didn't take long to locate five museums close by that sold the fake inro. To track the one left in my apartment was impossible. I also discovered the manufacturer, but with the company located overseas, it turned into a dead-end, like every other lead.

I sat back in my chair, took off my glasses, and rubbed my eyes. What was I missing? I didn't have anyone to discuss the case with. To protect them, I'd walled myself away from all my friends.

It was late, but I didn't feel like going to bed. I turned off the laptop, grabbed a coat from the closet, and slipped Betsy into its pocket. I unlocked the door, pried the rubber blocks from under it, and tucked them in a corner. A walk would help to clear my head.

The dark enhanced the peacefulness of Oak Grove. Dogs barked in the distance, and the muted sound of cars dragging a street proved someone besides me was still awake. The night chill made me zip up my coat partway. A stray tear trickled down my cheek, and I swiped it away. I wouldn't cry.

A motorcycle's revving engine caught my attention, and I slunk into the shadow of a large oak tree to hide. I didn't want anyone to see me.

The biker roared down the street and turned a corner. I lost sight of him, and the rumble ceased when he cut the engine. The only people in the neighborhood who rode lived down the block, the opposite direction from where this biker had gone. Curiosity got the best of me.

From shadow to shadow I slid, backtracking my earlier path. I stopped at the corner to scope out the situation. He'd parked between two cars and was talking on his phone. Only fragments of his conversation reached me. Something about 'lights on' and 'home.'

I wondered whose house he was casing and pulled out my phone to call the non-emergency line for the police. I didn't have enough evidence the biker planned to break into someone's house to dial 911, but they might send out an extra patrol. He hadn't spotted me, so I decided to monitor him while figuring out my next move.

While still on the phone, he dug into his saddlebag and pulled out a pair of binoculars. He raised them to his eyes. Who he was spying on? Had a curvaceous woman left her shades up as she got ready for bed? The police received occasional calls about a peeping tom and catching him would look good on an officer's resume.

I inched closer, trying to get a better vantage point and hear more of what he was saying.

"The curtains are closed. I can't see if she's there or not."

The back of my neck tingled. From the angle his head tilted, I drew a straight line. It ended at my bedroom window.

I patted my pocket, seeking the minimal comfort that Betsy provided.

"I'll move around to the other side," the biker said. "For all the good it will do. I can't cover every door from one spot. If she suspects she's being watched, she could sneak out, and I'd never know. But I'm betting she's tucked in for the night."

He had to be talking about me.

"I haven't spotted the car, but it might be in the garage."

He didn't mention which car, Dolores or the Charger.

"Yeah, I'll check. Anything else I should be on the lookout for, Chief?"

Chief? Did I catch that right? My first reaction was to confront the man and demand his identification. Was he working for one of the three-letter agencies and reporting to Chief Sorenson? He wasn't a local. That would explain why the chief had gone silent. And here I'd thought he was mad at me because I turned down his job offer.

My second instinct was to wait and learn more. Maybe it wasn't Chief Sorenson he worked for, but someone else with the title. Or just a nickname.

The entire time, he'd had his back to me. But

when he returned the binoculars to his saddlebag, I got a glimpse of his face. I shouldn't have been surprised.

It was the biker from the bar. Or rather, the fake biker. Or the biker faking to be something else. Had he recognized me? If he did, he hid it well. Until I knew the whole story, I'd treat him as a threat. And a suspect.

He shoved his cell phone into his vest pocket and, with a move made easy by practice, swung his leg over the bike's seat. If he wasn't an actual biker, he still rode regularly. Another piece of the puzzle. But where did it fit?

I waited until he drove away to release my breath, then followed the sound of the bike until he found his new place to park. Based on his conversation, I guessed he parked in a spot to watch the front of the house. Not wanting to count on it, I plotted a new path home. It took me through alleys and backyards. The riskiest part would be making sure I stayed out of his range of vision.

The path nearly doubled my return trip, but I didn't have a schedule. I slithered through a gauntlet of streets, alleys, and sidewalks, stopping each time a vehicle passed, hoping to stay unnoticed. I ended up half a block from home, facing the front of the house. All I'd run into were garbage cans and stray cats. I hoped they were cats, anyway. The raccoon didn't make an appearance.

I expected to find the biker in the alley, using it as cover. That's what I would have done. He wasn't there or in front of the house. Where was he?

The complication wore on my fading patience, but I didn't want to give up. If he parked on the side street with a view of the garage and the back gate, I wouldn't be able to spot him. The extra time I needed to get to a new vantage spot was worth the effort to screw with him.

Back down the alley to where it met the next street I went, dodging the same obstacles. I trekked the street to the corner, and from behind a telephone pole, peered towards the house. Still no sign of him or his bike. Had he given up his post already? I didn't believe it.

Unless he'd parked in Mrs. Axcel's driveway. Her house had been demolished after the fire, and only a decaying garage and an empty lot remained. If he parked in the garage's shadow, he'd be hard to spot unless I stood in front of the lot. Obviously, that wasn't in my playbook.

Temptation struck me. If I snuck down one more block and cut through the unfenced yards, I'd end up behind the garage. Turn the hunter into the hunted. Put me in the perfect position to sneak up and scare him. Or hold him at gunpoint and demand he tell me his mission. But, the night at the bar, I'd noticed the bulge under his left arm and suspected he carried. A gun, that is. Surprising him could end badly.

Instead, I tromped through other yards and a different alley, so I ended up on the side of the house away from the street. By entering the house through the basement, and taking the inside stairs all the way to the third floor, I'd get to my apartment without anyone knowing I'd been gone. That was my escape route, too. Until he proved different, the biker was an enemy.

Thank heavens I'd left a few lights on, and I didn't have to navigate through Joe and Luke's part of the house in total darkness. I detoured to the kitchen and its street-facing window to try to spot the biker. It had a better view of his suspected hiding place than any of the windows in my apartment. A car drove by at the perfect moment to reveal the bike sitting where I'd predicted it would be, but without its rider.

I stepped back and waited for my eyes to adjust to the semi-darkness, found an angle where the window didn't work as a mirror, then looked again. A shadow moved, and there he was, leaning against the corner of the garage. I almost felt sorry for him. If he planned to stand there the entire night, he'd be cold and tired long before the sun came up. Not quite the perfect revenge, but not bad.

Still, his presence made me restless and unable to sleep. If I called in a report to the police, I'd lose the slim advantage I'd gained in discovering his existence. Like a little kid staying up late to read, I made a blanket fort in my bedroom and surfed the internet until the battery in my laptop died. Then, finally, I fell asleep.

❆ ❆ ❆

I followed my morning routine—coffee, shower, sit on the steps and read the paper—but the simple joy had disappeared. The biker was gone, but he wasn't the problem. No, I still hadn't heard from Eli.

No requests for reports or research, not even a text to say hi. I missed him.

But he was more than my lover, he was my boss. Even if I didn't have a new assignment from him, I still had research to do. The topic was up to me. I could do it anywhere with an internet signal, but I chose to stick with my routine and go to the library. If the biker showed up, I'd know and could keep an eye on him while he kept an eye on me.

With no excuse to build a wall of books, I took a chair in the periodicals area. With the setup of the room, I'd be able to watch anyone coming or going from it. There'd be no sneaking up on me.

At least, that was true as far as the public knew. There was a secret way in and out. Out mostly, because it was hard to slide the last set of shelves from the backside to get in. But I wouldn't have to worry about getting stuck with no escape route.

Late morning, tired of lists and analysis of security vulnerabilities, I strolled through the stacks of the second floor to stretch my legs and give my eyes a break. I leaned against the balcony railing to survey the reading room below and gaze through the windows on the far wall.

That's when I spotted him—or not. It was hard to tell from the angle. Plus, he didn't look like a biker anymore. He'd adopted the persona of a frazzled businessman. White short-sleeved shirt, black pants, he looked like he came from the fifties. The beard was gone, too. I couldn't get a good look at his face, but the hint of a tattoo peeking out from under the sleeve of his shirt gave him away.

From the second floor, there wasn't a good place to study him further without exposing my presence. If I stood on the steps, I'd have a better chance, but they squeaked. If he looked up at just the right moment, he'd see me. I suppose it didn't matter; he knew I was in the library. So, how to mess with him?

Chapter 12

In the end, it was too easy. He knew I was in the library, so I didn't hide from him. And he wasn't familiar with the layout of the floors, which gave me an advantage.

I went down the stairs near the front entrance, so his back was toward me. With my phone in hand, I followed a path that wound through the tables and returned to the periodical room. In the process, I got several pictures of the man. Side shots, but enough of his face to assure me that, yes, he was the biker. Or his doppelganger.

That ended my illusion that he worked for one of the three-letter agencies. He wasn't good enough at disguising himself. It also moved him higher on the list of potential bad guys. But it didn't give me any clues as to why he was following me. It wasn't like I could ask him.

I couldn't eavesdrop on him, either. Not that he was talking to anyone. He pretended to read a paper out of New York while watching for me. Or waiting for me to leave the magazine area. But I wasn't there anymore. I was on the second floor, keeping an eye on him, having exited the secret way.

I wanted a full face shot to use for an internet search. The problem lay in capturing it without him noticing.

The arrival of a small group of our local firefighters in uniform saved me. They'd started to show up for story hour more often. Sometimes they even read to the kids instead of Danielle, the children's librarian. The kids loved it, and it gave her a break. On the pretext of taking their photo, I got a picture of the biker.

Now I had to plan my escape, wanting to rush home without being followed and see what the almighty internet would reveal. I didn't want to do the research at the library, with curious eyes peeking at my screen. I'd parked the Charger out back and not in my usual spot, so I could sneak out the rear door. That was easy. But the possibility he'd attached another tracker to the car worried me.

I drove a few blocks to a convenience store, topped off the gas, and tested the air pressure in the tires. That gave me the opportunity to check under the fenders. A long shot, because no one would be dumb enough to hide a tracker in the same place twice, right? But there it sat, on a different fender. If my memory served me correctly, it was a different model. I'd compare it to the first one when I got home and start a collection. Using a metal fingernail file, I unscrewed the cover and removed the battery. Then I took the long way home, staying vigilant for any followers.

❋ ❋ ❋

The picture was another dead end. I'd hoped, but not too hard. The biker's generic features made it hard to make an exact match. Middle-aged white guy with a few extra pounds, thinning brown hair and brown eyes. I didn't find him, but I discovered lots of photos of male models in various poses and clothing, or lack of clothing. I normally wouldn't waste my time looking at those pictures when I had Eli to admire, but it was all in the name of research.

Mid-afternoon, I took a break from the hard work. First, I wandered through Joe and Luke's part of the house, making sure everything remained locked and secure. I turned some lights off and others on so a diligent observer would think the boys were home. I spent a few minutes weeding Luke's vegetable patch while checking for a familiar motorcycle.

Although I often noticed traffic going by, I'd never specifically listened for motorcycles. I didn't spot any, but there was a constant rumble of them not far off. Too bad access to the DMV files wasn't part of my police records rights. I wanted to find out just how many motorcycles were registered in Oak Grove and the county.

As I sat back on my heels to admire my work, my phone came to life with the opening bars of 'Dream a Little Dream', my ringtone for Eli. It took a few seconds to dig the phone out of my jean's pocket, but I answered before voice mail.

"Hey, Sweetie. Long time no hear."

"You're not mad at me, are you?"

I grinned, prepared to make him worry. "Let me think about it. It's been a week and a half, and we've only talked once. You've ignored my messages. Hell, you didn't even call the night there was an alarm at your house. You were ghosting me. Do I have the right to be annoyed?"

He took a minute to answer. "What alarm? Wait, I should save that for last, shouldn't I? First I need to tell you how much I miss you and how sorry I am for not letting you into my secret."

My grin grew bigger. "You're learning."

"I really did miss you. I kept turning to tell you something or get your opinion on what somebody said and when you weren't there, I felt empty. And then at night, when I finally got to bed, I wanted to hold you while we talked about the day. But the way the meeting was set up, I couldn't have shared anything with you, anyway."

"Are you going to tell me about it now?"

"No, because I'm getting ready to hop on a flight home and can't discuss it in public. But I want you to do me a favor, and head over to the house in a couple of hours. I'll call you when I land, and as soon as I get in the door, we can make a video call." He paused for a moment. "Unless you have other plans?"

He made it too easy. "I thought about dragging the strip with the teenagers and showing off Dolores. Or hitting up the Outlaw. You remember, the bar on the edge of the county? It's the perfect place to pick up a one-night stand."

"How do you know?" he sputtered, then caught his breath. "You're teasing me."

"Of course I am. My plans include a glass of wine and a new book." I needed to hit up the bookstore. My shelves looked empty between the books I put in my safe-deposit box and the ones I'd been unable to repair. "The only thing that would make it better would be having you to snuggle with."

"I'd like to make that happen."

In a way, I was glad he wasn't here. I could lie to him on the phone, but not in person. Not even a lie of omission. I counted to three. I predicted what came next.

"How about flying down here?" he asked.

Bingo! Too bad I hadn't placed a bet on his response. I panicked for a moment, because I didn't have a handy excuse not to go, and I hadn't told him about my fear of flying yet. I was spared by a boarding announcement.

"That's me!" Amid the background noise, I heard Eli fumbling with his carry-on. "I'll call you when I get home."

"I'll be waiting. Love you," I said.

"Love you too, Buttercup. Bye." Then he was gone.

I stood, stretched, and stuffed the phone back into my pocket. There were plans to make and things to do.

I had enough time for a quick trip to the bookstore, my cousin Jane's liquor store, and to pick up groceries. When I got to Eli's, the gardener I'd hired to replace the rose bushes was there, so my schedule got delayed. Then the chicken I bought to cook took longer than expected to prepare. The carefully planned image of a carefree woman sitting by the fireplace reading a book and sipping on a glass of wine vanished in the wind.

He called as I put the last of the dirty pans into the kitchen sink. I wiped my hands on a dishtowel before putting him on speaker. "Hey, sweetie, you're home!"

He chuckled. "Not exactly. I'm at the office. I'm too keyed up to relax and want to get in a couple of hours of work."

"So, is this a business or a personal call?" I needed to set my expectations.

"Both. But business first to get it out of the way. You're the first person I'm telling about this. I haven't even talked to Kris about it."

Kris was the company lawyer. Eli sharing his news with me first made me feel appreciated, like a partner. And that scared me. Eli had mentioned it once, making me a partner, not just an employee, but I didn't think he was serious.

I set the thought aside to pay attention to what he was saying.

"Fire up the video system. I want to watch your face in life-size scale when I tell you the story."

It only took a few minutes until we connected, him in his office, me in what I called the library. In the original floor plan, it had been the parlor. The screen wasn't as big as the one on the computer in the front, but the room had a more intimate atmosphere and I preferred it.

There wasn't a polite way to put it. Eli looked rough. Not as bad as being run over by a truck, but not good. The long hours showed in the circles under his eyes and the scruff of a beard.

"You're a sight for sore eyes, Buttercup," he said.

"I wish I could say the same for you. You look like you need several weeks of vacation on a tropical island."

"Only if you come with me." He tapped a stack of papers on his desks. "In the meantime, I made the mistake of telling Darla I'd be back in the morning and she left paperwork for me to do." He grinned. "Remind me to set you up with signing authority the next time I go on a trip."

I didn't know how to react, so I ignored his last statement. "What were you doing in DC, anyway?"

"Well, the conference was advertised as a government-sponsored event to list bids that would soon open. Instead, a vendor tried to sell their services to get us on the list for future openings. In other words, a waste of time for those who know how the process works. I wasn't the only person who left after the afternoon break on the first day."

His face lit up. "And that's when it got interesting. You know how I've worried about not being able to supply businesses with complete packages? My software has nothing to do with HR or inventory, right? But in the hotel restaurant, I ran into a couple of other people who had been at the conference. Guy named Fairwood, lady named Lapahie. We got to talking, and it turns out they have the same problem.

Only in their case, they support inventory and bookkeeping programs.

"We got along pretty well and decided to get together the next day to talk about solutions to shared problems instead of going home. I rented a small conference room at the hotel and we practically lived in it for the next week."

I still wasn't sure where this was headed so I muttered "uh-huh" and let him keep talking.

"We ended up hammering out a basic agreement for a coalition of sorts, where we recommend each other to the folks we do business with. Nobody pays and nobody gets paid to be part of the group. The benefit of participating is an increased customer basis. As far as I can tell, no one has ever done this. We're breaking new ground!"

I hated to burst his bubble, but it was part of my job. "That sounds like a wonderful concept, but you've worked hard on your reputation. Do you trust it to these people?"

Eli smiled. "That's where you come in. I'm sending you an email with details of what we want to set up and who's involved. I want you to do your magic and find everything you can on both the people and the companies."

Chapter 13

Eli knew the way to my heart. The list of companies and people to check out would keep me busy for a week or more. Exactly what I needed to distract me from my troubles.

Which I didn't share with him. Things had settled down. No more car chases, no more vandalism, my life was looking up. Except for the biker, and maybe he played for the good guys.

Besides, we were too busy discussing 'other things.' I dared him to grow his beard out for real. He dared me to cut my hair. Neither was likely to happen.

We talked about Joe's operation and how I worried about the obvious signs that both Joe and Luke would need additional help soon. About his parents' upcoming wedding anniversary—forty years! The crazy things happening during this year's Spring Break.

What we didn't discuss was another story. I didn't want to worry him. He had enough on his plate. Even as we talked, he shuffled through the papers in front of him.

Talking to Eli made me feel safer, but the longer we talked, the more likely I'd slip up and spill my secret. So, when he mentioned calling his mom, I said I needed to wash the rest of the dishes, and we made our goodbyes.

I was torn between starting the research for Eli or taking advantage of my new dose of courage. Courage won.

Keys in hand, Taylor stepped out of the house and climbed into the Charger. Her multi-hued hair stirred in the evening breeze. She'd added a superhero T-shirt under the plaid one. She wrapped her jacket around her a little tighter, eying the dark green motorcycle parked across the street from the end of the driveway. Not the expected one, so it might be a coincidence.

Right. I didn't believe in coincidence.

I wouldn't allow it to stop my plan to head to Terry's. The bar should be back to normal, and I wanted to mingle with the college kids who frequented the place. If anyone knew of any threats to me on the dark web, Terry's would be the logical spot to hear about it. Its history of drug dealing and one-night stands made it edgy enough to satisfy the rebels in the crowd, even though it had been mostly cleaned up. Rumor had it drugs still could be bought there, but anyone wanting to use them had to go out back.

When I pulled into the street, the motorcycle didn't follow me. In fact, there was no sign of its rider. Either it was a coincidence, or another tracker had been attached to the car. I assumed the latter and pulled into the empty parking lot of Lakeview Elementary school. I had the wand for checking for bugs in the trunk and ran a quick scan but got no beeps. Still, I took the long way, keeping my eye on the rear-view mirror, but no one came along for the ride.

Only newbies parked in front of Terry's, but there was plenty of parking out back. Like one of the cool kids, I grabbed a spot and entered through the rear door. I ordered a mango-flavored vodka and lime soda, knowing I'd hate it, but I'd done my homework and it was the thing to drink. I'd fake it as long as possible.

Two guys battled it out in a racing game, and I hovered at the edge of the small group watching them. I debated the merits of challenging the winner of the round but worried it was too soon. If I pretended not to know how to use the controls, that would give one of them the opportunity to teach me. Then invite me to sit with them after I lost spectacularly.

They were near the end of the course, and it didn't take long for one of them to win. They headed back to their table, but I hung around the game. I sat in an empty chair and fiddled with the steering wheel. Someone stood behind me, but I didn't turn around.

"You have to put money in to make it work," a man said, chuckling.

"No duh. I just wanted to get a feel for the controls. They look different from what I'm used to," I answered.

He slid into the other chair. "You any good?"

I turned toward him and shrugged. "Better than some, worse than others. You?" It only took a glance to size him up. Short brown hair, brown eyes, anime t-shirt, faded jeans. Nothing out of the ordinary, except for his facial piercings. Just his eyebrows and nose, so unusual for Oak Grove, but not too outlandish.

"Wanna play and see?"

"Sure."

He dropped some coins in the slot and I dug into my pocket and added a couple of quarters.

"Ready?"

"In a sec." I took my time choosing my car. The game was more of a simulator than a cartoon, and my competitive nature rose to the surface. "Let's start with an easy course so I can warm up." And sucker him in by letting him win one or two rounds.

He won the first round fairly. I made a couple of bad gear changes as I learned the reaction of the pedals. He also won the second round by a hair. But I could tell he was bored.

"Let's move up a couple of notches," I said. "I'm Taylor."

He picked a game smack in the middle of the scale. "Andy. You from here?"

"Nope. Just visiting relatives. My mother asked me to help drive. She went on about all the things to do here. I don't think she realized how far it is from Pittsburgh."

"It's not too bad once you get used to it. Hell, I head down three days a week for classes. You ready?"

"Ready." I counted as the lights flashed to green and let my foot off the brake. It was time to give him a run for his money.

By now, four guys stood behind us, watching us race. I stayed behind Andy's car as we made the first round of the track. We passed the start line, and I pulled ahead, then fell back. I kept that up for the entire lap. The third lap I let loose and left him in the proverbial dust, gunning my way past the finish line.

The group behind us cheered. Andy shook his head. "I didn't expect that." He looked around. "Somebody else want to take a shot?"

"Look out, loser," one guy said and moved into the chair Andy vacated. "I'll show you how it's done." He grinned. "I'm Jordan."

Jordan's wardrobe matched Andy's, but his hair was deep black. I wasn't sure if it was dyed or natural. Instead of piercings, he sported a tattoo on his neck. At least, that's the only one I could see.

"Let's make it more interesting." I dropped more quarters in the slot and chose a higher level. "Will that work?"

His smile broadened. "Let's do this."

He was good. Real good. But I had more real-life experience. The first game, I 'accidentally' missed a shift, and he won. Second game, I barely edged by him to the finish line. I thought he'd win. Third lap, everything he tried didn't work. The sharp curve he crashed on, I successfully maneuvered by feathering the gas pedal just right. The drawbridge I sped across rose as he reached it, and he faltered before making the jump. I felt bad for him. "Play again?" I asked, after he crashed for the second time as I zoomed over the finish line.

"Naw, the game gods aren't with me tonight." He checked out my long-empty glass. "Want another drink?"

"Sure. I need a break." They seemed like a good group of guys to hang with. None of them set off any warning bells.

Four college-age girls sat at one of the other tables. They seemed intent on ignoring the guys, although they cast sideways glances my way. I wondered if I'd messed up a carefully laid plan on their part to get the guys to hit on them. But those were high school tactics, and I didn't play by their rules. They needed to step up their game a notch or two. Under other circumstances, I'd be willing to mentor them.

But tonight was about getting accepted. Not as a girl, as one of the guys. No flirting needed.

I made progress. Oak Grove gossip flowed freely. Most of it concerned who among their friends was seeing who, the various college professors, and making fun of their parents. It was interesting seeing the rumor mill in action from a different perspective since I'd spent most of my college years out of town. My name never came up, but it was only one night. I'd do this again.

Leaving earlier than everyone else was part of the plan, too. I didn't want to overstay my welcome. The group was in deep conversation discussing the latest superhero movie and I was out of my element. I got a couple of 'See ya's' as I left, and that was good enough.

I checked for any motorcycles in the parking lot before climbing into the Charger but didn't spot any. In fact, I made it back to Eli's house without a hint of being followed. I counted the night as a win.

❊ ❊ ❊

Four different notebooks lay scattered on the floor around me. I had too much information and was unable to visualize how to arrange it in a spreadsheet. Not wanting to lose track of it, I made copious notes about what I'd found, including the websites, on paper, by hand. If I needed to, I'd be able to tack the pages to the wall and rearrange them until I had an outline. It was a good thing I'd stayed at Eli's house, with more wall space to work with.

I didn't find any documentation of an organization like Eli envisioned. There were lots of partnerships of two or three sister companies and plenty of small companies that existed under the umbrella of a larger corporation. But his concept was unique as far as I could find. No wonder he'd been so excited and so focused. I forgave him for ignoring me.

I gathered basic information on each of the companies listed in his email. With the boring part over, I devoted my efforts to finding the dirt on each of them. There had to be a bad side to all of them. How bad was the question.

Even with the perfect working conditions—peace and quiet, all the technology I could imagine at my fingertips, a handy supply of munchies—my concentration was incomplete. When would Eli call? I'd sent him one swift update on the project, enough, I hoped, to spark his interest. Then there was the deep red motorcycle parked on the side street.

I spotted it when I went outside to water the new rose bushes. The red caught my eye because it matched the color of one flower in full bloom. And, like yesterday, no rider was in sight. I didn't get it. That wasn't any way to run a surveillance operation.

It wasn't like I could call Freddie and report a legally parked motorcycle. My fear kept me on edge. It isn't paranoia if someone is out to get you. But paranoia guided my steps to the third floor.

Not for two seconds did I believe that someone had parked a bike in eyeshot of the house and just left it there. The additional height of the third story would give me a broader view of the neighborhood and anything or anyone that didn't belong.

We hadn't installed curtains on the third floor yet. That meant if anyone happened to be monitoring the top floor, they might see me. I figured the chances were slim since I hadn't been up there recently. At least they wouldn't be alerted by me turning any lights on as sunshine lit up the rooms.

The first window sat low, halfway up the stairwell facing east, overlooking the rose garden. I knelt on the landing to get a better view. From there, the bushes that had been replaced stuck out, identified by the fresh dirt piles. I hoped they'd survive being transplanted.

The next window I checked out overlooked the backyard and the wooded area. This was the room where Eli and I had been held captive when things between us were just getting started. The one I planned to turn into an office someday. The woods were the obvious place for a stalker to hide, except there wasn't anything to see except someone in the kitchen. And I hadn't opened the kitchen curtains this morning, so he couldn't see inside. Unless he hid in the shadow of the trees where I'd be unable to spot him, he wasn't there.

The next room had the largest window. In fact, it took up a third of one wall and had replaced two smaller windows. Jake had suggested the change when we first started remodeling the house. It provided a sweeping view of the lights of the city at night. Daytime, it became a sad reminder of what the city was losing piece by piece as shown by empty lots and houses in need of repair. Now, it didn't reveal anyone where they didn't belong. The motorcycle remained where I'd spotted it earlier.

I called the last room, with a window facing the main street, the ghost's room. I'd never seen the ghost, but I'd heard it plenty of times. Some days when I pulled up to the house, I saw the curtains in this window move, despite all the repairs. I'd left the thin and faded curtains up, so the ghost would feel safe.

The curtains provided enough cover so, from the outside looking in, I'd be a shadowy figure. That they would think I was the ghost made me grin. But my grin vanished when I spotted the figure sitting at the base of the big old oak tree at the edge of the yard.

Chapter 14

From this angle, I couldn't identify the trespasser or tell if he was technically on Eli's property. He may have been on the city setback, owned by the town. But it was a guy as proven by the long beard. So, not the man I had named "Biker," unless he wore a different disguise.

Confused, I stepped away from the window and sat on the top step to think. I had no evidence that the bikers were doing anything but watching. In fact, the bad things happening to me had stopped at the same time as I spotted the first guy.

Were they protecting me? But why? And who asked them to? They weren't professionals, that much was clear.

I didn't have much to work with. Hell, I didn't have anything to work with except speculation. I'd risk too much by confronting the man under the tree and demanding the truth. But grouchy old Auntie Hilda could.

Auntie Hilda pounded her cane on the concrete. "You," she—I—barked. "Wake up! What are you doing here?"

Biker number two—or was it three?—jerked his head up from his chest where it had been resting. "Huh?"

I tapped the tip of the cane against the toe of his black boot. "This isn't a hotel. Find somewhere else to take a nap."

He hopped to his feet and backed away a few steps. "Hey, lady, leave me alone. I'm just waiting for a friend to bring gas for my bike. The tank's empty."

He was at least an inch and a half too short to be the original guy. I arched an eyebrow. "Good story. Your friend seems to have forgotten you because you've been here for over an hour. Vagrancy is still against the law and you're lucky I haven't called the cops."

"I wonder what happened to him." He pulled his cell phone out of his pocket and pretended to scroll thru his messages. His acting was as bad as his lying.

"Maybe his dealer didn't make his connection." I waved my cane in the air. "We don't need your kind here. You and your friend I saw last night. Now git and don't come back."

"You're one of those people who watches everything that goes on, aren't you?"

"Yeah. What's wrong with that?"

He shifted from one foot to the other. He was out of his league. "You can help."

I hadn't expected the conversation to go this way. "What do you mean?"

He pointed toward Eli's house. "Have you met the folks who live there?"

"Nobody lives there. There's a couple of people who come and go, but they don't live there. The lady always says hi, but I've never talked to the man."

"You ever see anyone else there?"

"Sure. But like I said, they come and go."

He tugged on his beard. "Look. I shouldn't say this, but here's the deal. Someone is giving the lady a hard time. Me and a few of my friends were asked to keep an eye on her and the place. But she doesn't make it easy. And she's not aware we're here, and we can't tell her. We could use more help."

"What do you want from me?" I leaned on the cane, pretending to be worn out. "I can't sit out here all day. There are my shows to watch and my cats to take care of."

"I get it. And I need to clear it with the guy in charge. But if you can call him when you see something unusual, someone who doesn't belong, it'll help us-and her. Figure out who her friends are and who might be looking for trouble."

"Who are you working for?" I asked, trying to sound only slightly interested, while I was dying to know.

"Can't tell you." He shrugged. "I have no idea. It's a favor for a friend of a friend."

"Sounds fishy to me. I think I should call the cops. You look like a bunch of peeping toms."

"That's what I said when I was asked to do this.

But the guy in charge is an ex-cop if that makes you feel any better."

Not at all. I had helped to bust a crooked cop a few years ago. But then, the guy in front of me looked like an ex-cop in disguise. "His name isn't Clear something, is it?"

He looked puzzled. "Who?"

I sighed loudly. "You aren't from around here, are you?" I waited until he shook his head to continue. "We had a dirty cop a while back. If I remember it right, his name was Clear something. Clear. Clearsky, no, Clearman, no, Clear, Clear, Clearmont! That's the name. Clearmont." I stabbed my cane at the biker and he backed up a few more steps. "Is that who you're working for?"

He tugged at his beard and shook his head. "Don't know anyone by that name. Look, forget I said anything, okay? Me and my friends are here to help. We won't bother anybody unless they go to hurt the lady and we can't wait for the cops."

"I should call the police, anyway. I don't trust you further than I can spit. And let me tell you, I can't spit worth a hill of beans with these damn dentures."

The hint of a smile reached his mouth and then vanished. Perfect. I didn't want him to see me as an actual threat.

"Let's make a deal. We'll stay out of your hair and you stay out of ours. Okay?"

"I'll be keeping my eye on you. Don't think you'll get away with anything."

"Right. Now, I'll go back to being a watchdog. You've distracted me long enough."

"Huh. Like taking a nap is doing your job." I waved my cane at him again. "She's a nice lady. Whatever is going on, if you're supposed to protect her, you better get to it." As I turned around slowly and limped down the sidewalk, I caught a few bad words in the mix he muttered, just loud enough for me to hear.

❈ ❈ ❈

An analysis of the risks versus the rewards proved a night at Hot Wheels, Oak Grove's biker bar, was out of the question. No matter what personality I adopted, the possibility of getting caught was too high. I didn't know enough about the biker culture to fit in.

At least I'd learned a few things. Being watched wasn't a figment of my imagination. And the bikers appeared to be on my side, but that didn't mean I trusted them.

Their amateur status resulted in a toss-up. On the plus side, I could get around their watchfulness. If I left as myself and came back as Taylor, they wouldn't know it was me. On the downside, if I was able to confuse them, so could someone else.

And I planned to confuse them. Taylor needed to make another appearance at Terry's. I had the feeling something would happen tonight.

❈ ❈ ❈

The atmosphere at Terry's had changed. The guys huddled around the games and the girls sat at

117

their table, and no one laughed. I wondered if one of the new faces at the bar was responsible for the tense atmosphere.

I got my drink—the rum and coke was meant as a statement—and peered over Andy's shoulder as he played a video game. His timing was off, and I wondered again what was wrong. Jordan had equally bad luck with the racing game.

Andy pounded his fist on the game's dashboard and turned to me. "Hey, Taylor. You came back."

"Yeah, you guys were fun to hang out with last night. What happened?"

"See that blond guy at the bar? He's Marly's ex, Kody. Kody Vinrod. Every time he shows up, he causes problems."

"Don't you stick up for her?" Marly was the girl with long brown hair who talked about her philosophy class the previous night.

"We try. We run interference when we can and we've complained to management. But he's related to Butch, and Butch doesn't want to get involved. We hate to call the cops and start trouble."

Butch was the bartender. I'd heard about him from Jake. Jake didn't like him, and now I understood why.

"He seems to be behaving himself." From the corner of my eye, I sized up Kody. He looked like the all talk and no action type.

"So far. Things will change after he gets a couple of drinks in him. I've tried to convince Marly to leave, but she refuses to let him run her off."

Good for her. But a mean drunk was never predictable. My hero complex kicked in full steam.

"Anyway," Andy went on, "Trouble's brewing. You might want to go."

"Or I can stick around for the show." And do what I could to fix the situation.

I nursed my first drink to make it last longer and switched to straight soda for my second, not wanting to dull my reflexes. So far, Kody, while not exactly behaving himself, hadn't interacted with Marly. He'd played a couple of games, badly, talked too loud and drank too much, but none of those demanded any action from me.

He ignored me, and I didn't challenge him to any games, as badly as I wanted to embarrass him by making him lose. Instead, I switched things up and chatted with the other girls on and off. They weren't very talkative, and nothing I tried to draw them out worked.

I was sitting beside Marly when Kody strolled by on his way to the back and tugged on her hair. She put her hand to her head. "Ouch! That hurt. Don't do that!"

He laughed. "Poor baby. You used to like it."

"You never listened to me when I said it hurt. Now, leave me alone."

I gave her points for standing her ground. Maybe she wouldn't need my help. But he reached out and grabbed a bigger handful of hair and tugged harder. "Who's going to stop me?"

I swiveled out of my chair and pushed my way between them. "She said to leave her alone."

Andy hissed. "He's got a gun, Taylor."

So did I. But I wouldn't resort to using it if I didn't need to.

"Don't stick your nose where it doesn't belong, girly," Kody snarled.

"Didn't your mama teach you to keep your hands to yourself?" I asked, syrupy-sweet. "You should go back to kindergarten."

"You need someone to bring you down a peg or two. Learn your place."

"How original. Is that the best you can do?"

Faster than I expected, Kody raised his open hand to slap me. I thought all the drinks would have slowed him down. But my training kicked in, and I sidestepped the blow.

"You've got to do better than that," I said calmly.

One of the girls laughed nervously. From behind the bar, Butch said, "Go home, Kody. You've had enough for the night."

Coward. He hadn't done anything to calm down the situation.

"Not unless Marly comes with me. You coming, Marly?" Kody asked. His angry eyes locked on mine.

"No. I've told you no before and I'm telling you again. No."

I read his intentions and was prepared when he reached for her shoulder. With a quick thrust, I knocked his hand away. "She said no."

If he had known what was good for him, he would have backed down. He wasn't that smart. He swung at me. In a classic move, I grabbed his arm and used his own power to toss him to the floor. "Not cool," I said.

He should've stayed down but wasn't that smart. He wobbled as he half-rose and lunged at me. I moved aside and kicked him in the rear as he sailed by. The alcohol didn't do him any favors.

"Enough is enough. Give it up. Go home." I wondered how everyone else was reacting and if I'd need to defend myself from any of his friends, but didn't dare take my eyes off him. I backed up until I bumped into the bar.

It took him longer to get up the second time. For a minute, I thought he'd finally gotten smart and was giving up. I was wrong.

Chapter 13

I'd never been in an actual bar fight. It wasn't like the movies. No one else joined in. It was just me and Kody. Where was Butch with the shotgun kept behind the bar for stopping fights? I mean, that's what happened in every book. But as far as I could tell, he wasn't even going to call the cops.

One of the girls had. A part of my brain processed she was on the phone and talking to 911. Good. I bounced on my toes, waiting for Kody's next move.

I hadn't tried to hurt him. Yet. Only to embarrass him. I'd hoped that would be enough to get him to stop. At the moment, I didn't think my strategy had worked.

Holding on to a chair, he dragged himself off the floor. As he reached behind his back, the world slowed down. I'd already figured out where he stashed his gun. If he got to his, and I got to mine, innocent people might get hurt.

I didn't have time for pretty. Or graceful. I threw myself at him.

His head 'thunked' as we smashed into the floor. Metal screeched as his gun slid across the tile. I hoped someone kicked it out of the way. He kept swinging. I avoided a punch but took a hard elbow to the cheek.

I couldn't win this on a physical level. He was bigger and stronger. I needed to at least stay on top. If he rolled us over, I was done for. My best bet was to abandon the fight and pray the cavalry came to the rescue.

He struck wildly, and I dodged it by rolling to the right. Then kept on rolling until I was a few feet away. A rush of cold air hit me as I got to my knees.

"Police! Freeze!"

I recognized that voice. I would have gladly frozen, but I had to dodge a charge from Kody first. I may have 'accidentally' caught him with an elbow as I crawled out of his way, but I didn't feel bad about it. Then, I raised my open hands shoulder-high and froze.

"Interior jacket pocket, left side," I told Officer Sloan. While he and Sergeant Kinchloe had struggled to subdue Kody, I'd taken a seat in the nearest chair. I adjusted all the bits and pieces of my wardrobe, including my wig, folded my hands in my lap and waited. "It's a 9mm Beretta. The chamber is loaded, but the safety is on." With Kody on his way to the police station, it was my turn to be grilled. "My concealed carry permit is in my purse, wherever that got to."

As far as I could tell, Sloan didn't recognize me. Neither did Kinchloe, although he'd barely looked my way. I blamed it on the bad lighting. And the fact they didn't expect me to be there. The disguise wasn't *that* good.

"Take your coat off slowly and hand it to me," he replied. I was the enemy until I proved otherwise.

"Right." I peeled off my jacket, grimacing as I squirmed out of the left sleeve. Kody must have caught me with a blow I didn't remember on my shoulder. I'd sport a major bruise in no time flat.

"You okay?" Sloane asked.

"I think so." I handed him the jacket. "But an ice pack wouldn't hurt."

"You sure you don't need medical attention?"

I'd turned down an ambulance—twice. "I'm sure."

"Be right back." Sloane headed to the bar, taking my coat with him. He returned with a stingy bag of small cubes. "Bartender isn't much help," he grumbled.

"That's what I said."

"What do you mean?"

"He should have gotten involved and put an end to the situation long before this. He's either a coward or an abuser himself. I can't make that judgment."

Sloane looked at me suspiciously. "Are you a PI?"

I held the bag of ice to my cheek. "Come on, really? You don't know who I am?"

"Should I? I'd remember that hair."

I had so many pins and glue holding the wig into place that it wouldn't be easy getting it off. "It'll be easier to give you my ID. Where's my purse?"

Only a few people remained in the bar. Marly had gone with her parents to the police station to give her statement. From what I gathered, she hadn't told them about her troubles with Kody, wanting to stand on her own two feet. But one of the other girls called them and when they showed up, Marly had wilted in her mother's arms. At Kinchloe's suggestion, they planned to apply for a restraining order.

But Andy stayed behind and so did Sammie, Marly's best friend. She brought my purse. "I kept it safe, Taylor," she said. "I wish I could do what you did."

"Thanks." I worried that she might not like me so much in a couple of minutes.

"I don't have any weapons in here," I held my purse out towards Sloane. "No sharp objects except a nail file. Do you want to retrieve my wallet or should I?"

He cocked his head as if trying to figure out why I was so familiar with the proper procedure. Without a word, he took it, pulled out my wallet and handed it to me.

I dug out my license and concealed carry permit and passed them to him.

He studied them, whistled, and looked again. "We need to continue this at the station. Sergeant, can you finish up here?"

Kinchloe, who was interviewing Butch, strolled over. "What's up?"

Sloan handed him my paperwork. Kinchloe studied it and then peered at me. "Well, I'll be… yeah, I'll meet you there. Things are about wrapped up here."

Sloan gave me back my paperwork. "I'll keep your gun for now."

I nodded. "Can I have my jacket?"

"Sure." Sloan pulled out Betsy and tucked her into his waistband. I doubted it was proper procedure, but there wasn't anywhere else to put her until he got back to the police car. Andy's eyes nearly bugged out of his head when he saw the gun. Sloan handed me my jacket, and I tugged it on, wincing when I moved wrong.

"My car is out back. Do I need to go with you, or can I meet you there?" I asked. I'd play by whatever rules they set.

Sloan and Kinchloe exchanged a glance. Kinchloe shrugged. "It's you. We'll see you there."

❀ ❀ ❀

I didn't expect the parking lot at the station to be so full when I drove up. I guess they'd called in extra officers. And I didn't expect to see Freddie's Mustang, but there it was. Maybe he'd been brought in for something else. The lump in the pit of my stomach doubted it.

But I grabbed the melting bag of ice, pretended nothing was wrong, and strolled in the front door. Bo manned the front desk. He looked up as I walked in and I saw no recognition in his eyes.

"Can I help you?" he asked.

"I'm here to meet with Officer Sloan."

He got to his feet. "Holy heck. Really? Sloan warned me you didn't look like you but didn't tell me anything else. I'm impressed."

"Thanks," I said lamely.

"You and my sister ought to get together and trade secrets. You remember, she's the one who's into steampunk."

I remembered. "Sure. After this gets straightened out."

He caught himself. "Business first, right?" He jerked his head towards the back. "You know the way to Detective Thomason's office?"

I did. Too well. The door stood open. I stopped in the hallway to gather my courage.

"Come in, Harmony," Freddie called.

Bo must have ratted me out. I drew a deep breath and took the four needed steps to face down Freddie and Sloan.

And Chief Sorenson.

And the biker.

I should have guessed.

"Shit," said Freddie.

"God damn," said the biker. "That's not who you asked us to watch out for."

Sloan chuckled.

"Good evening, Miss Duprie," said Chief Sorenson.

"Good evening, Chief. It's crowded in here, isn't it?" I asked.

"You're dismissed, Officer Sloan," said the Chief. "We've got it from here."

Sloan took Betsy from his duty belt and laid her on the desk. He nodded, and as he brushed by me on his way out, he winked.

"Take a seat, Miss Duprie," the chief said. "This is not the discussion I expected to have with you. You've gone rogue."

"What do you expect, Chief? For me to sit back and wait for the next bad thing to happen?" I sat in the only empty chair in the room. Unfortunately, it meant I sat beside the chief. Even this late at night, he dressed in a business suit. Next to him was the biker. Minus the beard, but with a bit of scruff on his chin. Freddie, in jeans and a polo shirt, was in his chair behind the desk. I leaned past the chief to talk to the biker. "We haven't been introduced. I guess you're Dawson?" I held out my hand.

"How do you... Never mind. Yes, I'm Dawson. You can call me Drew."

We shook, me making sure to use a firm grip. Now that I knew, I picked up on the signs he was an ex-cop. The cargo pants. The boots, more military than biker style. I was outnumbered. If I didn't take charge of the meeting immediately, it would go badly.

"So, how long have you had your eye on this Kody dude?" It was a stretch, but logic told me it was more than my appearance that had the men upset.

"What do you know about him?" Chief Sorenson asked, a sharp edge on his words.

"Nothing but presumptions. Tonight was the first time I had the displeasure of meeting him."

"I'd like to hear your assumptions," Freddie said, leaning forward.

I took a minute to gather my thoughts. "He was the charming high school bully and hasn't changed since graduation. The kids tolerated him because he had access to booze and drugs. He's good looking enough that girls were flattered by his attention— especially the ones with low self-esteem that he could manipulate. He's still trying to get by on his connections. But now his high school friends are out of his sphere of influence and he's doing what he can to maintain his control."

I took a breath. "Have I gone too far? Your only concern is that he's selling drugs, right? And I saw no evidence of that. But you've got plenty of other charges to hit him with."

Drew chuckled and swiveled his chair to face me. "And you thought me and my friends could get away without her seeing us, Chief? When did you first pick up on the fact we were watching you, Miss Duprie?"

"I wondered on Monday, suspected on Tuesday when I caught you scoping out my place, and was positive on Wednesday when you showed up at the library. I just wasn't sure if you were good or bad guys until tonight. And call me Harmony."

His eyebrows scrunched. "Wednesday I get, but Monday? I didn't get my instructions until Tuesday morning."

"You picked a really good bar for your introduction to Oak Grove, then. Or are you doing double duty and hoped to pick up a drug sale or two at the Red Door? Because despite its rough appearance, I hear it's legit, that the new owners are cleaning up the place."

Drew grinned and shook his head. "We're doing this all wrong, Chief. She should have been informed and involved from the beginning. Tell me how you know I was at the Red Door, Harmony."

I wanted to test his memory. "Your choice of beer is a lager. I don't drink light beer."

All three men looked at me like I'd lost it. I ignored them and continued.

"My kid sister went to the party, and I was her ride."

The Chief and Freddie still looked puzzled, but Drew's face cleared and he laughed. "That was you? How many personalities do you have?"

"Only one." I tapped my forehead. "Everything else is just a big kid's version of dress-up." Born out of desperation, not fun or playtime.

"Seems like a safe way to do it," Drew said. "I'm having trouble switching between two."

"This isn't a game," Chief Sorenson snapped. "Let's get back on track here. Miss Duprie, what *were* you doing at Terry's tonight?"

Chapter 16

"What was I doing at Terry's? Besides playing Wonder Woman?" I put the bag of ice, now mostly water, in the garbage can. "Research. I figured if someone on the internet is playing games with my life, college kids would be the ones to know about it. That's why I'm dressed this way. I didn't count on Kody messing up my plans."

"Tonight was your first night there?" Freddie asked.

"No. I went last night. Played a few games, hung out, broke the ice. Didn't learn anything, but I didn't expect to. I'm using the story I'm in town visiting for a few days. That way, if I don't show up some night, no one will think anything about it."

"And if someone recognizes you?"

"Oh, well." I shrugged. "Nothing ventured, nothing gained. It's better than sitting around and waiting for something to happen."

"We're doing everything we can, Harmony. You should know that better than anyone."

"I understand. I also realize the department

doesn't have the resources or the time to devote to my case. It's not like you can call the state police in to investigate someone vandalizing rosebushes."

"What?" Chief Sorenson stiffened.

"I didn't bother reporting it. Someone sprayed about a third of the rosebushes at Eli's with weed killer. At least, that's what the master gardener said. I had to get several of the bushes replaced."

"What else haven't you told us, Miss Duprie?"

I considered the question. "I didn't mention the times I was followed. And the trackers on the rental car. Of course, I found the first one after you showed up, Drew. I figured you were responsible."

Drew looked at Chief Sorenson and shook his head. "Not me."

"You said the first one. How many have you found?" the chief asked.

"Two. I started a collection and stuck them both on the garage door. It's been a couple of days, so I should check if there's a new one."

Sorenson slammed his fist on the top of Freddie's desk hard enough that the coffee in Freddie's cup nearly sloshed over the rim. Freddie pushed his chair back until it met the windowsill. I jerked backward, taken by surprise by the force of their reactions.

Drew stood and placed his hand on Sorenson's shoulder. "This is bigger than me and my friends can handle. I'm the only one with a law enforcement background. The guys are just my club buddies, looking for something to do. You knew that when you called me. If Harmony can get past us, so can the bad guys, whoever they are."

He looked at me. "I'm sure you've guessed, but I worked for the Chief in his position before he came to Oak Grove. We've kept in touch. In fact, he invited me to join the force here. I turned him down, liking where I was. But about six months ago, I was forced to retire. Got injured on the job. I think he took pity on me and invited me here to give me something to do."

"Once a cop, always a cop," I said. "But I wasn't looking for the signs, so I didn't spot them until tonight."

"Was that a compliment? I'll take it." His grin didn't quite convince me of its sincerity.

"You're looking for a compliment? Here's one. Nothing new has happened since you showed up. It may be a coincidence, or because you and your friends served as a deterrent, but I've had a normal week. Excluding the party on Monday, because there's no proof it had anything to do with me."

"I don't believe in coincidence," Drew growled.

"Neither do I. That's what makes this so frustrating. There has to be a person or persons behind all the events, but I've been unable to make a connection. And I don't believe for a second they've given up."

Freddie pulled a stack of manila file folders to the middle of his desk. "We've been tracking the offenders Harmony is associated with. Most of them are still incarcerated. A few are on the street, but not around here."

Drew's eyes widened and picked up the one on the top of the stack. "Those are all connected to her? That's impressive. But just because someone is behind bars doesn't mean they don't have access to the internet. And isn't there a theory about her being targeted by an on-line group?"

"We're going in circles here. That's why I was at Terry's. And I'll go back, if my identity can remain a secret. None of you are capable of going in undercover, and I'm not sure anyone on the force could."

"Detective?" Chief Sorenson asked.

Freddie shook his head. "The only officer we have that might pull it off is Hunt."

I snorted. "As fresh from the academy as he is? He's as stiff as a log."

"I can't allow you, as a civilian, to do this, Miss Duprie," the chief said.

"You don't have the authority to stop me, either," I said quietly.

"Try me. I can come up with a laundry list of things to charge you with after tonight. Hold you while the department investigates."

"And Dan would have me out on the street so fast heads would spin. The DA would question every charge, drop them, and ruin your credibility."

He took a deep breath and opened his mouth, but I didn't give him time to get the words out. I turned to look directly in his eyes.

"I know you want to protect me. And I appreciate it more than I can say. But I have to stand up for myself. No one else can."

"Who's Dan?" Drew whispered to Freddie.

"Her lawyer. She has his personal number on speed dial," Freddie whispered back.

My eyes never moved from the Chief's. It was a match to see who would give in first. Except Drew 'accidentally' dropped the file he held, and we both looked as papers tumbled to the desk and the floor.

"Oops, let me get those." Drew knelt and started retrieving the documents. Naturally, my eyes followed the movement. When I looked back up, Chief Sorenson was helping to straighten the papers on Freddie's desk.

Crisis adverted. For the moment. I'd thank Drew later.

"One thing we haven't addressed," Chief Sorenson said, once everything was back in order, "Is motive. Other than revenge. Which, so far, isn't panning out."

I didn't know what the three of them did next, but I suspected they plotted my future while I spent a good half hour with Officer Sloan. After being summoned by Chief Sorenson, he took me aside to give him my official statement about what happened at Terry's. By the time we finished, I was more than ready to head home. I hadn't decided which home.

Another night, it would be fun to slip away without any of them realizing I'd gone. But tonight, it sounded like too much effort. When Sloan excused himself and asked me to wait for a moment, I placed bets on who would come back with him. My hope was for Freddie. I guessed wrong.

Drew walked out with Sloan, his helmet in one hand and Betsy in the other. I wondered if it was he or Freddie who'd talked Chief Sorenson into giving her back to me. "I get the honor of escorting you home tonight," he said as he handed her to me.

"Honor? Did anyone tell you how I hate bodyguards?" I shook my head and slid Betsy into my jacket's pocket. "This isn't the first time I've played hide-and-go-seek with someone who thought I was helpless."

His grin was real this time. "The Chief told me a few stories. I didn't believe him until tonight. But I volunteered to make sure you got home safely. Another of the guys has the task of making sure no one bothers you so you can get some sleep."

I cocked my head. "And if I leave?"

"You'll be followed. And since you have the advantage of knowing the town, you could lose him. But we've all had enough excitement for one night, so how about you play along and stay home?"

I nodded. It was late, and I couldn't do any more damage. All I wanted was to wash the layers of makeup off my face, get rid of the wig, and crawl into bed.

Drew held the door open for me as we exited the station. He stood a bit too close for my liking, but he was new at this bodyguard gig. It would take a while to break him in. I checked my phone while we walked the short distance to the parking lot, wondering if Eli had tried to contact me.

"Shit!" Drew grabbed me and spun me around.

My first instinct was to seize his arm and flip him

to the ground. The second was to make sure I kept a tight grip on my phone because I had a new message from Eli and didn't want to lose it. My third was to turn and identify the problem.

I rotated my body enough to see the parking lot. There were fewer cars than earlier, with the task of processing Kody finished and things settled down. The Charger was right where I'd parked it, second row back, near an overhead light. With the letters "bitc" scrawled across the windshield in what appeared to be white paint.

We reconvened in the small conference room where everyone could review the security tapes at the same time on the TV mounted on the wall. That made room for Sloan, Kinchloe, and Bo to join us. They left an old-fashioned bell to ring for help at the front desk.

While they retrieved the security camera footage, I dashed to the restroom to wipe as much of the gunk off my face as possible, emptying the paper towel holder. That way, it wasn't as easy to see the tracks of my tears. I also shed the wig, wanting to be the authentic me again.

They had the file queued up when I returned. "We waited for you," Freddie said. "We're just at the spot where you got here."

Drew studied me, then nodded without saying a word. I didn't know what that meant, so I ignored it.

It was weird watching Taylor-me walk up to the door and disappear inside. Then it was like watching paint dry as nothing moved for a long time except the leaves on the trees. An older car pulled into the parking lot, stopped for a minute, then left.

"What was that about?" I asked.

"It happens now and then," Kinchloe answered. "The theory is someone wants to make a call and is smart enough to pull off the street to do it."

That made sense. We went back to drying paint. Occasionally, there would be a flare of light as a car drove down the street. One time it was a pickup with the left front headlight out. Bo spotted it first.

"Freeze it," he said, got out of his chair, and walked up and tapped the edge of the screen. "See this? It looks like someone walking in the shadows."

Freddie restarted the video. I thought Bo was wrong; it was only the leaves on a bush moving in the breeze, but kept my mouth shut. The world moved into slow motion as we waited for something to happen.

"There," Chief Sorenson said. "At the edge of the sidewalk."

Freddie stopped the video.

"I see it, too," Drew said. I still couldn't identify anything. Was Drew just flattering the chief?

Bo, standing near the screen, tapped a dark spot. "Is this what you spotted?"

"Yes. Advance a few frames, Thomason."

Freddie started and stopped the replay. Car lights flashed by and the shadow disappeared, replaced by the trunk of one of Oak Grove's big old oak trees. He hit the play button.

I dug into my purse for my glasses and swapped

them out for my contacts. My eyes were tired and maybe I'd see what everyone else was seeing with my glasses on.

Another thirty seconds of nothing happening. Then, a figure darted from behind the oak tree and disappeared behind the nearest car.

"Stop!" the Chief roared. Freddie backed up the playback.

Nothing new showed up in the replay. Just a slim figure dressed in dark clothing, including a hoodie pulled over their face. Truth was, I couldn't tell if it was male or female.

Freddie kept the video going.

Half a minute later, the person popped up at the front of the same vehicle. They made a quick dash over to Freddie's car and dropped to the ground again.

"Get your car checked out, Freddie," I said. "Make sure they didn't mess with it." He was smart enough to know that, but I needed to break the oppressive silence.

It was only a few seconds but seemed much longer for the suspect to show themselves. They half-crawled through the gap between Freddie's car and the Charger. Then, hopped onto the hood and pulled a can out of the hoodie's front pocket.

I clenched my fists as they sprayed each letter on the windshield. B. I. T. When they got to the C, they stopped and shook the can. Then started again. It took them two more tries to finish the C. They rolled off the Charger as lights flashed into the parking lot.

Watching them retrace their path to the sidewalk was anticlimactic. Freddie stopped the video as the figure walked behind the oak tree and out of the camera's range.

"Comments? Observations?" Chief Sorenson asked in the hush that followed.

"It's a good thing they ran out of paint," I said.

Chapter 17

My attempt at humor fell flat, even to my ears, but it was a way to calm my rattled nerves. There was no doubt in my mind what the missing letter was. I pressed on. "And a better thing it's a rental and not Dolores."

"Dolores?" Drew asked.

"My car. She's in storage for protection."

"Harmony names everything," Freddie explained. "If she mentions Betsy, that's her Beretta. What she calls me depends upon how upset she is with me at the moment."

Heat rose in my cheeks. I didn't realize he'd noticed.

"Back to business, people," Chief Sorenson said.

"He was wearing gloves," Freddie said. "No hope for fingerprints."

"He took the paint can with him, so we can't trace it back to the store he bought it from," Kinchloe added.

"You might get shoe prints off the hood of the car," Drew said.

Sorenson nodded. "Keep it going."

"I'll request security footage from the businesses across the street. See if we can figure out whether he was on foot or caught a ride." Freddie restarted the video and let it play as he talked. "That will have to wait until the morning."

"I don't see any distinctive markings on the clothing." Bo stared at the screen. "No logos, no slogans, nothing to identify the brand."

The rookie was good.

"What else about him?" Sorenson planted his elbows on the table, locked his fingers together, and rested his chin on them.

"Why do you keep saying him?" I was truly curious. "That could be a teenage girl."

"True. We shouldn't make any assumptions," Freddie said. "His—or her—build is androgynous. But males commit most graffiti crimes."

"But this was a targeted attack," Drew pointed out. "Specifically aimed at Harmony and her car. Not a crime of opportunity."

"Take the video to the spot right after he jumped off the hood," Sorenson ordered. "Watch the body language."

What was he looking for? I didn't catch anything new in the footage. No one else seemed to either.

"See how he reaches down and adjusts himself?" Sorenson asked. "That's a guy or a very well-trained female pretending to be a guy."

Freddie reset the video so we could watch again.

Sure enough, like Sorenson pointed out, the perpetrator pulled a classic male move, like a baseball player putting things where they belonged.

"Go back again," Bo said. "I spotted something else."

"How far?" Freddie asked.

"When he jumps off the hood. Look chest level. Is that a reflection or a flaw in the recording?"

I took off my glasses, rubbed my eyes, and put them back on. They were starting to play tricks on me. When we got to the spot Bo had requested, the flash of light was obvious, now that I knew to look for it.

"What is it?" I asked.

"A badge of some sort? Or a mirror?" Freddie suggested.

"Or a body cam," Drew said. "Recording the deed to show off to his friends."

Oh, shit. "Chief, do you still get emails about that internet channel that posted the fire videos?"

He shook his head. "It got shut down shortly after your friends figured out who was starting the fires. But I agree with your train of thought."

"Revenge videos?" Bo asked.

"Except I was never associated with the investigation," I pointed out.

"What?" Drew asked. "What am I missing?"

"A few months back," Chief Sorenson said, "We investigated a rash of small fires in the community. Videos of them were posted on a social site. Harmony got in touch with some friends who, using their computer skills, identified the teenagers responsible."

Which had skirted the boundaries of legality, but the Chief didn't know that.

"All I did was contact the experts," I explained. "They did the work. My name doesn't appear in any of the police reports, and neither do the names of my friends."

"Officially," Freddie said. "But rumors spread."

"So why isn't anyone spreading any rumors about what's going on now?"

"Because only one person is responsible and they aren't talking?" suggested Sloan.

It made as much sense as everything I could think of.

"We need to pursue the video angle," the chief said. "Thomason, I want you to be the lead, but choose someone to assist you if needed."

"No offense to our more experienced officers," Freddie said, "But Hunt here knows his way around the internet better than most."

"Kinchloe, can you rearrange the schedule and make it work?"

"Consider it done," Kinchloe said.

I was itching to return to Eli's and start a search. I stood. "If there's nothing else, I should get going."

"You can't go yet," Freddie said. "We need to process the Charger first. Scour it for evidence. Once we're done, I'll try to get the paint off the windshield before the sun hits it."

"Who's available to give her a ride?" Drew asked. "I don't have a spare helmet."

Sloan raised his hand. "I will. With your permission, Chief. All of us aren't needed to handle the report. We'd be in each other's way."

Sorenson nodded. "Dawson, you'll follow and make sure there are no more surprises."

I felt as if some hidden message had exchanged between them, but was too tired to worry about it. I yawned and dug the Charger's key out of my purse and put it on the table. "You might need this. I can get it back in the morning before I return the car to the rental agency. I don't want to drive it anymore."

❀ ❀ ❀

"Nice place," Sloan said as we pulled up to the house. Drew, on his motorcycle, was right behind us.

"You should have seen it before it was remodeled."

"Oh, is this the Victorian you fixed up? My mom told me about it."

There it was, the good ol' gossip mill in action. So why wasn't it working for me?

"Would you like to come inside and see how it turned out? That way you can make your mother jealous." I didn't remember leaving a mess anywhere.

"If you don't mind. It would give me something to talk to her about at Sunday dinner. I should verify nobody's hiding behind any doors to jump out at you."

"Unless they crawled in a second or third-story window, we're clear." I'd checked my phone on the way. I also finally read Eli's message and texted I'd call in the morning. "The security system is reporting everything is good to go."

"Those doorbell cameras are nice, but don't cover enough."

"Who said anything about a doorbell system? This is a custom-designed program that covers the entire first floor with the possibility of expansion to the upper floors." Sure, I was bragging, but Eli's work deserved it. I swung open the car door without looking and almost hit Drew.

He jumped back to avoid being knocked over.

"Why don't you wait in the car until Sloan and I clear the house," he said. "Give me your keys."

"That's not the way it works. I have to disable the alarm first." I held up my phone. "It's an app. It tells me every time someone even tries to get into the house."

"Cool! You can explain how it works after we check out the premises. Will you turn off the alarm, please?"

I waited in the car with the doors closed while Sloan and Drew made sure it was safe inside. Not that I had any doubt, but I'd let them satisfy their training. And it gave Sloan something to talk about with his mother.

Drew sat in one of the leather chairs, looking as if he planned to settle in after I watched Sloan leave. That wasn't in my plans.

"Don't you have someplace to be? Guys to talk to, suspects to follow, something?"

He grinned and leaned back in the chair. "Nope. I'm staying here tonight and every night until we catch this guy."

I arched an eyebrow. "Did I ask you to do that?"

"You didn't. I'm staying anyway."

I reopened the front door. "Go patrol the perimeter or something. You aren't welcome here. And stay off the porch or you'll set off the alarm."

"One of the guys will be here in a few minutes to do just that." He reached for his phone. "I'll pass on the message about the porch."

"You didn't get the memo, did you? I don't do bodyguards." Especially ones that invite themselves in without asking first.

"When have you ever needed a bodyguard?"

I held up my hand and counted on my fingers. Then I closed my fist and started over. His eyes got wider each time I raised a finger.

"But I've only had one professional," I opened the door further. "I made him stay in his van most of the time. You're not a professional."

"Close the door, Harmony. You're a target standing there."

He was right. I shut it most of the way.

"Good advice. That still doesn't make you a pro."

He shook his head. "The Chief told me you might be a handful. He didn't warn me you'd be this obstinate."

"What is your relationship with Sorenson? I mean, I know you worked for him, but there's more to it, isn't there?" With a lot of digging, I might figure it out, but it would save a lot of work if he told me.

He tilted his chin. "I'll trade you. Shut and lock the door, come sit down, and I'll tell you about it."

I took my time to consider the offer. Long enough to make him twitch. "You get ten minutes. If I'm not sold by then, you're out." I closed the door and locked it. "Start talking."

He followed me into the kitchen when I went to get some water. "We were on the force together up in Buffalo. He started a year before me, but we ended up as partners and friends. He was always a step or two ahead of me, made detective first, but deserved it.

"I took assignments where I wouldn't be in his direct line of supervision so we could stay friends as he moved up through the ranks. I didn't want even the shadow of conflict of interest to interfere with his rise to glory.

"Politics took care of that. He didn't play along with some particularly nasty pressure coming from the City Council, one member in particular who didn't like cops."

I had a zillion questions, but sipped on my water and settled into the other chair. I'd given him ten minutes. He hadn't sold me yet.

His back to me and his hands stuffed in his pockets, he stared at the empty fireplace. "When the opportunity here opened up, he applied, expecting his chances were next to nothing. Figured a local guy would get the position. Couldn't believe it when he landed an interview. Thought it was a joke when they offered him the job. But he took a chance and accepted."

"He's done a good job here," I said. "As far as I know, no one on the force resents him getting the spot." We'd lost a couple of officers shortly after he started, but rumor had it they needed to leave.

He turned, shoving his hands deeper into his pockets. "Did I pass? Will you let me stay?"

"You haven't told me about his personal life. Wife? Family?"

"And I won't. It's not my story to tell."

I could live with that. I checked my phone. "You have two minutes left to tell me why he called you."

"Easy. I got injured on the job and won't take a desk assignment. I'm not ready to spend my days fishing, so I've been playing with the idea of starting a bodyguard business. He thought this would give me practical experience." Drew grinned. "I have to say, it's not what I anticipated. You defy my expectations."

"Which were?" I felt oddly flattered. I gave him a bonus point.

"He's told me stories about you without ever mentioning your name. When he asked me to be a watchdog for a librarian, I expected a little old gray-haired lady."

He lost points. "You don't go to the library much, do you?"

"Honestly?" He scratched his chin. "I can't tell you the last time I read a book that wasn't police or crime-related."

At least he was reading.

I was still undecided, uncomfortable offering another man a bed in Eli's house. But it was too cold to make Drew sleep on the porch, and he had no van to banish him to.

"I didn't convince you," Drew said, interrupting my musings.

"There are other factors." I quirked my mouth. "This house isn't mine. And I'm in a relationship. It just feels weird having you here overnight. But I don't see another way."

Chapter 18

I hated Drew being in the house. I considered tucking a rolled-up blanket in the crack between the floor and the door for extra security. Although Chief Sorenson did, I didn't trust Drew. Not completely. I couldn't figure out why.

From the comfort of Eli's bed, I listened to Drew's movements downstairs. He walked from room to room, in what I assumed was a final check before settling on the couch. Just by checking the app, I saw that everything was locked up tight. But if it made him feel useful, I'd let the charade play out.

I curled up on my side and tucked Eli's pillow to my chest. It was as close as I could get to him.

❈ ❈ ❈

I woke to the smell of coffee and toast and rolled over to look at the bedside clock. No matter what the numbers said, it was too early. But I needed to get up and go to work.

That was its own problem. Without the Charger, I wouldn't be going to the library. And I didn't want Drew in the house while I worked on confidential research for Eli. He'd be relegated to patrolling the perimeter with his friends. That didn't break my heart.

Fully dressed, I headed downstairs.

"Good morning," he said. "There are scrambled eggs in the pan on the stove. They should still be warm. I couldn't find any bacon to cook."

"I'm not a big bacon eater." Eli had tried to convert me with no luck.

"And there's a box of doughnuts waiting on the porch. I didn't want to open the door because I worried it would set off the alarm."

It sounded as if he was making himself at home. I'd have to put an end to that. "I'll grab one before you go."

"Just like that, you're throwing me out?"

Wow, he'd gotten the hint in one. "Yes. Unless the Charger makes an appearance, I'll be here working on private material. No company and no watchdog required."

"And if the car shows up?"

"I'll be making a trip to Pittsburgh to swap it."

"You think that will do any good?"

"For a day or two. Maybe longer now that you and your friends are keeping an eye on me." I tapped the proper sequence on my phone. "The front door is unsecure now. You can get your doughnuts. I'll even let you sit here and finish your coffee while you eat one."

"Wait a minute. Only the front door?"

I nodded. "Yes. The first floor is divided into four sectors, each controlled individually. It also reports on potential intrusion by sector."

"Nice system. Where did you get it? Can you install the app for me?"

"Nope. It's Eli's prototype. I don't have access to the base code." I wouldn't have given him a copy, anyway.

"What happens if someone attempts to break in when you aren't here?"

"And I don't confirm that everything is fine within a few minutes? An automated call goes out to 911." I grinned. "And a small army of angry geeks descends upon Oak Grove."

Drew pursed his mouth and walked outside. He returned with the flimsy box balanced in both hands. Under his arm, he'd tucked a newspaper.

"The guys brought it over from your apartment," he said. I followed him to the kitchen where he set everything on the counter. "You're the only one with access to the security?" he asked as he opened the box and pulled out a glazed doughnut.

"Nope. Eli and two of his guys see the same thing as me." I debated between eating a doughnut, or the scrambled eggs that Drew had cooked. The doughnut won. I chose a creme-filled one to go with my coffee. "Tell your guys thanks for the goodies and the paper. It's just what I need to start my day. But you can leave anytime now."

"Just like that?"

"Yep. You're welcome to park at the end of the

driveway, but it looks as if it's going to be a gorgeous day. You should go for a ride. Enjoy it while the weather lasts."

He hesitated. "As much fun as that sounds, I've got a job to do."

"Then go do it." I took a second doughnut and placed it on a napkin, then picked up the box and handed it to him. "Take these with you."

Alone.

Finally.

I brought up the John Denver music site and set my computer to play through the big screen TV. Then I plopped into a recliner and opened the paper. It wasn't as good as sitting on my bottom step at home with Piper to keep me company, but it was okay.

With the second doughnut and a fresh cup of coffee on the coaster on the end table, I was set. For a change, I started with the police blotter. The way our newspaper worked, Kody's arrest report would be in tomorrow's edition, but I wanted to catch up on everything else happening in town.

Jonas Pritchard got picked up for littering—again. Mrs. Reed was caught jaywalking. Now, the police don't worry about a little bit of jaywalking, but she's blind as a bat and can't see when cars are coming. They get the judge to yell at her to get her to stop. It works for a couple of weeks, and then she's back at it.

My need for gossip satisfied, I moved on to serious business—the comics. After a chuckle or two, I'd be prepared to face the world. I was perusing the sports section when I thought my phone beeped. With no new message notification, I assumed the weather app had updated.

I switched to state news—not much happening there, either. The Legislature was out of session, thank heavens, so they couldn't create any new unneeded laws. The only section left was local news, and I didn't care about the small list of engagements and weddings.

I imagined the back door opened and closed, but that was ridiculous. The door was locked. The noise must have been part of whatever ad was playing between songs. I returned to the story about the high school band preparing for the Fourth of July parade.

"You need your coffee refilled, Angel?" called a voice.

Shit, that was no ad. I picked up Betsy from the coffee table. "Jake?"

He poked his head around the kitchen door frame, looking just like I remembered him, from the short brown hair to the scruff on his chin. And, of course, the devilish grin on his face. "Good morning. You look comfy. Don't get up. I'll join you as soon as my coffee is ready."

"Jake? How did you…?"

"How did I get in? Eli set me up with a copy of the security app on his last trip here. He figured someone should have access to the house when you make trips to Florida. That was before I got the job. Didn't he tell you?"

That was a better explanation than the one I'd concocted. "But…" I started again.

"Who are those guys out there? They made it fun. Getting by them without being caught, that is. I haven't done something like that for ages. But they aren't very good. I could teach them a thing or two. You aren't in trouble again, are you?"

By now he was standing in front of me. He put his cup on another coaster and leaned over and kissed me on the forehead before sitting in the other chair.

"By the way, where's Dolores? I checked your place before I came here."

I finally found my voice. "Dolores is in secure storage. My life has been interesting the last few weeks."

It was a relief to let the story spill to someone I didn't have to censor it for. He listened and absorbed every detail without interrupting, his face getting more troubled at the mention of each incident. His fists clenched until his knuckles turned white when I recited last night's events.

"So where is Eli?" he asked when I got done.

"He doesn't know," I answered, avoiding Jake's eyes. "He's involved in a big business deal and didn't need the extra worry."

"You should have called me, Angel."

"I didn't want to bug you when you were getting set up in your job. What are you doing here, anyway? And where's your car?"

"I had a day off and thought I'd come by and say hi. The car is parked a few blocks away. I drove past and noticed the biker out front, so I figured I'd check out what was going on before coming in. If you're paying them, you should get your money back."

I sighed. "Chief Sorenson hired them. The guy in charge is an old friend of his."

He stood and held out his hand. "Come on, we're going for a ride."

I shook my head. "I have work to do."

"It'll still be here for you when you get back." He knelt in front of me and stared at me with his big, brown, puppy-dog eyes. I never could resist them. "Please?"

I was done for. "Where?"

"To talk to an old friend. After that, I want to discuss this with Thomason."

I didn't even have my shoes on. And the jeans I'd grabbed were one of my old pairs. "I need to change clothes."

"For where we're going? You're practically overdressed. Stop stalling."

We made a deal. I went with him, but I got to drive his car, a souped-up Charger. It was like falling back in love with an old friend. Jake had taught me everything I knew about defensive driving in it.

Drew and his men about had a collective heart attack when Jake and I strolled out of the house. Jake wanted to sneak out the way he came in, but I vetoed the suggestion. I didn't want to risk one of them being trigger-happy. I asked Drew not to follow us, but he did. It took a good fifteen minutes to lose him.

Once we were by ourselves, Jake directed me to a part of town I avoided. Even Oak Grove had an area that wasn't safe. Sadly, it made sense that Jake wasn't worried about going there.

I'd seen the name 'The Purple Onion' in police reports a time or two or three, but had never dropped by. Never planned on going there, either. Still, I held my tongue when Jake told me to park right out front of the dingy entrance.

What remained of the paint on the 'Purple Onion' sign over the entrance appeared more brown than purple. The 'NE' in the open sign flickered wildly. Fingerprints, outdated flyers, and ads covered the glass in the door. The stench of stale beer assaulted my nose as I opened the car door. Despite the sign, it looked dark inside and I wondered if the bar was really open. Who started drinking this early in the morning, anyway?

But Jake was at the front door waiting for me. I swung my legs out of the car and stood. "Are you sure about this?"

"Trust me, Angel."

I did trust him. Most of the time. I'd give him the benefit of the doubt.

Inside, it took a moment for my eyes to adjust to the dim lighting. I thought I knew all the worst bars of Oak Grove, but suddenly I was an expert. The walls were stained with years of cigarette smoke and every seat at the bar had been patched with duct tape. How they managed to maintain their liquor license was beyond me. I stuck close to Jake as he strode toward the back as if he owned the place.

He stopped to talk to two old men at the end of the counter. They each had a beer in front of them, proving there was a reason the bar opened before ten in the morning. While the two men stared at me, making my skin crawl, they mumbled greetings to Jake and discussed the weather.

I was tempted to abandon ship and make a break for the door when Jake slipped his arm around my waist, leading me to a table in the back. I didn't object, figuring it was part of his plan. Whatever that was.

"Be right back, Angel," he said. "Have a seat."

He didn't even offer to pull one out for me. There wasn't a napkin in sight I could use to wipe the chair off, so I swallowed my pride and sat next to the wall. The spot made it easier for me to keep an eye on everyone else.

Jake took his time at the bar. I guess he and the bartender had a few weeks of catching up to do. For a minute, I wondered why Jake had never mentioned this place in our conversations about bars in Oak Grove, but just as quickly I knew the answer. I'd disapprove of it and would tell him so.

"It's not your brand, but at least pretend to drink it," he said, sitting a beer in front of me.

I could play his game. And I did better than pretend, I drank a little. It wasn't all bad, but I didn't make a habit of drinking before lunch, so everything after that was only a sip. Jake, on the other hand, had half of his gone in no time flat.

"What are we doing here?" I leaned toward Jake and whispered.

"Be patient," he whispered back. "And drink your beer."

I took a sip, and another. And tried to be patient. But until Jake put his hand on my knee and pushed on it, I didn't realize I was bouncing my foot. I stopped and concentrated on not starting again. I paid attention to that and not my surroundings and didn't realize another man joined us until he pulled out a chair and sat beside me.

"Hennessey," he said.

"Carl," Jake said.

I figured it was impolite to stare, so I studied him from the corner of my eye. Older, balding, probably black hair at one time, but now mostly gray. His beer belly was not-quite-hidden under the too-tight t-shirt he wore.

"I heard you asked for me."

"I need a favor," Jake said.

"Figures. That job fall through? I don't have an opening, although Terry's might. Or does it have to do with your companion?" Carl studied me. I stared back.

Jake finished his beer. "The job is fine. I need information."

Carl leaned back and raised his hand in a peace sign. In a minute, the bartender came over with two beers, put one in front of Carl and one in front of Jake.

"Go on," Carl said.

Jake jerked his chin towards me. "Do you know who this lady is?"

"I've never seen her before, but I can make a guess since she's with you."

"Then you know about the problems she's been having?"

Carl lifted his beer to his lips and took a deep drink. "I've heard a rumor or two."

"Have any of my old friends been in town looking for me?"

Chapter 19

Old friends? What was Jake talking about? I picked up my glass and pretended to drink, trying to fit in, and failing miserably.

"A few of the regulars have asked about you, but that's not who you mean," Carl responded.

"No." Jake tapped one finger on the table. "Friends from before."

Carl nodded. He understood, even if I didn't.

"I haven't heard of any newcomers in town." Carl grinned, the gaps in his teeth showing. "Not since the last one we chased away." He picked up his glass and held it out in front of him. Jake clanked his glass against it, in a toast.

"That was fun, wasn't it? I owe you for that. And I owe you again for the information. It relieves my mind on the current problem."

Carl glanced at me. "You thought someone was using her to get back at you?"

"Or at least as a way to get me back here. Except she didn't do her part and come begging me for help.

I didn't want to hang around Cleveland on my day off and came back to say hi. Walked into the situation with no warning."

"And no preparation."

Jake nodded, his mouth a tight line. "Playing it by ear."

"It's what you're good at."

I finally figured out what they were talking about. Several months ago, Jake referred to men he'd been in prison with coming after him to correct various slights, imagined or real. And how he had to protect me from them. Back then, I thought he'd been lying to manipulate me. Now, it seemed all too real. Goosebumps rose on my arm.

Jake drained his glass. "Wish I could hang out, but I've got things to do." He took out his wallet and slapped three twenties on the table. Too much for the beer. I figured he was paying for the information. "Let's go, Angel."

I dutifully followed him back outside, the sunlight making me squint.

He held out his hand. "Give me the keys."

The beers weren't the problem. I sensed his mood. The calm he'd shown in the bar was a sham. If I let him drive, it would be dangerous for both of us. And everyone in his path.

"No. The last thing you need is to get busted for a dumb traffic violation," I said. I turned his words back on him. "Trust me, Jake."

He took a deep breath that was almost a shudder and opened the passenger side door. "Only you."

It broke my heart, but I couldn't deal with it. Not

now, and maybe never. I got into the driver's seat and asked, "Where to?"

"Thomason's office if he's there. Call him. Don't say I'm with you."

From one fire into another.

"Hennessey," Freddie said when we walked into his office. "Harmony didn't mention you."

Jake was back in form. He hated police stations but wasn't allowing it to show. "Detective," he said as if greeting an old friend, "Nice to see you, too."

"What do you want?"

Jake didn't wait for an invitation. He held a chair for me, then took a seat himself. When he crossed his legs and arms, I had a flash of Eli in business mode.

"How can I assist the Oak Grove Police in ensuring Harmony's safety?" he asked.

Freddie's mouth dropped open. "What are you insinuating?"

"It seems clear to me. Even here she's not safe from attack. And I snuck by the so-called bodyguards Chief Sorenson brought in. If I can do it, so can someone else."

Freddie slammed his fist on his desk. "Damn it, don't you think we're doing everything we can? And I heard about your little trick this morning. What the hell were you trying to prove?"

Jake looked as calm as a windless day. "Nothing. Until she told me her story, I had no intention of doing anything besides dropping in for a visit. Now, I'm considering abducting her and taking her to

Cleveland with me. Because we both are aware she won't go willingly." The ends of his lips curled up, but it was the ghost of a smile. "She can bunk with me and I'll get her a job at the bar. If she gets paid under the table and pays for everything she wants with the cash from her tips, she'll be nearly untraceable."

His idea was better than the plan I'd played with.

"I won't allow you to drag her off into a potentially dangerous position where you can't protect her. I seem to remember that you're a convicted felon who can't legally carry a gun. Hell, if it comes down to it, I can find a reason to hold you on potential charges. Breaking and entering is one possibility. How did you get in Eli's house this morning?"

Jake reached in his pocket, pulled out his phone, and waved it in the air. "I have the key. And the code. Eli gave it to me. Try again."

"There's an unsolved burglary you're a suspect in."

I'd mentioned the Cookes when I told Jake about everything else.

"The old couples' house?" Jake arched his eyebrows. "There are security tapes to prove I was in Cleveland."

"You have an answer for everything."

Jake uncrossed his legs and leaned forward. "Not everything. I have no idea why someone is preying on Harmony. I thought perhaps it was her association with me, but my sources have debunked that theory. It makes me wonder, Detective, is there any chance the real target is you or Chief Sorenson and picking on her is a way to make you look incompetent?"

Shit. I hadn't thought of that. It made the most sense of anything anyone had suggested.

Freddie's face lost its color. He pushed his chair back and stood. "Wait here," he ordered before striding out the door.

I had no plans to go anywhere. "Where did you get that idea?" I asked Jake.

"A flash of inspiration. I don't know if it's true, but it's worth checking out. Freddie or someone on the force should have an informant that can find out. They just aren't asking the right questions."

It was a different angle at least.

Freddie returned, accompanied by Sorenson. And, no surprise, Drew. The two of them glared at the two of us.

Drew spoke first. "You didn't mention your driving skills."

I fluttered my eyelashes. "There are lots of things you don't know about me."

"Like you hang out with a convicted felon?"

I supposed to an ex-cop that would be an issue. "Who has served his time. And helped bust a few bad guys. Drew, this is my friend, Jake Hennessey. Jake, this is Drew Dawson, an old friend of Chief Sorenson."

Drew turned to Sorenson. "Does he have to be here?"

Freddie interrupted. "It was his idea."

"And if you throw him out, I go, too," I said, rising from my chair.

"Everyone, settle," Sorenson said in his command voice. "I want to hear what Hennessey has to say."

"As you can guess," Jake said, choosing his words carefully, "I wasn't the popular guy in prison. I was a loner and didn't play well with the gangs. When I came back here, I worried that I'd be the target of retribution from outside connections. And I was concerned Harmony would become collateral damage. While I prevented that, it always bothered me. I figured leaving Oak Grove would be the best way to protect her.

"When she told me what was happening, I assumed someone didn't get the message. Like I told Thomason, the idea didn't pan out."

"So, you're going to throw the blame on us?" Sorenson asked.

"Do you have another idea? From what Harmony told me, you're scrambling and can't keep up with everything that's happening. Her car getting vandalized in the station's parking lot doesn't exactly inspire confidence in the department."

Had Jake gone too far?

I couldn't catch all three reactions, so I concentrated on Chief Sorenson. His was the important one. An expression of sadness flashed across his face, quickly replaced by his normal authoritative demeanor.

"Your point has been noted and taken into consideration," he said. "We'll put out feelers to see if it holds water."

"And in the meantime?" Jake asked.

"In the meantime, perhaps you can persuade Miss Duprie to cooperate with our efforts to keep her safe."

I didn't even try to defend myself.

"Or you can adapt your efforts to meet Angel's peculiarities." Jake winked at me.

"Angel?" Drew asked.

"Later," Chief Sorenson said. "It's complicated."

Now *that* was a true statement.

"You're her friend. What do you suggest?" the Chief asked.

"I rather like the idea of her bunking with me." Jake turned to me and wiggled his eyebrows. "Just like old times."

I knew exactly what he was talking about. It wouldn't happen.

"Jake," I started.

"Yeah, yeah, your heart belongs to Eli. So, why isn't he here?"

Because he'd been wrapped up in a project and I didn't want to get in his way.

Because the time hadn't been right.

Because he'd be upset I hadn't told him before.

Because I had something to prove. That I could do this myself.

But I couldn't. And I didn't like it. Not one bit.

I stuck with the standard line. "He's in the middle of a big deal and I don't want to distract him."

"For two weeks?" Jake tilted his head. "He has serious issues with ignoring the rest of the world when he's involved in a project, but two weeks?"

"He's working on the legal stuff now, fleshing out the details."

"You're making excuses. For him or for you?"

Or both of us.

"Okay, I'll call him. Tonight." Did the promise count if I crossed my fingers?

"I have to head back to Cleveland soon. I'll take you to lunch and hang out as long as I can." Jake pointed a finger at Drew. "Then you take over. There's no way Eli will get here before I have to leave."

He twisted to point to Sorenson and Freddie. "And you two keep doing what you are good at and get to the bottom of this."

"Jake," I said and put my hand on his knee in warning.

"What, Angel?" He took my hand. "I'd do anything to protect you. But I can't. These fine gentlemen would lock me up the minute I touched a gun. And I'm afraid that's what it will come down to."

"No one has tried to hurt Harmony yet," Freddie pointed out.

"Yet is the operative word." Drew pulled at his waistband as if adjusting the duty belt he no longer wore. "It's a logical next step."

"Except none of this is logical," I said. "I'm not anyone important. If Jake's theory is correct, wouldn't it make more sense to target the Mayor or a member of the City Council?"

Chief Sorenson held up one hand, palm out. "Don't put yourself down, Miss Duprie. Your unofficial service to our community is appreciated by those who need to know about it."

That sounded like a campaign speech, but he meant it. At least, I hoped he did. Still, I wasn't convinced it was enough to make me a target for someone with a vendetta against the police.

"Now that we have that much of a plan, I owe Harmony lunch." Jake stood. "Angel, do you have Drew's number?"

I had his number, all right. I was already trying to figure out how to get away from him once Jake left. "Is the rental ready to be released yet? I'd like to get it cleaned so I can return it. Were you able to pull any clues from it?"

"The bad news," Freddie said. "Is that we weren't able to get any evidence from the vehicle, not even a footprint. The good news is, it was sprayed with a water-based paint and our maintenance people washed it off before it dried."

A trip to Pittsburgh was in order. After lunch. And after giving Jake a run for his money, car to car, to help him blow off some steam.

Chapter 20

Food came first. Drew followed Jake and me to the Dairy Barn, and we let him. At least he had the decency to not sit with us or even in the next booth. He picked a table across the room where he could watch us and everyone else. Since it was past prime lunchtime, the restaurant wasn't that busy making his job easier.

Getting rid of him afterward worked out smoother than we expected. Timing was everything. We lingered over our drinks long after Jake paid the bill. The minute Drew headed to the restroom, we dashed out the door.

We switched cars and took different routes to our destination—a lonely patch of county road where we'd go when Jake was teaching me how to *really* drive. Then we swapped again.

Like a pair of giddy teenagers, we matched trick for trick in our cars, always on the lookout for traffic. It was just what we both needed to help forget the stress. He drifted, I did a J-turn. He did a ninety-degree turn. I pulled off a 360. He won because I never dared to try the driving on two wheels stunt.

As a pickup drove by, the passenger staring at us longer than necessary, we climbed out of our cars and leaned against his.

"I should head back," Jake said.

"And I should call Drew and tell him I'm safe and will be back in a few."

"Don't give him a hard time. He's trying to help."

So far, Drew's trying hadn't done any good. "I know."

Jake put his hands on my shoulders and fixed his eyes on mine. "And call Eli tonight. Promise me, Angel. I don't like this. It feels all wrong."

To me, too. "I promise, Jake. I'll cooperate with Drew and call Eli." I didn't cross my fingers, either.

He leaned in and kissed my forehead. "Call me if you need me. Or if there are leads in Cleveland you want me to track down."

"Don't be afraid to call me. The phones work both ways." I moved so he could open his car door.

"Is that a hint?" he asked. "Because you know how bad I am about that."

Yes, I knew. He climbed in and pulled the door shut. I stood back when he started the engine and took off, going the wrong direction. A short distance down the road, he did a J turn and reverse J turn, honking his horn as he blew by me, leaving me in his proverbial dust.

I waited until he was out of sight before pulling out my phone and calling Drew.

"Where are you?" he yelled without even a hello when he answered.

"About ten miles northeast of town. It'll take me twenty minutes to get back. I'm headed to my apartment, not the house. I'll meet you there." I hit the button to end the call and turned the ringer off before tossing the phone into the passenger seat. Reality would return all too soon.

I took my time, deciding where I wanted to stay. It was too late for a trip to Pittsburgh to swap out the car, and I needed to get some work done before I called Eli. My place would give me more privacy, but I wouldn't be able to see him almost life-size on the big screen.

But I wanted to check on the apartment, water the flowers, and see how my African violet was doing. I'd start there and make my final decision later.

Three motorcycles were parked in front of the house when I pulled into the driveway. Great. Now I had to deal with three men with chips on their shoulders instead of one. I braced myself for what was coming.

Drew got to me first. He pulled on the door handle, but the door was locked. Another thing Jake taught me to always check. "Open up, Harmony," he roared.

I rolled the window down a slit. "Back away from the car, Drew. And tell your buddies to do the same. I'm here, but I'm capable of driving off."

He raised one fist, and for a moment I thought he was going to pound on the window. Or the roof. Instead, he opened his hand and ran it across the top of his head, then backed away three steps. With a jerk of his chin, the other two men also moved away from the car.

With a smile planted on my face, I swung the door open. "Well, hello, boys."

Drew grabbed the top of the door as if he was afraid I'd close it again. "You promised you'd cooperate."

I got out of the car and smiled bigger. "So, I lied. I'm here now. And I'll tell you how this is going down."

His lips tightened. "You've got it wrong. You take orders from me. I'm the expert."

"Really?" I put one hand on my hip and cocked my head. "Really?"

"The lady's got you there, Dawson," said one of the men. I had my back to them and didn't recognize the voice. When I pulled in, I'd identified the guy I fooled with my Auntie Hilda act. I didn't know the other one. It was time to name them. Bob One and Bob Two. I was pretty sure there was a Bob Three somewhere.

"I'll make you a deal. I'll unlock the apartment and let you go in first to make sure it's safe. After that, I need to go downstairs and water the landlord's flowers, and I'm not comfortable letting you into their part of the house. Your friends," and I pointed over my shoulder, "Can cover the outside exits to make sure I don't escape. You hang at the top of the stairs and I'll give you a running commentary of what I'm up to. Sound fair?"

He hesitated long enough that I wasn't sure he'd agree. I focused my eyes on him, not blinking, trying to make him uncomfortable. It worked.

"Agreed. But no pulling any of your tricks. I don't trust you."

"You shouldn't." I reached over the driver's seat and retrieved my purse. I dug through it until I found my keys, buried in the bottom under a comb, Betsy, and a pack of tissues. "Follow me."

I counted the steps as I walked up them to calm myself, even with Drew close behind. The numbers never changed, but the simple act of counting made it feel like coming home. When we reached the top, I verified the tape was still in place—it was—before unlocking the door.

I stepped aside. "After you."

With his gun clutched in his hands, he bumped the door open with his shoulder. He disappeared inside, and I counted backward from one hundred until he returned. I got to ten.

"It's clear," he said. "Go on in."

A faint, familiar scent met me. It wasn't Drew's aftershave, but Jake's custom formula. I should have known. He said he'd checked out my place before going to Eli's. I wondered what other surprises he left behind. But I wouldn't look for them while Drew watched my every move.

I removed Betsy from my handbag and tucked her in my waistband, then hung the purse on its hook. After a quick stroll through my favorite place in the world, I opened the interior door leading downstairs.

"Come stand here," I ordered Drew, "So I won't have to yell as loud." It gave me a mischievous joy to see the scowl on his face.

As soon as I reached the first landing, I started my commentary. I planned to bore him with the details. "Okay, there are six steps to the bottom. Now I'm opening the door to the second-floor hallway." The door creaked in accompaniment to my words. Joe needed to oil the hinges.

I kept it up. "This floor has four rooms, including the bathroom. There's a pitcher in the front room with the plants. I'm going there first. Okay, got it. Now I'll head to the bathroom to fill it. The water pressure is a little low, but Joe and Luke don't seem to mind. Anyway, it will take a minute to fill the pitcher."

While I waited, I sang a few snatches from the first song that came to mind. One of those terrible pop songs with only one verse and a chorus that wormed its way into the listener's brain. He'd fall asleep hearing it in his head. Subtle revenge.

"Okay, I'm back in the front room," I said. "And the plants are looking good." The African violet had a few more shoots of new growth. It would survive.

"Now I'm going downstairs to make sure no one has bothered anything on the first floor." I worried someone would involve Joe and Luke in their plot against me, but with Drew's men watching the place, that shouldn't happen. At least, I hoped they kept their eye on it even when I was at Eli's. I'd have to ask Drew.

I sang the same silly song as I peeked into each room. Everything looked the same as it did the last time. One less thing to worry about. I wondered when Joe and Luke were coming back. I didn't think they'd planned to stay in Pittsburgh this long.

"I'm on my way up," I announced and started singing again.

He waited for me on the landing. Not quite in Joe and Luke's part of the house, but that wasn't our deal. "You were supposed to stay upstairs," I said. "You're an ex-cop. You know how to take orders."

"Did anyone ever tell you, you can sing?" he asked ignoring my words.

"No."

"Good. There's a reason for that."

I learned long ago I couldn't carry a tune. He didn't hurt my feelings, not one little bit. Well, maybe a tiny bit. I returned the favor by ignoring him. "Now you get to do what my last bodyguard did. Go sit at the bottom of the steps and be bored. I'll hang out here and read for a while." I'd left my laptop at Eli's, so I'd have to head over there, eventually.

"You've got a chair and a loveseat. I'll just sit in whichever one you don't."

"Drew, Drew," I sighed. "No. Just no. I like my privacy. Besides, isn't it better to stop a bad guy before he gets in here?" I had him on that one. "At least it's not raining."

I'd missed this. Sitting in my recliner, a cup of mint tea on the coffee table and a book in my hand. I'd never admit it out loud, but having Drew and his men watching out for me made me feel safe. But I couldn't hide out forever. I'd promised Jake I'd tell Eli what was happening.

That's when I found Jake's message. As I put away my teacup, I spotted the paper stuck in a drinking glass. I knew where it came from—Jake had a unique way of folding his notes. It reminded me of the paper footballs me and my friends played with as kids in the school cafeteria.

After making sure I was still alone, I unfolded it. Sometimes his notes were nothing more than a simple drawing of flowers, or a few words of support. They were more of a way for him to say hello when he didn't have time to hang around.

This one was a single word. 'HI!' Jake being Jake. Still, it was all I needed.

With a spring in my step, I headed downstairs to meet up with Drew and get back to business.

Chapter 21

The video screen did nothing to hide the dark circles under Eli's eyes. They revealed how hard he'd been working and how little sleep he'd been getting. I hated adding to his worries, but I'd made promises.

I sent Drew out of Eli's house for the first part of the call, making him wait on the porch. I wanted time alone with Eli. Drew didn't even argue.

"Hey," I said when his face appeared on the big screen.

"Hey, yourself." He smiled, and some tiredness disappeared. "Man, you're a sight for sore eyes."

"And you look like you need a few days off. Have you gotten any sleep since you've been home?"

He groaned. "Not enough. I'll try to catch up tomorrow. But the reports you sent saved me hours of work."

I was about to destroy his plans. I hated myself. Maybe I should wait a day or two. "Hmm. I've got a suggestion for what you could do with a few of those hours."

He grinned. "Oh, yeah? Tell me about it."

It was too easy. "Joe and Luke are out of town," I told him.

His eyes widened. "We can be as noisy as we want."

Oh, yeah. "And I have access to the whole house. And you left a couple of your ties here."

His grin broadened. "What do you have in mind?"

There were lots of possibilities, but as much as I wanted to, I couldn't keep up the playful banter. "Help me figure something out first."

He caught the shift in my attitude. "What's that?"

The carefully plotted words didn't come. "There's someone you need to meet," I said instead. I walked over and opened the front door. "Come in, Drew."

I pulled him into camera range. "Drew, this is Eli Hennessey, my boyfriend." I hated using that word, it sounded so juvenile, but there wasn't another one that fit. "Eli, meet Drew Dawson. He's an ex-cop. Drew is acting as a bodyguard at Chief Sorenson's request."

Eli opened his mouth, but nothing came out. He picked up his glass of water and drained it. "Tell me what's going on."

Drew butted in. "Somebody has it in for Harmony, but the police haven't been able to develop any leads as to who or why. They don't have the resources to protect her, and I'm considering starting my own agency, so Chief thought this would be good experience for me."

Eli was moving in and out of camera range, and I

couldn't tell what he was doing. "How's that working for you?" he asked. "This is Harmony we're talking about."

"Chief severely underestimated her independent streak."

I was over the male bonding act. "Whatever. I can take care of myself."

"What kinds of incidents are we talking about?" Eli paused in front of the camera long enough for me to see that he was holding three shirts. What was he doing?

"Oh, the typical stuff. Car chases and car thefts, random vandalism, trashing my apartment..." my voice trailed off.

"How long has this been happening? And why didn't you tell me before?" Eli moved off-camera again and I couldn't gauge his reaction.

"The first incident happened the day you started your conference in DC. But it didn't really affect me, so I wasn't going to bother you. Then a pattern developed. By then you were buried so deep in your project I didn't have the heart to interrupt you. You know how you get when you're in the middle of a big job."

"I'm never too busy for you."

Good words, but I knew better.

"The last incident happened in the parking lot of the police station," Drew said. "It's been suggested that Harmony is being used to make the Oak Grove Police Department look bad. It's as good of a theory as any. That's the angle currently being investigated."

"What other theories are there?"

It was my turn to answer. "I guessed I was the subject of one of those dark web games, like SWATing. But I can't find any proof of it. Jake thought it was a way to get revenge against him, but that didn't pan out either."

"You called Jake before me?"

"He showed up today as a surprise. He yelled at me for not calling you."

"At least he did something right. Is he still with you?"

"No, he headed back to Cleveland. Said he had opening duties tomorrow. But I suspect the real reason is that hanging out with cops and ex-cops made him nervous."

That earned a chuckle from Eli. He came into camera range. "Drew, are you staying with Harmony tonight?"

"If she lets me. She forced me to sit on her steps this afternoon."

Eli laughed. "At least she didn't make you stay in a van across the street!"

"I would have, but all he has is a motorcycle," I grumbled. "I let him sleep here last night, but I wasn't happy about it."

"And you'll let him stay tonight because I'm asking you to," Eli said.

"Yeah, yeah. But he has to sleep on the couch again."

"The couch is more comfortable than a lot of places I've slept." Drew rubbed his neck. "It makes me hurt just to remember Army cots."

"Or worse yet, a foxhole," Eli said.

"Okay, let's not turn this into a king-of-the-hill male bonding session." I shook my finger at Eli. "But I've done what I promised and told you. Now I'll chase Drew outside so you and I can talk in private." I turned so Drew couldn't see my face and waggled my eyebrows. "I found the train of thought I lost earlier."

Eli shook his head. "As much as I'd like that, it won't happen. I need to talk logistics with Dawson and then make reservations. I'm already half-packed."

My heart dropped to the pit of my stomach. "You're going on another trip? So soon?"

"Why? Are you coming here?"

"No. I have to get this figured out. If my original theory about me being the target of some twisted internet game is correct, the trouble will follow me wherever I go."

"And that's why I'm coming to you, Buttercup."

I didn't know Eli had spent so much time figuring out ways to break into the house, and the best way to defend it. He must have walked the neighborhood, determining where hedges and trees provided cover, and which windows provided the best views of different spots of the yard. I guessed the training he received as an Army Ranger was responsible. Drew took notes in one of those little notebooks cops always carry, and, in my head, so did I. They were trying to stop people from getting in and I was figuring ways to get out unnoticed. I'd proven the knowledge could come in handy.

"You need more guys to do this right," Eli said. "Especially if you plan to monitor Harmony's apartment. Which you should."

"I didn't have enough information when I started this project." Drew rubbed his chin. "I'll add it to my list of lessons learned. A bodyguard gig seemed easy compared to being a street cop, but this assignment has proven me wrong."

"It'll be easier when I get there. I'll stay with Harmony, so you and your men can provide perimeter security."

"This is a job for professionals, Mr. Hennessey, despite Harmony's opinion."

Eli's eyes glinted. "I'm more dangerous than I seem, Dawson. We'll discuss it tomorrow."

Eli didn't like to talk about his time in the Rangers. I'd pried some information out of him, but that was between the two of us and I wouldn't share.

"If you send me your flight information, I'll meet you at the airport. I have to swap out the rental car," I said.

"In Pittsburgh? Why aren't you using the place in town?" Eli asked.

I frowned. "There's a possibility that someone at the agency is part of this. I rented two vehicles from there and got followed in both. The second time, the person following me was driving a vehicle with the rental company, too. It may be a coincidence, but I wanted to avoid the risk.

"And there's not enough evidence to involve the police so they can get a warrant. I can't prove it wasn't someone who just happened to be going the same direction as me."

"Why Pittsburgh?" Drew asked.

I gave him a one-shoulder shrug. "Anonymity. How many people pass through the airport in a day? I made sure I fit in with the crowd. Easily forgettable. And it worked. For a few days, anyway."

"I wouldn't call a Charger anonymous," Drew said.

Eli chuckled. "Compared to Dolores? Slumming it, Buttercup?"

Drew cocked his head. "Dolores?"

"My car. She's a salsa-red Jaguar. F-Type. She's in secure storage for now. I didn't want to risk losing her after the first two car thefts."

"Excuse me, but you're an out-of-work librarian. How do you afford a Jaguar?"

Technically, he was right. About the librarian part. "I have a new job. I'm a research analyst." That was the non-flowery title Eli and I had come up with for my position. Still, I'd bought Dolores long before Eli hired me. It wasn't like I needed to work, but I wanted to. I had more than enough money to live on without a job, I just didn't like to spend it.

And why didn't he know about Dolores? Was Chief Sorenson withholding information or did Drew not ask the correct questions? He was an ex-cop, after all.

"You'll bring Dawson with you when you come, right?" Eli asked.

There went my plan of a long, quiet drive, accompanied by my favorite playlist. "Sure."

"That way I can add him as an extra driver on my rental. You and I can come back in your car, and he can drive mine."

That part of the plan I liked. It would give Eli and I much-needed time alone.

"See any problems with this, Dawson?"

"No, sir," Drew said.

"Good. Get my phone number from Harmony and call me so I can add you to my contacts. I presume you've given your number to her."

"She has mine. I don't have hers. She wouldn't give it to me."

That way he couldn't call me when I didn't want him too. Or track me. That had been a good thing when I'd been with Jake.

"I'll make sure that changes. Tonight. Now go outside so I can talk to Harmony in private."

Then it struck me. Just like that, Eli had taken charge, as natural as breathing. Drew was answering to him, not the other way around. I'd seen it happen in the office, and now that I thought about it, there were other times. I'd have to watch my step to keep our relationship on equal footing.

We waited until the door closed with a distinctive click. "Are you okay, Buttercup?" Eli asked.

"Yes. No. I'm pretending to be. I don't like anything about this. And I don't get it. But mostly I'm mad. Mad that they hurt my friends to make a point. Mad that they killed the roses I worked so hard on. And yes, mad that there's nothing me or anyone else has been able to do about it." I fought back the tears and held on to my anger. I would not cry.

❀ ❀ ❀

With a glance in the rear-view mirror, I yanked the steering wheel to the left. From the corner of my eye, I spotted Drew grabbing the dashboard. So much for my quiet little trip to Pittsburgh. How had they known?

"A warning might be nice," he grumbled.

I was too busy checking for an opening to answer. I found it between a semi and a silver sedan and moved into the farthest left lane of the road.

"Don't you believe in turn signals?" Drew asked. "If there was a trooper behind us, you'd get pulled over for a traffic violation."

I ignored his remark. "Watch for a dark blue pickup. It's been with us for five miles or so. Maybe it's just going our way. All roads lead to Pittsburgh or something."

He twisted as far as possible in his seat. Which wasn't far, because the seatbelt stopped him. "Someone you know?"

"Nope. It was hanging three or four cars back. Never getting too close." I applied the brakes to create room between me and the semi.

"Then what makes you think they are following us?"

"Instinct. Experience. Take your pick. I expect it will come up alongside of us and then drop back."

"You've done this before."

Too many times. "Yes."

"There are lots of things I don't know about you."

I eyed my mirror. "Three cars behind. This lane. Coincidence?"

Chapter 22

Drew swore and leaned forward so he could get to his gun, tucked under the seat. "You're sure it's the same vehicle?"

"The lights on top are the giveaway. Who puts smiley face lights on their truck anymore?"

At least it wasn't a game day, and the traffic flowed smoothly towards Pittsburgh. And the Charger had enough power to handle my demands.

"You need to get to an exit," he said.

"And what? Pull into a gas station where they can confront us? You aren't a cop anymore and if you pull your gun on them, you'll be the one getting arrested. They haven't done anything illegal. I can't even tell how many people are in the truck and what odds we'd face."

"And I can't call for backup. I don't like working this way."

"Welcome to the real world." I spotted an opening spanning two lanes, floored the gas pedal and punched through the traffic. Once in my chosen spot, I slowed to mingle with the other vehicles.

"Holy shit!" Drew braced himself with one hand on the car's ceiling.

"How many tickets was that trick worth?" I joked.

"Enough to put you in a jail cell next to mine."

"Why, Drew, you made a joke!" I smiled, despite the situation.

"It was a statement of fact. Not a joke." But I saw the ends of his lips twitch upward.

The maneuver put us in the slower traffic, which placed the truck in front of us. They'd moved over a lane, the perfect position for me to keep an eye on them. I was pretty sure it was *them*, and that I'd spotted more than one person in the vehicle.

"The high seat backs make it hard to tell," I said. "How many people do you count in the truck?"

Drew leaned forward. "Two, no, three? No, two and a dog."

"A dog. That makes this interesting. Who brings along a dog on a car chase?"

"A couple of kids in it for the fun?"

"Then why us and how? No one else knew we were heading to Pittsburgh today." I scanned the Charger with my magic wand before we left and hadn't found a tracking device. "Who's the leak? Who did you tell?"

"Chief Sorenson and my guys. No leaks there."

He might trust his men, but I didn't know them. Especially the new ones he'd added to provide additional coverage. Therefore, I didn't trust them. But I wouldn't say it out loud. I didn't want to insult him. "Then what are we missing?"

"A neighbor spying on you? Normally I'd suggest a co-worker, but you don't have any."

I didn't have time to answer. I was in the middle of an evasive action because the blue truck pulled in front of us and slammed on its brakes. A quick tap of my brakes and a swift move into the empty spot in the next lane, and we ended up side-by-side.

But I was too close to the vehicle in front of us, so I had to use my brakes again while keeping my eyes on the road. "Did you get the plates?"

"Temp tag. And no, I didn't get the number."

"Did they have a video recorder?"

"I can't tell. You think they are recording this to post somewhere?"

"Maybe. I'll drop back. Try to get a picture of the tag." I slowed. The driver behind us honked and veered into the fast lane. As he zoomed by, still honking, he gave us the one-finger salute. I didn't blame him.

"Give me a few more feet," Drew hissed.

It should have been easy peasy. But things didn't go my way. A furniture company vehicle filled in the space next to us, blocking Drew's view of the rear of the pickup.

"I vote we disappear," I said. "I can make it happen. There's an exit not far ahead. If we stick behind the delivery truck, we can jump off and they'll be stuck. The GPS can find back roads to the airport."

"You don't want to follow them and get their information?"

"I do. But if we keep this up, we'll cause an accident."

"Yeah." Drew stared out the side window. "I don't like it but it's the safe thing to do."

Even taking residential streets part of the way, we got to the airport early. Which was good, because it gave me time to turn in the Charger. And bad, because it gave Drew a chance to grill me while we hung out in the coffee shop near baggage claim.

"Where did you learn to drive?" he asked. "It's rare to run across a civilian with your skills."

I concentrated on my tea, fiddling with the tag hanging from the rim of the cup. "A friend taught me."

"Another thing Chief Sorenson didn't tell me."

"I doubt he knows." I looked up. "And I'd prefer if you could keep the secret."

He stared at me, then slowly smiled. "You're not a proper librarian at all. You drive like no one's business, you transform into different people, and carry a gun. I hope I never have to see you use it."

He forgot my self-defense skills, as minor as they were. "I'll take you to the range sometime so we can practice."

"It's different aiming at a target than shooting a person." Drew stirred his coffee and his eyes got blank.

I wondered what memories haunted him.

"I've never gotten the hang of aiming for center mass," I said. "It's less stressful to shoot for an arm or a leg or something."

His head jerked up. "You've shot someone?"

It was my time to stare at the table. "A couple of times. Always in self-defense. I didn't like it."

"Does the chief know?"

"Yes." I took a sip of my tea. "It's hard to hide something like that in Oak Grove."

"I got that impression. Can any of these people you shot be responsible for your current misfortune?"

"Chief Sorenson and Freddie tell me no, that they are still in the tender care of the prison system."

"Freddie?"

"Detective Thomason. We became friends after he arrested me." We even dated for a short time, but I decided not to share that tidbit.

Drew almost spit out the swallow of coffee he'd just taken. "And what were you arrested for?"

I grimaced. "Drug trafficking. It was a trumped-up charge, and the DA shouldn't have pursued it. But you know how election-year politics are. It was a great big black mark on the Oak Grove Police Department's record when the jury of my peers found me not guilty."

"And were you? Not guilty, that is?"

"Innocent as a baby." In more ways than one, back then. How times had changed. "There are still a few cops on the force who don't believe it."

His eyes darkened. "Could one of them be responsible? I hate to think of the officers I've met being involved, but I've worked a case with a bad cop."

And I'd helped get one busted. "I won't suggest that to the Chief. Our relationship has been off-balance since I turned down his job offer."

Drew set down his coffee cup and stared at me. "He offered you a job?"

"Not as a cop. As a research assistant. An expansion on the reports I do for him every month. I take what the department has accomplished and make it fancy to impress the City Council. He didn't tell you any of this?"

"I'm beginning to feel like my dear old friend has set me up for failure on this case."

We stared at each other. "No way," I said.

He shoved his coffee cup to the middle of the table. "You're right. No way,"

My phone beeped, and I grabbed it. Anything to break the uncomfortable storm cloud that had rolled in.

"It's Eli. His plane has landed." I pushed away from the table and stood.

Drew didn't move. "It'll be twenty minutes or more before he gets here."

True. And those minutes would creep by like hours. But getting up and moving would help burn off my nervous energy. I was a grown woman. It was silly that the promise of seeing Eli made me feel like a kid in line for the ice cream truck. But it did.

Eli's arms wrapped around me made it worth the wait. Which turned out to be closer to forty minutes. Because his flight didn't get to a gate for ten minutes after it landed. And he was at the back of the plane, the only spot available when he bought his ticket. Even the first-class seats were sold out.

Eli held out his right hand, leaving his left arm wrapped around my waist. "Dawson," he said.

Drew stood about five feet away from us. He had to step forward to grasp Eli's hand. Just another way Eli made clear who was in charge.

"Hennessey," Drew said. They gripped hands a moment too long. I had no doubt who won that exchange because Drew let go first.

"How was your flight?" I asked Eli as we threaded a path through the crowd headed to the luggage carousel.

"Between crying kids, sitting in the middle seat, and the odors drifting out of the restrooms? Hell. But I got here, and that's what matters. I would have taken the jet, but with Andy's wife due to have a baby, I couldn't ask him to leave home."

Andy was Eli's occasional pilot. Although the company owned a jet, Eli only used it when he had to impress potential big-ticket customers. Or tend to a last-minute emergency. And I was proud that Eli put Andy's family ahead of his own comfort.

"How was the traffic on the way down?"

"Not too bad. Had a little excitement, but nothing I couldn't handle."

"We had a tail," Drew said. "Harmony shook them."

Eli paused for a second, losing his hold on me. I stopped and waited for him to catch up.

"Who else knew you were coming?" Eli asked.

"We already dissected the list," Drew answered. "Couldn't come up with a suspect. I have a theory a neighbor is spying on her and reporting to someone else."

"Seems farfetched, but so does everything about this." Eli led us to the proper carousal, and we waited until his solo suitcase came into view. He let go of me long enough to grab it. It was a standard black, but the gold-colored luggage strap wrapped around it made it stand out from the others. I'd given it to him as a joke, but secretly, I liked that he used it.

It took extra time to get our rental cars since we used different agencies and had to wait in line both places. Eli ended up with a boring black sedan, while I got a white Camaro. Blending in hadn't worked, so I went with what I wanted. Drew was on Eli's agreement, and Eli was on mine.

Eli and I both wanted to drive the Camaro back to Oak Grove, leaving Drew to drive the sedan. We flipped a coin—Eli won. As a consolation prize, I got to choose the restaurant for supper. I didn't go with my first choice, a romantic little Italian place I'd heard about, because with Drew along as a third wheel it just wouldn't work. Instead, I settled on a chain restaurant with a good reputation right off the interstate.

I banned any conversation relating to my problems. Instead, I got treated to long discussions about the upcoming baseball season and the best handgun for police work. Typical male bonding. I pretended to pay attention, but, in reality, I studied the other patrons, wondering if any of them was a plant sent to keep track of me.

But we made it through supper without an issue— except the argument over who got to pay the bill. Eli won that one, too. When I teased him about it, telling him he should buy a lottery ticket, he just winked and whispered he hoped his luck lasted once we got home. I predicted it would, but I'd make him work for it.

We made it back to Oak Grove without a problem. Although it was weird not to worry about the headlights of the black sedan sticking behind us the whole way. Eli didn't take it easy on Drew either, as he tested the Camaro's handling. I longed to get it out to my favorite almost deserted road and give it a workout.

"I'm tired, but I'm not ready to call it a night," I said as we pulled up to Eli's house.

He reached over and rubbed the back of my neck. "I know what you mean. I'd like to test Dawson and see how good he is."

"Not as good as he wishes," I said. "He hasn't transitioned from cop to robber yet. He can't think like a bad guy. Plus, I have the homefield advantage."

Eli grinned. "What do you have in mind?"

"Your choice…we take off from here and see how fast we can lose him and his friends, or head inside and try to sneak out on foot."

He pulled me in for a kiss. "My choice?"

Chapter 23

Like teenagers, Eli and I pulled apart at the glare of headlights in front of us as a vehicle entered the circular drive.

"Curses, foiled again," Eli groaned. Then his mood shifted. "You have Betsy? My gun is still in my luggage." Which was in the trunk of the sedan parked behind us.

I reached for my purse. "Why did Drew's men let them through?"

"One way to find out." Eli swung open his door. "You wait here."

Before he could climb out, Drew showed up. He leaned in the open door. "It's safe. That's Detective Thomason."

Well, so much for our plans. Freddie wouldn't show up this late unless it was important.

Eli grimaced. "Business before pleasure."

Or not. "You want to give them a show? Come here."

"I like the way you think."

We leaned into one another. Our lips met. Fireworks blasted into the sky. Time stopped. Well, metaphorically.

Someone cleared their throat. "Don't forget where we left off," Eli whispered, his lips still touching mine. He caressed my cheek before we separated.

He climbed out, pulling himself up with one hand on the door. "Hey, Freddie, I didn't expect to see you so soon."

Freddie nodded. "Glad you're here. Can we go inside and talk?"

Shit, this sounded bad. I opened my door, swung my legs out, and stood. "What's up, Freddie?"

He didn't meet my eyes. "I've got a few questions to ask. I'd rather not do it where someone can hear."

Drew and Freddie took the easy chairs, while Eli and I sat on the couch, his arm wrapped around my shoulders. He'd gone into alpha mode, a king protecting his queen. At least, that's the way he made me feel.

"Before you start," Eli said, "Does Harmony need her lawyer?"

Freddie shook his head. "No, not her. Hennessey—Jake—might."

"What happened?" I hadn't caught the local news for several days.

"Can you tell me where you and Hennessey went after you left the restaurant? Drew says you lost him."

"Park Lane off Highway 20. You remember, where the developer had visions of a big new housing complex, put in the streets, and then went bankrupt?" I answered without hesitation. "We were testing the handling of the Charger. The pavement is rough, so it was a good test. We were there for a couple of hours. Then he headed back to Cleveland."

"You'll vouch for him?"

"Absolutely! Why?"

"Seems funny that there was another major robbery the day he was in town."

Damn. I glared at Freddie. "So, you think Jake came to your office to talk, had lunch with me and Drew, an ex-cop, then took his flashy car and robbed someone? In broad daylight? How logical is that? Who got hit?"

"Have you met the Hardens?"

"No. They must not use the library."

Eli chuckled. I jabbed him with my elbow. This was serious.

Freddie frowned. "Couple, mid-thirties, dual-income, no kids. Live on the west side of town. Wife came home from work early, didn't see anything out of place. But when the husband got home, he discovered half of his expensive whiskey collection missing."

"And how does Jake tie into this?"

"His reputation. The Hardens' security system didn't alert them to a break-in."

"Sounds like you have a new player in town. And that Jake's source was wrong. It may be someone trying to get to him."

"That the security didn't pick up the intruder bothers me," Drew said. "Could it be a case of insurance fraud? I assume homeowner's insurance will cover the loss."

Freddie nodded. "I would have considered it—except for two things. One, the wife noticed ice cream bars missing from the freezer and the husband claims he didn't eat them. Two…" He pulled out his phone, fiddled with it, and leaned forward to hand it to me. "This was in the locked cabinet where he keeps his whiskey."

I took his phone and studied the screen. "Is this the right picture? It looks like the inro found in my place."

"It is. Same manufacturer, same model."

I'd laughed when Eli bought a whiteboard. It remained stashed in a closet ever since. But as I stared at it now, I admitted to myself that it worked for what we needed. But as often as we rearranged the events, nothing clicked, especially when we included the two thefts. Even using different colors for the various events didn't provoke any breakthroughs.

A growing stack of beer cans attested to the time spent and the heat of the discussion. Freddie had switched to coffee after one, but I'd had one too many. Which was good, because I was relaxing for the first time in several weeks. Which was bad, because I wouldn't be up to full capacity if something went wrong. But why was I worried when I had three men ready to protect me?

And that was the problem. Down deep, I wanted

to be the person to figure this out. I stared at the whiteboard, hoping for a revelation.

"So, who in town drives a new blue pickup with smiley face lights?" I asked when the conversation hit a dead spot.

"I don't work traffic anymore," Freddie said. "But it'll stick out like a sore thumb. I'll put out the word for the officers to watch for it. But it could have come from anywhere."

True. Which led me back to my original theory about me being the target of an internet scavenger hunt. But where did the burglaries fit in?

And what if they didn't? Fit, that is, with everything else?

"Eli," I said, "You once told me that when you're solving difficult coding issues, you take everything in small bits instead of trying to resolve the overall issue. What if we applied that same principle here? Take the two burglaries for starters. What are the commonalities between them?"

"Besides the ice cream?" Drew asked.

I blocked off a new section on the upper right corner of the whiteboard. "Start there. Freddie, have you asked if anyone else has encountered the suspect in a break-in eating food?"

"If it happened here, it didn't get included in the official report. I'll put out the request to other departments in the area."

"What else?"

"The security systems," Drew said. "What brand and how old were they?"

I added it to the board.

"The Cookes' is about a year old. The Hardens had theirs installed six months ago," Freddie said. "I don't remember the brands."

I starred the entry to look up later.

"This is interesting," Freddie said. "But we need to list the differences, too. The Cookes' house was vandalized, the Hardens' wasn't."

He had a point. I started a new column.

"The burglaries appear targeted, like the culprit planned ahead what he or she was looking for," Freddie continued. "Valuable electronics weren't touched. Shoot, at the Cookes, an old milk jug filled with coins got tipped over but the money was left on the floor."

The space was getting crowded. I erased an old scribble to make more room.

"The Cookes were on a trip, the Hardens at work. That suggests the suspect kept track of their movements," I said. No one argued the point, so it got written down.

"I sure wish we knew who made the security systems," Drew said.

"What are you thinking, Drew?" Freddie asked.

"A few years ago, a company took heat when it turned out they contracted with a prison to have inmates work the call center monitoring their alarms. They had to change their operations when the press got wind of it."

I added a second star next to the entry. "When we run out of ideas, we can go back to that. I have access to the reports. The info should be in them, right, Freddie?"

"You have access to the reports?" Drew's jaw dropped.

"And several national and state crime databases. Courtesy of Chief Sorenson. But their information isn't up-to-date enough for our purposes. They are aggregates over months and years."

"I know the ones you're referring to. And you're right, they won't help us."

Eli had been unusually quiet. "This isn't your expertise, Eli, but can you think of something we're missing?" I asked.

"Cars," he said. "Freddie, did the neighbors identify any suspicious vehicles?"

"We're still questioning the Hardens' neighbors," Freddie said. "But no one had any useful information in the Cookes' incident."

I wrote 'cars' anyway.

"What was the overall value of the stolen whiskey?" I asked after a minute of silence.

"He had one priced close to a thousand bucks," Freddie answered, "But most of them were in the three to five hundred range. Harden values the loss around four thousand dollars, based on the prices he paid."

Memories of my father savoring his whiskey on special occasions came to mind, but I'd never acquired the taste for it. He drank it on the rocks, but with two, and only two, ice cubes. I wondered if any of his bottles were that pricey. I'd given them away when he died.

"That's a lot of bottles to come up to that amount. The thief must have been prepared with a cardboard box or bags or something," Drew speculated.

"The cameras were disabled, so there's no way to tell," Freddie explained.

Unless the culprit found the home's stash of grocery store plastic bags. If it was like mine, I'd never notice a few missing.

"Do we consider all the bottles as one item?" I asked, juggling the marker. "The inro was the only thing taken from the Cookes. How do I classify the whiskey?"

"We list each bottle as a separate item. Mr. Harden had an inventory, so he told us exactly which bottles were stolen and their original cost, as well as how they rated for flavor." Freddie grinned. "He even tracked which bottles had been sampled and which ones were still sealed. He's a bit of a fanatic."

We all had our hobbies. I wouldn't judge Harden's.

"That leads us back to the inro. I mean, one was stolen and one left behind, but there has to be a tie-in. Which puts us back to the vandalism at my place, but nothing was taken, so it doesn't fit." I put the marker on the ledge of the whiteboard and sat beside Eli, leaning against his shoulder. "It's a big circle."

"Or copycat." Eli draped his arm around my shoulders and tugged me closer. "The famous Oak Grove rumor mill at work."

"And leads back to my original theory that there's a site on the internet handing out imaginary points for targeting me."

"Why you?" Eli asked.

"Jake suggested it's to make the police appear incompetent. Whoever is doing this is too chicken to mess with an actual cop, so they are picking on me as a substitute."

"We're checking in with our sources but haven't found any basis for it yet," Freddie said. "It's only been a day and these things take time."

The sudden absence of Eli's arm surprised me. He put his elbows on his knees, clasped his hands, and leaned forward.

"If we're thinking along those lines," he said. "There is one more theory we should consider. Whoever is responsible is out to get me."

❊ ❊ ❊

"You never mentioned having enemies," I said later, when Eli and I were alone. Well, alone as we would get. Freddie had gone home, but Drew was on the couch downstairs.

"I don't call them enemies. I call them competitors." Eli sat on the edge of the bed to take off his shoes and socks. I did the same on the other side.

"You never talk about them."

"Nope. And I don't intend to now. That's work, and this isn't." He walked over and put a hand on my cheek. "I fell in love with your brain before we officially met. Tonight, when you were analyzing the connections and puzzle pieces, and seeing them in a way that two police professionals didn't, I remembered that. I fell in love with you all over."

He leaned in and kissed me, a kiss so deep it reached into my soul. He groaned as he pulled away.

"Now," he said. "We can do this one of two ways. Fast and as many times as we can stand, or slow and easy and pray no one interrupts. Either way, I plan to get my fill because I have a feeling life is about to throw us a curveball or two."

I knew what I needed, and hoped it was what he wanted, too. "What if," I said, tugging at his polo shirt, "We go fast and hard the first time and then take our time getting to know each other again?"

He pushed away my hands and peeled off his shirt, revealing his broad shoulders and muscled chest. "You," he said, taking the pins out of my bun, "I definitely love the way you think."

Chapter 24

"Thanks, R.B., I'll be in touch." Eli closed the call, and we stared at the screen asking us to rate the quality of the connection. "That's zero for five. No one has heard a whisper."

"Welcome to my world." We'd slept most of the morning. Eli was devoting the afternoon to video calling his business associates to see if any of them had caught any rumors. I stayed out of frame and listened in as I scoured the internet for a new channel devoted to Oak Grove. "It's one dead end after another."

"Did anyone ever check on the security systems installed in the houses that got robbed?"

"Two different companies. IHouseSecurity and ClearChoice Home Security. Another lead that goes nowhere."

Eli tapped aimlessly on the keyboard. "I'm glad I'm finding dead ends. That makes it less likely I'm responsible for hurting you. That's been playing on my conscience."

"Are you ever going to tell me about your competitors?"

"I need to get out of the house. Do you want to go for a walk?"

It had turned into a lovely day after an early morning rain, one reason Eli and I had stayed cuddled in bed for so long. "Sure," I said. "Should we let Drew follow us or do you want to sneak out?"

His eyes twinkled. "Do you have a way to leave with no one noticing?"

"Through the basement door. It's at an odd angle that I don't think they have covered. The inside is barricaded, so no one can use it to sneak in."

"It's tempting. I want to check it out later. I've only gone into the basement once, to do some wiring. But I don't want to get on Drew's bad side just yet."

I was so far on the bad side I couldn't get any worse. Still, there was no point in antagonizing Drew needlessly.

He hung ten feet back, far enough that he couldn't listen in on our conversation. I wasn't sure how he'd save us from an attack at that distance. Not that we would need help unless they outnumbered us. We both carried our guns.

I didn't push Eli to talk. He'd tell me when he was ready. We held hands and walked the first three blocks in silence, drinking in the fresh air and reveling in the sun's warmth. And, in my case, no mosquitoes or heavy humidity, which would have hassled us in Florida.

"I got into the software business late," Eli said as we watched a pileated woodpecker searching for bugs in an old maple tree. "Long after the dot-com boom and bust. That put me at a disadvantage in the market.

"What I had going for me was my experience with the Rangers. I had a different perspective on security than the folks who only understood software. My supposed hero status gave me an in to clients that no one else had. They didn't like it."

"I was a small player at first. When I hired Lando, that changed. With his skills combined with mine, I was able to break into bigger markets. I've made friends, but I helped put a few guys out of business." He grinned. "They deserved to be out of business. Their products were garbage."

"And how does this play into the new deal you're working on?"

In his excitement, Eli bounced on his toes, like a boxer warming up. "Can you imagine the market share a coalition of small software developers can capture? A lot of business people are tired of either being ignored by big companies or priced out of the market. If we can tap into that, we'll benefit everyone."

"You mean you aren't in it for the money?" I teased.

"The money won't hurt." He grabbed my hand and started walking again. "We're making Drew nervous by staying in one spot too long."

I'd been focused on Eli and hadn't noticed.

"Was anyone interested that didn't get invited to your meetings?" I asked.

"Nobody beyond the select group knows about it. There is always a chance for leaks, but we kept them to a minimum. We'd even stop talking when we had food delivered."

"And when you compare timelines, Thalia's car was stolen the first night of the conference. That eliminates your activities as part of the plot."

"All right, we leave out the new project. Which still doesn't clear me as a source of the issue, although it seems unlikely." Eli moved closer to me to make room for two teenage boys coming from the opposite direction. "I feel better, even if it doesn't solve the problem."

The boys tossed a basketball back and forth, sometimes dropping it, laughing as they scrambled to catch it. Normal behavior, but something seemed off. Maybe they were trying too hard to look like they were having fun, but there was a certain tension in their posture. Stiff, not natural. I bumped Eli with my elbow.

He leaned in as if to kiss my cheek. "I'm with you. Stay sharp."

We slowed our pace. I pointed out a blue jay flying by, squawking. Eli used the moment to casually push his jacket to one side and put his hand on his waist. Close to where his gun sat.

One boy dropped the ball, and they both bent to retrieve it. They whispered to each other, but I couldn't hear the words. Suddenly, the first boy grabbed the ball and took off running across the street. The other stared at us for a moment, then rushed to follow his friend.

Heavy footsteps thudded on the sidewalk behind us, and we turned to face Drew.

"What was that all about?" he asked.

"I'm not sure." Eli readjusted his jacket to hide his gun. "Whatever, it didn't go the way they wanted."

"What was the plan?" Drew clasped his hands on top of his head and asked for the fourth time. Not that I was counting.

I refused to lock myself in the house, so we sat on the porch, watching the grass grow. As tempting as a beer—or something stronger—sounded, I stuck to water. Eli and Drew were drinking sodas. Eli's stock of beer was almost gone, anyway.

We'd speculated on the various possibilities. One of the boys would toss the ball and try to hit my face. Or try to trip me. Or ram me with his shoulder and knock me down. Nothing illegal, nothing that couldn't be written off as an accident. They chickened out when Eli revealed his gun, and suddenly they weren't so tough.

None of which got us anywhere.

"I should have chased after them, made then talk," Drew grumbled.

Except the longer I was around him, the more noticeable the weakness in his left side became. He didn't limp, exactly, but it was like his body forgot how to move sometimes. Which explained why he wasn't on active duty. And why he wouldn't have been able to catch up to the boys.

"On what grounds?" Eli asked. "Bouncing a

basketball? Jaywalking? You'd get charged for unlawfully detaining a minor."

I emptied my glass of water and stood to go get more. "What bugs me," I said, "Is how they knew where we were. It's not like they bugged the car since we didn't take it. And Eli has verified there's no tracking app on my phone." Except for the locked-down one he developed and was password protected and usable by only three people, including me.

"Which leads us to an old-fashioned method." Drew looked up and down the street. "Give me a high window and binoculars and I'll find out everyone's business in a day or two. Are any of these houses empty?"

I thought about it as I got my water. I thought about it more, sitting on the front steps, listening to Eli and Drew comparing notes and analyzing the situation one more time. Every house was lived in, except for one, and it was being renovated. But I didn't know the neighbors. Probably because I didn't spend much time at Eli's and when I did, I was working or taking care of the yard. It was a sad excuse.

"What do you think, Buttercup?" Eli asked.

"Sorry, I wasn't paying attention. What do I think about what?"

"Were we boring you?"

"It's not that. I was stuck on Drew's question. About houses being empty. Except for the one being fixed up, the answer is no. The houses north of here have folks who have lived here forever. The rentals to the south have constant turnover, but they are a single story and down the hill, so they don't have a good view of this place."

"I haven't noticed many kids in the neighborhood," Drew said.

"Most kids who grow up here leave when they become adults unless they get jobs in the Pittsburgh area and commute. There's not much industry left in Oak Grove. A family moved in about a month ago, but I'm betting they won't stay long. The house is in rough shape and they haven't made any repairs."

Drew hissed. "A month ago? Shit. Don't point and try not to look. Can you describe the house?"

I closed my eyes to remember. "Three stories, white, peeling paint, faded green accents. The front porch tilts to one side. The yard is in decent shape. I've seen a man mowing it." I popped my eyes open. "Why?"

"Remember, don't look. What is the name of the family?"

The temptation was strong to check out the house, so I turned to Drew instead. "I haven't met them. Why?"

"It may be a coincidence, but your troubles started shortly after they moved in. I'd like to know more about your new neighbors."

I reminded myself I didn't believe in coincidence. "Seems like a longshot."

"It's as good as anything else we've got."

"This window will give you the best view. We can haul a chair up here for you. The curtains don't provide much cover, but if you stay a ways back, it should be fine." The third floor provided a different view of the house across the street.

"You didn't remodel this room at all. Run out of cash?" Drew asked.

Behind us, Eli chuckled. He knew money wasn't an issue in my life.

"It's the ghost's room. I didn't want to touch anything."

Drew swiveled on one foot. "Ghost?"

"It's an old house. Of course, there's a ghost. I've never seen it, but I hear it. If you watch, you can see these curtains move when no one is here. The windows are sealed, there isn't a draft, there's no logical way to explain it."

Drew grinned. "You ever see this ghost, Eli?"

"It only shows up when Harmony is alone. She's dared me to stay here by myself some night, but that's never happened." He wrapped an arm around me. "And I'm okay with that."

"Well, a ghost isn't responsible for what's been going on, so I hope it doesn't mind sharing the room for a day or two."

I hoped the ghost would show itself and wipe that smile off Drew's face. "It likes company. Just talk to it and it'll settle down."

"Or we could set up a video cam and you wouldn't need to waste hours waiting for something to happen," Eli suggested.

"It won't give me the flexibility I need or the

ability to respond immediately. I've done this before," Drew said.

I had other ways to get the information but didn't want to burst Drew's bubble. "At least the Wi-Fi signal reaches up here, so when you are bored you can always surf the internet."

"That's not the way I work. Don't worry, I'll be fine."

Chapter 23

"I give him one day max," I said, filling a thermos with coffee to take upstairs to Drew. "He doesn't realize how little happens around here."

"I give him two. Just because he seems like the kind of guy who hates to admit he's wrong." Eli's smile reached ear to ear. "What are we betting for?"

"My choice?" I fluttered my eyelashes. "Loser has to wash the dishes by hand for a week?"

I hated using the dishwasher, and Eli didn't understand why I wouldn't run it when it was only half-filled. I didn't want to waste water.

"Nope, if I win, you use the dishwasher. We've got more dishes with Drew here, anyway."

It was fair, but I frowned and sighed loudly. "Okay. Whatever."

"You realize there's an added benefit to having Drew on the third floor, don't you?"

I hadn't thought about it. "What?"

He took the thermos from me and set in on the table. Then he picked me up, pushed his lips to mine, and twirled us around. "He's also at the opposite end of the house. It's almost like we get to be by ourselves."

Almost. But not quite. If that's all I could get for now, I'd take it.

❋ ❋ ❋

By the time I wandered downstairs in the morning, showered, dressed, and ready to go to work, Drew had disappeared back to his appointed station. I'd heard him head downstairs sometime around midnight, but the only sign of his presence was the blankets he'd pulled off the couch and tossed, unfolded, into a corner. Eli, already hard at work, glanced up and grinned.

"You're late for work, Miss Duprie."

I yawned and stretched. "Sorry. I had a late night last night."

His grin widened. "Then I did my job well."

"Are you fishing for a compliment, Mr. Hennessey?" I sashayed my way over to him, swinging my hips, and placed a kiss on the top of his head. "You were in fine form last night. If I wasn't on the clock, I'd suggest another round."

He groaned and grabbed my hand. "And if Darla wasn't on my back about some contracts needing reviewed, I'd take you up on that. But I have a phone conference in half an hour and I'd like you to take part. So, we both have to be on our best behavior."

I switched into business mode. "Who are we meeting with? Any information you need before the meeting?"

218

"The police chiefs of three small towns in Maine. They want to pool resources and use a shared database. None of them have the budget to use my software on their own. It's not something I've ever tried, but I can make it work."

"And I guess you need as much information about the towns and their police forces as I can get my hands on in the next twenty-five minutes." I already had my laptop fired up and my browser on the big screen. "Give me the names and let me do my magic."

The planned half-hour introductory meeting ended up lasting an hour. The chiefs were as impressed with Eli's understanding of their needs as he was with their level of cooperation with each other. At the end of the meeting, when they asked about pricing, the number he gave as an estimate was well below his standard price. Jan in sales would give him heck about it, and Eli would do it anyway, not for the first time.

It was too soon for a celebration, but I offered to take Eli out for lunch. Figured I'd kill two birds with one stone and invite Janine and Sarah too. If we ate at the diner down the street from the library, I wouldn't have to worry about anyone's car getting stolen. I hoped.

Drew wasn't happy about it naturally, because he wanted to stay and monitor the house across the street. Eli and I convinced him that Eli was enough of a bodyguard for the short outing and we would call him if we needed backup. Which we shouldn't.

Freddie didn't come with Sarah. It made me worried and happy at the same time. Worried because I feared he was working too hard to take a break, and happy because Sarah felt comfortable enough to come on her own.

I warned Eli that Janine and Sarah didn't know everything. At least, I hadn't shared everything. I didn't know what they'd gathered from the rumor mill.

"We miss you at the library," Janine said, once we'd settled in and ordered. "I keep looking for you when I'm working at the desk."

The diner had seen better days, and I squirmed to find a spot where I wasn't sitting on the rip in the booth's seat. "It'll be at least a few more days until I'm back. I'm working on a big project for Eli."

"Ah uh. Sure. Big project. I'm surprised the two of you even left the house," Janine giggled.

My cheeks burned, but Eli took it in stride. "I have to make good use of what little time I have with Harmony," he said smugly. Under the table, he put his hand on my thigh. "But she persuaded me that the two of you would be upset if I came to town and didn't at least say hi."

Sarah smiled. "Good story. I don't believe for a second she doesn't have another reason for this lunch. You want to spill the beans now or later?"

I was saved for a moment by the waitress bringing our drinks. It gave me time to recover my mental balance.

"It was the only excuse I could come up with to escape my slave driver boss." I put my hand to my forehead. "Work, work, work. He's working just as hard. You guys are the perfect reason to turn off our computers and take a break."

"I noticed you're driving your car again, Sarah. Is it okay?" A quick switch of topics was my best bet.

"Better than ever, actually. It had been having problems, and Freddie's mechanic fixed them. It'll last me a couple more years."

Well, something good had come out of the mess. Then our food came, and conversation lagged while we filled our stomachs.

When Sarah's phone pinged, she slid it into her lap to check it. Like any of us wouldn't notice. I don't know why she felt guilty, Eli had checked his phone twice.

"Any good news to share?" I asked. I had an agenda, and this might give me my opening.

She exhaled. "No, I was hoping to get word on a house I'm this close to selling." She held her thumb and forefinger together. "I thought the couple I showed it to this morning would put in an offer, but nothing yet."

"Speaking of houses, do you know anything about the white one on Vale Street across from Eli's? I thought it was empty, but I saw someone mowing a few days ago."

Eli kicked me. I ignored him. "It doesn't look like it would take much work to whip into shape. At least, not from the outside."

"If you're looking for a new project to tackle, I'll find you a house. But not that one."

"What's wrong with it?"

"Nothing major, except it's tied up in litigation. Mrs. McInerney, who lived there for years, had to go into a nursing home a few years back. The kids lived out of town and didn't maintain it. When she died, the son and his family moved in. But the estate isn't settled yet." Sarah shrugged. "Anything could happen when it finally gets to a judge. There isn't a will."

"Sounds messy. But I'm not ready to commit myself to anything. I'll let you know if I change my mind."

"If you've got that much free time, then I should find you a few more projects." Eli winked.

"Or you could volunteer at the library a few hours a week." Janine nodded her head. "I have the perfect slot for you."

I held up my hands to fend off any more suggestions. "Nope, and nope. As much as I love the library and you, Janine, you don't need me in your way. And you…" I poked Eli with one finger, "I do plenty extra for you. Don't push it."

Sarah hid her mouth with her napkin and giggled. Janine chuckled. Eli grinned widely enough to nearly break his face and raised his eyebrows. "On or off working hours, Buttercup?"

That did it. The three of them erupted in laughter. I punched Eli in the shoulder and scrunched down in my seat until I couldn't help myself and joined them.

"That was mean," I said as we drove home.

"What?" Eli asked, glancing at me but keeping

both hands on the steering wheel. He'd won the coin toss for the right to drive the Camaro home.

"The thing you said in the restaurant."

"About you doing extra after hours? I was doing you a favor."

"How?"

"Two favors, really. First, you take yourself too seriously and you needed to laugh. Second, I wanted to distract your friends and you from the conversation about the house across the street. You were gearing up to push Sarah for more information, and I didn't want too much attention drawn to it. Especially as instinct says it has nothing to do with anything."

He was probably right. I had the same impression. "Are we going to tell Drew he's wasting his time?"

"Then neither of us will win our bet. And I'm looking forward to watching you load the dishwasher. I can see it now, you bending over to put the dishes in the lower rack, wiggling your butt— yeah, I'm going to like it."

"Maybe you should wash the dishes naked."

He almost missed a red light. The brakes squeaked as we came to a stop. "That wasn't part of the deal."

He was right. I'd blown my chance. "Care to up the stakes?"

"Hold that thought and hold on," he said. "Things are about to get hairy."

At the next intersection, he made a sudden right turn. My seat belt kept me from hitting the door. I peered in the side-view mirror but couldn't see anything. "Where?"

"Huh." Eli eased off the gas pedal. "Never mind. He didn't follow. Guess I was being paranoid."

I didn't believe it. I don't think he did, either.

Drew clattered down the stairs as we walked in the front door.

"Making any progress?" I asked as he grabbed a soda from the fridge.

"I've been on boring stakeouts," he said, popping open the can. "But this is ridiculous. The most excitement I've had all day was when a car almost didn't stop for the school bus picking up kids."

My chances of winning the bet went up. I avoided Eli's eyes, not wanting to laugh and then having to explain to Drew why. "Welcome to the real Oak Grove. We should have warnings attached to the city's Welcome sign telling adrenalin junkies that staying here is a hazard to their health."

Drew chuckled. "But you are still here. And don't tell me you didn't get a thrill out of the car chase on the way to Pittsburgh."

I'd never admit it.

"Did you have any problems at lunch?"

"No cars got stolen, no one called me a bad name, the food was good and the friends even better. Couldn't ask for more than that." And I was waiting for the other shoe to drop and all hell to break loose.

Drew just nodded. "In that case, I'm heading back upstairs. Don't worry if you hear me talking, it'll just be me and the ghost passing time."

"You've met the ghost?"

He winked. "Just joking. There is no such thing. See you later."

I waited until he vanished before turning to Eli. "He's in for it now. The ghost doesn't like being ignored."

Eli was turning on his laptop and getting ready for an afternoon full of work. "What will the ghost do?" he asked, humoring me.

I didn't have any idea. "I guess we'll find out when Drew comes down for supper."

Chapter 26

Eli was in the kitchen, pulling something together for supper. It was a better choice than making yet another run to Mama D's—I hoped. As much as I loved Mama's food, it was more appreciated in small doses. Eli didn't tell me what he planned on cooking, but we didn't have the ingredients for anything complicated.

I tried to ignore the banging of the pots and pans and the occasional curses. He'd assured me he had it covered.

I put the spare moment to good use with another search on myself. Had anything new popped up? I still wasn't convinced that I wasn't the subject of a twisted game. Especially after the confrontation on the way to the airport.

But the most promising links were purple, showing I'd already visited them. I scrolled further into the list with little hope. Even finding the census records of a woman from the 1800s who shared my name didn't catch my interest.

My phone pinged, and I picked it up to see a new message from Freddie.

'*Can I come over?*'

That he asked made me suspect bad news. I was tempted to tell him no, but I sent back '*Sure. See you in a few.*'

"I hope you made extra," I called, heading towards the kitchen.

"Does it smell that good?" Eli asked.

"Fishing for a compliment again? It smells good, but that's not why I asked. Freddie is on his way."

"Bad news?"

"Is there any other kind lately?"

Freddie turned down the offer to join us for supper. "Sarah's waiting for me, but I didn't want to hold off on updating you with the latest information."

"Your face isn't the one of a cop who arrested the villain," I said.

"Not me. But those guys who hassled you on the interstate? They're from Washington County. You aren't the only people they've bothered. It's a game they've been playing for a couple of weeks. State cops caught up with them today." He crossed the incident off the list on the whiteboard.

It didn't solve the rest of my problems, but it made the overall picture less complex. Everything else happened here in town. A bit of weight lifted from my shoulders.

"What will happen to them?" Eli asked.

"Depends upon what charges the DA can come up with. Reckless driving will be the easiest. I've given them your name and phone number, Harmony. The investigators may want to question you."

"I'll be glad to help."

"I gave them Drew's contact information, too. Where is he?"

Eli and I grinned at each other. "On the third floor, maintaining surveillance on the surroundings. He thinks he'll be able to spot someone spying on us and turn things around on them," I explained.

"I offered to put a camera up there, but he wanted to try it the old-school way," Eli added.

Freddie's mouth twitched. "I've done that a few times. I'll take the camera. If you'll pass the word along, I'd appreciate it."

We did just that over a meal of jazzed-up scrambled eggs and toast. Sometimes breakfast for supper hit the spot, and tonight was one of those nights. There was a touch of everything in the eggs, including onion, green peppers, and diced tomatoes. Oh, and the pepperjack cheese I'd bought on a whim. Eli had done himself proud.

And since he'd cooked, I did the dishes. He had more work to do. Work he wouldn't allow me to help with, saying I'd already put in my eight hours for the day. So, after Drew disappeared back to the third floor, and I'd cleaned the kitchen, I settled myself in an armchair to check my email. Now and then, I still got requests for independent research jobs.

But all that was in my inbox was spam. I took care of it and stared at emptiness. It seemed lonely.

I'd been thinking about springing for a security system for Luke and Joe's house, a way to ease my conscience about all the trouble I brought their way. Researching the reputations of the two companies whose systems had failed seemed as good of a place to start as any. Maybe it would give me a clue about what to avoid.

It was logical to start with ClearChoice because it came first in the alphabet. Despite trying various sites, I only found a few negative reviews. And two of them were obvious fakes. Either they had a great **PR** team, or their products were as good as claimed.

I moved on to IHouse. Their reviews were mostly positive as well. A few seemed familiar, but how much could a reviewer say? But when I checked out the negative remarks, I hit pay dirt. Two of them were, word for word, the same as ones for ClearChoice. That sent me on a hunt for other security companies and their reviews. Sure enough, almost all of them had the same negative comments.

But now I wondered about the positive reviews. And with Eli buried in his work, I had the time to dig. But it required at least one cup of coffee.

I made two. One for me and one for Eli. I set a cup by his left hand and laid my hand on his shoulder. He stopped typing long enough to pull it to his lips and kiss it. That was enough, for the moment.

We were still working when Drew came downstairs. "I hate to break this up," he said. "But it's bedtime for me."

"Hold on, this will take me a minute to finish," Eli said. "What are you working on, Buttercup?"

"Look at what I found. You, too, Drew." I shared my findings on the big screen. "I was checking out the two companies that made the security systems that were breached. And guess what?"

Eli put his hands on my shoulders and kissed the top of my head before studying the images in front of us. He whistled. "Imagine that."

"What?" Drew asked.

I switched to a different web page. "This is Harlington, Incorporated's website. They say their roots are from a family business in the 1930s that specialized in protecting Americans' constitutional rights. I did some digging and found out the family specialty back then was moonshine. Now, they are 'dedicated to providing safety and security in a modern era.' Ironic, isn't it?"

I switched to the 'about' tab. "Here's a list of their subsidiaries. See anything interesting?"

It was Drew's turn to whistle. "Both companies involved in the burglaries are mentioned."

"Exactly. What they are doing is marketing several variations of their product to different audiences. IHouseSecurity is aimed at the lower end of the market. ClearChoice is a step above."

"So, you think someone from the security company is breaking into homes with the systems they installed? That only happens in books and movies."

I'd thought of it and come to the same conclusion. "I'm more worried that someone found a flaw in their software and is exploiting it. I don't know how they figure out who to target unless they've hacked the company's computer systems."

"It hardly seems worth it to go to that trouble for what they've been taking."

"You'd be surprised." Eli massaged my shoulders, and the tightness in them flowed away. "We get infiltration attempts several times a day. We've hardened the systems, but my network gurus still have to watch out for malicious login attempts. And we're small potatoes compared to other companies in our field."

I understood most of what he said.

"If you're correct," Drew said. "We need to take this to Detective Thomason."

"But not tonight," I said. "It's late and everything we have can wait until the morning. The only people working at this time of day for the companies are the folks monitoring the alarms and they won't be able to tell him anything."

"I wonder if the person is breaking into other places not around here? Is there a way for you to find out?"

Eli cleared his throat. "I could, but it wouldn't be legal. Freddie will need to handle it through the proper channels."

Drew blinked. Several times. "You freak me out. The both of you. I'm just a kid in a pool filled with sharks. I'm used to facing down bad guys and have the scars to prove it, but this is a whole different playing field. If I walked by the two of you on the sidewalk, I'd never even give you a second glance."

And that was the way I liked it.

"I feel sorry for Drew," I said as Eli and I cuddled in his bed.

"Why?"

"I bet he was great as a street cop. Got to know the neighborhood, knew who belonged and who didn't. Probably made sergeant and nothing higher. Told himself it was so Chief Sorenson could keep moving up. He knows how to use a smart phone, but the idea it's a computer doesn't click. He hasn't transitioned to the modern world. And that's sad, because he'll never be able to have his own agency unless he's lucky enough to hire the right people to do the background work."

"Do you think that's why Sorenson brought him here?"

"Drew thinks it was to give him some practical experience."

"Right. And show him he needs to rethink his plans."

Made sense. "How can we help him?"

"I don't know that we can. This is something he'll have to figure out for himself."

❋ ❋ ❋

I left Freddie a message at the cop shop first thing in the morning. Well, first thing after I woke up and had my coffee. I didn't call his personal number because it wasn't an emergency.

Eli and I were debating the best way to set up a

shared database for those three towns in Maine when Freddie showed up. I brought up the pages I'd saved, and he spotted the connection right away.

"You know this doesn't solve your problems, Harmony," he said after I sent him an email with the links. "Not if your theory about the burglaries being separate is correct."

"Truth is, I wasn't looking for this when I started. I just wondered how much the systems cost. But, if it helps you out, I'm good."

"If it gets the City Council off the Chief's back, we'll all be better. An unhappy Chief makes for lots of unhappy officers down the chain."

I'd seen that in action. And experienced it myself when I covered for Janine at the library.

"Where's Dawson?" Freddie asked. "Still up on the third floor?"

"Yes," Eli said. "And that means I win our bet."

A grin spread across Freddie's face. "You two had a bet going about how long he'd last on his stakeout? What did you win?"

"Harmony has to use the dishwasher for a week and I get to watch her load it."

"That's it? I would have gone for higher stakes. Like she has to cook for the week."

"She likes cooking."

I did, but I liked it when Eli cooked, too. And, once in a rare while, we cooked together. That was the best.

"What's he so fixated on?"

"A house across the street. He thinks it's suspicious because the people moved in about a month ago.

Sarah said that's when Mrs. McInerney died and her son and his family showed up."

"Dawson is barking up the wrong tree. I've heard about the house. The sister is harassing them with bogus wellness and CPS calls. The guy is trying to ride it out until probate is over and then he plans to file a restraining order against her." Freddie shook his head. "Some families. I'll break it to Dawson so it comes from an official source."

Chapter 27

"We've got a tail." Eli twisted to peer out the back window. He'd caught me checking the rear-view mirror too many times.

"A motorcycle. I'm pretty sure it's one of Drew's guys. That explains why he didn't put up a fight when we told him we were leaving."

"Or demand he come with us. Even though we're just going to your place."

I'd gotten a text from Joe that he and Luke were home. So, we were heading there to visit and see how Joe felt. And check on the African violet. I hoped to move it back to my apartment.

I glanced in the mirror again. "Should I play nice and pretend he isn't there or lose him? If he's one of Drew's, he knows where we're headed." The bike bothered me. It didn't look like the right model, but I wasn't an expert.

"Let's see what Drew knows." Eli had his phone in his hand, scrolling through his contacts.

Until we'd received confirmation from Drew that

he'd sent our follower, I wouldn't take it easy on him. I made a quick left while Eli waited for Drew to pick up. The rider came with us, as expected. I didn't expect to lose him that fast.

And some of my tricks wouldn't work against a motorcycle. They had a built-in advantage based on their size and maneuverability. I couldn't throw him by ducking down an alley.

"Drew wants a description of the bike," Eli said. "He didn't assign anyone to come with us, but he thinks he knows who it could be."

"I'll make a right at the light. That should give you a view of the bike and rider." I even turned on my signal to make sure that the rider would stick with us.

"Green and black bike, helmet is black with fluorescent green stripes, rider is wearing a black jacket with lime green accents. There's not much more I can tell you," Eli said, as much to me as to Drew.

I tried but couldn't hear Drew's side of the conversation.

"We can shake him," Eli said. "Or bring him back to the house. Your call."

I strained to catch Drew's response.

"I'll put you on speaker." Eli pushed the button.

"Can you hear me, Harmony?" Drew's voice came from the phone.

"Yes. What's the story?"

"Kid's name is Saunders. Johnny Saunders. He's a wanna-be. He's been hanging around with my guys in their off—hours, being a nuisance."

"What's he want?" While I waited for an answer, I slid into a dirt alley. If he didn't have a dual-purpose bike, the dirt and ruts would slow him down. And if my tires spit up a few rocks, he'd have to back off.

"He wants to be part of the action, trying to make himself a reputation. The guys have been managing him by sending him on minor errands to keep him occupied."

"What have you learned about him?"

"That he's full of shit. He knows lots of good words and understands basic police procedures. You know, the kind you pick up from watching cop shows. But he thinks that makes him an expert."

Been there, done that. "You want me to take him down a peg or two?"

Drew hesitated. "Let me handle it. Lead him here. I'll have the guys use professional moves to cut him off and teach him a lesson."

I exchanged a glance with Eli. Drew's proposal made sense but destroyed the fun factor.

Eli read my mind. "We'll take the long way back, Drew," he said. "Give your men more time to get set up."

"10-4. See you in a few."

Eli ended the call. "What are you planning, Buttercup?"

"How does a slow tour through the newest residential areas with the most stop signs sound? Staying under the speed limit and braking for every squirrel and other living thing?"

"The exact opposite of what he expects. I like it."

I stretched out a trip that should have taken five minutes to fifteen, going through two school zones, watching for Mrs. VanWey. She'd been a crossing guard forever. Then I remembered she'd finally 'retired' after forty years of being a volunteer. I followed a bus for a mile or so. The stop and go traffic would tax Saunders' skills. I got him stuck at a school crossing but drove slow enough for him to catch up.

"How can he not tell that you're jerking him around?" Eli asked, leaning forward to see in his side-view mirror.

"He knows. He's waiting for the opportunity to pull some fancy trick and show me up."

"And he doesn't dare try it when there's the possibility of a cop nearby."

"That's what I'm hoping. To tell the truth, it's fun watching him get frustrated."

"How far are we from the house? I don't recognize this street."

"Five blocks. We're on Ash. It's only four blocks long and ends when it joins Maple. The only people who use it are the folks who live along it. It'll put us right where Drew wants us."

Not only was Ash the shortest street in town, it included a ninety-degree turn, confusing anyone who didn't drive it regularly. I counted on the assumption that Saunders was in that group.

I braked for the curve and made it easily. Saunders wobbled as he straightened up. A couple of years ago, the city had installed a rumble strip to slow people down. The Camaro handled it flawlessly, a motorcycle not so much, no matter how good the rider.

Right where they were supposed to be, I spotted four motorcycles at the intersection. The 'correct' kind of bikes. Bulky and sitting low to the ground compared to the one behind me. It was the first time I'd seen all four of Drew's men together. Bobs One, Two, Three and Four. He must have woken up the night shift to join in the fun. I wondered if he'd ever introduce them to me.

"Here we go," I said, fluttering my foot on the gas pedal. As I passed the first man in the cluster of bikes, I raised my hand in salute. It was their move.

He pulled out behind me and a second man behind him. I turned onto Blue Spruce Drive, and my view got blocked by a six-foot-high hedge. It didn't matter; it was up to Drew now. Joe and Luke would wonder if we didn't get to their place soon.

❋ ❋ ❋

"I'm worried about Joe," I said, placing the African Violet back onto its little stand, positioned to get the perfect amount of sunlight.

Eli was busy getting the iced tea from the fridge. "Why?"

"He's had plenty of time to recover from his surgery, but he looked pale." And distracted. And uneasy.

"I didn't notice, but you're closer to him than me."

"It's like the spark disappeared. He's always been so full of life, and today he got tired walking up one flight of stairs. He's keeping a secret from me, and I'm concerned something is wrong with him."

"Or he was worn out after a busy week." Eli handed me my tea and bestowed a soft kiss on my cheek. "You have enough to worry about, don't go imagining things to make it worse."

He was right. And wrong at the same time. I didn't believe I was mistaken, but until Joe told me what was going on, I needed to pretend I didn't know.

With my head on Eli's shoulder, I sipped on my tea and looked out the kitchen window. Piper darted back and forth near the rear fence, sometimes throwing himself against it, frantically barking. He wasn't celebrating being home.

"Eli," I hissed.

In a seamless motion, he set down his glass and pulled out his gun. Because I had to stop to pull Betsy from my purse, he made it to the first landing before I got to the door. He waited for me to catch up and we reached the bottom side by side.

Piper barked a few more times, then trotted over to greet us, slobber drooling from the sides of his mouth. About the same time, Luke dashed out the back door. "What's going on?"

Eli lowered his gun. "Don't know. I didn't spot anything. But something upset him." He reached down to pat Piper's head.

"Any chance that raccoon came back?" I asked.

Joe shook his head. "Not likely in the middle of the day. A stray dog or a cat, I'd believe, but you didn't spot one."

We hadn't seen a person, either. I felt foolish as I tucked Betsy into my jean's pocket. "Whatever it was, is gone now."

"I'll keep a watch out for a few days," Luke said. "In case someone's pet ran away."

It was as good of an explanation as any. Too bad I didn't believe it.

"Were we overreacting?" Luke had taken Piper inside, and Eli and I had climbed the stairs to my apartment. We sat on the loveseat sipping our teas and staring at the wall. Eli had a call scheduled, and we had a few minutes to kill.

He put his glass on a coaster, leaned against the back cushion and took his gun out of his pocket to examine it. The metal gleamed in a beam of sunlight that snuck in through the front window. "I've never seen Piper that upset."

Several years ago, I had, when the police maintained surveillance on my place, trying to prove I was a drug dealer. "I can't convince myself it was only another dog."

He snapped on the safety. "We can fake it for Luke and Joe. And that's all it will be—pretending."

I'd gotten good at pretending. Too good. And it might be time for another act because I needed to find out whatever I could about Johnny Saunders. I doubted I'd uncover the information on the internet. Eli would hate Taylor, but her reappearance seemed to be our best shot.

While Eli talked on the phone, I started my research. In between quick jobs for him, that was. He'd scribble something on a notepad and pass it to me. I'd find the answer, add it to the sheet, and give it back. The tactic worked like a charm. It made him seem more of an expert than he already was while giving him the ability to use his considerable appeal on the people at the other end.

In between his quick questions, I started my search. Assuming Johnny was a local, I began with recent high school yearbooks to figure out how old he was. I didn't have any luck with the first few I checked, but I wasn't sure if I was spelling his name correctly or what he looked like. I gave it up as bad methodology.

Next, I ran general searches trying to figure out how to spell his name. I quickly discovered it was too common of a name to narrow down to the right person without additional information. There were at least three men living within an hour of Oak Grove with slight variations. Or, they were the same guy using different spellings for different things. I couldn't decide.

I was about to text Drew and see what more he knew about Johnny when Eli slipped the notebook back to me. The question he posed would take more than a minute to answer, and I was on his time.

Chapter 28

Eli double-checked the lock on every window and the door before we headed back to his place. It did nothing to relieve the irrational guilt that I was putting Joe and Luke in danger. With the extra police patrols and Drew's men stationed in the neighborhood, they'd be safe. I hoped.

I lost the coin toss, so Eli got to drive. Halfway to the house, he made a sudden turn to the right, throwing me against the door.

"What color is the car?" I asked, twisting to look behind us.

"No one is following," He gripped the steering wheel. "But I'm not ready to go back to the house where we'll be watched." The right side of his mouth lifted. "Now I understand why you hate bodyguards. Call Drew and tell him we're going for a drive and not to worry."

I cheated. I sent a text instead. That way Drew couldn't yell at me. Then I followed it with a second message to say we wouldn't be answering his calls and don't bother trying.

With that chore finished, I sat back and prepared to enjoy the ride. "Where are we going?"

"It's too soon for star-gazing, but do you suppose anyone is up at the point?"

"Sounds good." The point was the 'parking spot' for Oak Grove's teenagers. And by parking, I meant make-out. Because it sat on a hill above the city lights, it made a great place for stargazing. No kids would be there this close to suppertime. Even the sheriff's deputies wouldn't run patrols there until later.

We passed a car going down the hill as we went up. True to my prediction, we had the overlook area to ourselves. The Camero wasn't a convertible, so Eli and I leaned against the driver's side and each other and watched fluffy white clouds float across the sky. Leaning turned into hugs and soft kisses. It was perfect, but it wouldn't last forever.

"Come back to Florida with me," Eli whispered, "Where I can protect you." He pulled back to stare into my eyes. "Besides, I enjoy having you sit by me when we are working together. I fall deeper in love with you each time."

My heart fluttered. Truth was, we'd crossed every boundary we'd set for ourselves to separate our work and love lives. And I didn't regret it a second. But I couldn't commit myself to Florida. I fell back on an old discussion. "We'd be fighting off mosquitoes there."

He chuckled and stole my next line. "There aren't any hills, either."

A small plane passed by overhead and we stopped to watch until it was only a sparkle in the sky. The sound lingered on, mingling with the faint rumble of semi-trucks on the unseen highway.

"Have you seen a therapist about your fear of flying?" Eli asked out of nowhere.

I'd never told him I was afraid of traveling in planes. I hadn't told anyone. "Where did you get that idea?"

He stroked my back. "Call it a hunch. It's the way you react every time I mention you coming to Florida. And how you clung to me when we took the company jet from here to Orlando."

Yeah, I'd barely made it through the flight, even with him to hold on to. I opened my mouth to tell him I'd seen a professional about my problem when there was a loud 'POP' nearby.

Eli shoved me against the car. His hard body covered mine. "That was a gunshot. Are you okay?"

I was fine. But if someone put a bullet hole in the rental vehicle, I'd be pissed. "It didn't sound close."

Now and then, Eli would get a haunted look in his eyes, as if remembering something terrible. This was one of those times. What nightmare was he reliving?

Another 'POP,' nearer this time, and he pushed me to the ground, laying on top of me. "I can't tell where they're coming from." His hand rubbed my thigh, but he was only reaching for his gun.

Betsy and my phone were in the car. "How can we be sure they're shooting at us?" I asked quietly.

"You see anyone else?" he snapped.

I was thinking in terms of squirrels or birds. The

gun didn't sound loud enough to be someone poaching deer. But Eli knew more about weapons than I ever would.

I snaked my hand to the middle of his chest. "Give me your phone."

"I left it in the car."

Which sat too close to the ground for me to crawl under and get to the other side. Hell, I didn't even know which side the shots came from. "If you jump up long enough to open the door, I can crawl in and snag our phones." And Betsy.

"No."

I'd expected that answer. "What's your plan?"

Another shot rang out. It whistled in the air as it flew by.

"He's downhill from us," Eli said with a note of satisfaction in his voice. "In the trees. And the upward slope is throwing his aim. He's shooting high."

I guessed that was a good thing.

Without warning, he rolled off me. "I'm going to stand up. After the next shot, I'll run around to the other side of the car. I don't think he's good enough to get two shots off that quickly. He sure as hell can't hit a moving target."

"Then what?"

"You'll join me. I'll tell you the rest then. Trust me."

I did. "I'm ready when you are."

His muscles tensed. He took a deep breath and nodded at me. As swift as a rattlesnake's strike, he sprung into a half-crouch at the rear of the car. Then he disappeared.

My turn. But where was the shot—my cue? I was tempted to make my move without waiting.

I heard the hiss of the bullet cutting through the air before the gun's report. On my feet, I pushed one foot in front of the other. I counted each time my shoes met the hard dirt surface. One. Two. Three.

My hand slid over the smooth surface of the car's trunk as I made my turn. A second shot rang out. Closer. Too close. What had Eli said about the guy not being good enough to get two shots off? Then I realized it was Eli giving me cover. Like a runner headed for home, I dove the last few feet into Eli's waiting arms.

We ended up tangled in a heap. But safe. For the moment. I took a minute to catch my breath. And to kiss Eli once or twice.

"What's the plan?" I asked. He was the ex-super soldier, after all. This was in his area of expertise, and I was more than happy to let him take the lead.

"First, I'll get the phones and your gun out of the car. Then you'll call Drew and 911. Drew first, because once 911 answers your call, you won't be able to hang up. Drew can't do anything but rally the troops because he won't know where we are."

Made sense so far. The emergency line would be dispatched to the sheriff's department. Drew would inform Sorenson, who would reach out unofficially to make sure our situation was taken seriously. No chance for failure there.

"Then we wait?"

"Then *you* wait. While you keep the 911 operator entertained, I'll drop over the edge of the cliff and circle around. I want to come in behind this guy's position and take him out. He won't have a chance to escape."

I should have told him to let the professionals handle it. That it was too dangerous. But the precipice was only ten feet high, and kids jumped down for dares all the time. And he was the professional. The haunted look in his eyes had been replaced by that of a hunter. There was no point in arguing.

The attacker fired again. The shot must have been wildly off-target because I didn't hear it strike anything. "What are we waiting for?" I asked.

"This." He cupped my face in his hands and leaned in for a deep kiss. One that sent warmth flooding through my body. It meant 'I'll see you later,' but my fear made it feel like 'goodbye.'

He got to his knees and yanked open the car's door. My purse was behind the passenger's seat, and he struggled to get it out of the small space. He passed it to me. I retrieved Betsy and nestled her in my hands. It may have been a false sense of security, but I felt more confident.

Next came my phone. It had been in the cupholder. Luckily, it still had a full charge because I might need it for my call to 911.

Eli wiggled his way back to the ground beside me. For just a moment, we leaned against the car.

"I wish I had more ammo," I said, checking to make sure there was a cartridge in the chamber.

"You shouldn't need to use Betsy. She doesn't have the range to be effective. If the bad guy gets close enough to put her in action, aim for center mass."

We both knew how that would turn out.

"Make the calls, Buttercup. I'm going silent. I'll see you soon."

Phone in hand, I watched as he ran a few steps and disappeared over the edge of the outlook.

I opted out of the call with Drew and skipped right to emergency services.

"911. Where's your emergency?" said a female voice.

"I don't have an address. I'm at the point."

Her keyboard rattled. "The hangout spot?"

"Yes."

"Is this a medical emergency?"

Not yet. "No. Someone is shooting at us. They've missed, so far."

"May I have your name, please?"

"Duprie. Harmony Duprie."

"Holy… Hang on."

I didn't think 911 operators put callers on hold. Then I realized people were talking in the background and I wondered what was going on.

"Miss Duprie?" a man asked.

The voice sounded familiar, but I couldn't place it.

"Yes?"

"This is Deputy Nelson. Remember me? I understand you are at the point and shots have been fired?"

I remembered him. He'd suspected me of murder

but was glad to admit he was wrong. "That's correct. Nobody has been hit. The guy can't hit a barn door."

"Are you there alone?"

"It's too early for the high school kids. We're the only ones up here. Eli Hennessey is with me. Do you remember him?"

"Yes. Are you in a safe place?"

As safe as possible. "I've taken cover behind my car. It's a rental—a white Camaro." I didn't want him looking for Dolores and not finding her.

"Deputy Chicos is on his way to your location. We received a bulletin from Chief Sorenson concerning your situation a few days ago. What else can you tell me?"

"I'm armed and so is Eli. But we don't have a visual on the shooter. He's hiding in the woods." And took that moment to fire again, hitting nothing.

"Are you all right, Miss Duprie?"

"Fine. Like I said, he's a rotten shot." Either that or he was trying to keep us pinned down.

The line went dead for a moment. "I've patched in Deputy Chicos," Nelson said. "He'll be there soon. Keep talking so he can monitor the situation."

I couldn't hear sirens yet. "Eli is circling in behind the shooter. His phone is silenced, so we can't communicate."

"What's he wearing?"

"Eli? Tan khakis and a light blue polo shirt." One of my favorite colors on him, but it wouldn't do much in the way of camouflage.

"What's his number? We need to call him and tell him to back off and let us do our jobs."

"His phone is off, remember? And he won't quit. He's afraid the suspect will take off before law enforcement arrives. Your sirens will be the giveaway."

"We're coming in as a Code 2, Miss Duprie. Lights, but no siren."

That explained why I didn't hear anything except for the ever-present rumble from the freeway. The crows weren't cawing, the robins weren't chirping. Their absence made me realize I was alone—and terrified. What if the bad guy crept up on me? What if that shot had been him shooting Eli? Did I dare to peek out from behind the car to check out the area?

I gulped, fighting back a wave of nausea. I could do this. The cavalry was on its way, and Eli was nearby. And okay.

I had to believe it.

Chapter 29

"Miss Duprie? Miss Duprie!" Deputy Nelson's voice broke through my trance.

"Sorry. I was listening for Deputy Chicos' car," I lied.

"He's still a couple of miles out. Sit tight."

Patience is a virtue, just not one of mine. There had to be something to do besides wait to be shot. I was tempted to stick my head out from behind the Camaro to survey the territory. But if the bad guy got lucky, I'd be toast. Instead, I laid flat on my stomach and peered through the slight space under it.

I didn't see much. Sticks and rocks and dirt. Litter left by careless people. A lot of wild bushes and small trees at the edge of the parking area. The trunks of larger trees beyond that. A smattering of pines mingled in with oaks and maples. No signs of a man's legs and shoes. That was a good thing.

A breeze rustled through the leaves of several bushes. But that seemed wrong. More of the branches should have been moving. And higher up, not only next to the ground.

"How close is Chicos?" I whispered into my phone.

"What's happening?"

"I'm seeing movement at the edge of the clearing. It doesn't look like the wind. But nobody's there."

"Is it staying in one place?"

I hadn't been paying good enough attention. "No. It's moved. Not by much, but a bit."

"Keep your eyes on the area."

They were glued to the spot. Nothing stirred. A sudden gust whipped up the dirt, and every tree and bush responded. I covered my face with my arm to block the dust.

Then it strutted out from under the cover of an azalea. The one that got away last fall. A wild turkey.

I'd heard a few lived in the woods surrounding Oak Grove but had never seen one. It wasn't that impressive with its wings tucked in close to its breast, but it amazed me anyway. The way it waggled its head made me grin despite the situation. "Miss Duprie?" Nelson asked.

"When's hunting season?"

"Not until the fall. Why?"

"I'm no wildlife expert, but it looks like a turkey to me, red neck and all. And I think he knows he's safe because he's strutting like he's got nothing in the world to worry about."

"A turkey?" There were some loud voices in the

background, and he came back to me. "The experts here say it's possible. Unlikely, but possible."

I wanted a picture of it to prove I wasn't imagining things. I stretched my arms out under the car and pushed the button on my phone. Several times, moving the focus a little each time and hoping one of them would do the trick.

As I checked the results, more movement caught my eye from the edge of the clearing. Another turkey? Did they hang out in flocks?

But no. Whatever it was, it was too big to be a bird. "Deputy," I whispered. "There's something else out there. How close is Chicos?"

"At the bottom of the hill. He's located an old pickup. No tags. We're running it based on the VIN."

"We may not have time to wait." The bushes rustled again. I switched my phone to my left hand and gripped Betsy in my right. I wasn't the only one scared by the noise because my friend, the turkey, ran back into the forest.

"Stay where you're hidden."

That was the plan. I kept my eye on the trees. A large bush, browner than the rest, moved out from the edge of the woods. Wait, what?

The bush stood. The underside was a mottled green and tan pattern. Then the bush shook itself and fell to the ground. A man in camouflage with green stripes painted on his cheeks studied the surroundings. One gun hung in a shoulder harness and a rifle was slung across his back. I snapped a picture. If something happened to me, there would be evidence of who had done it.

His eyes settled on the Camaro. At least, that's what it seemed like from my viewpoint. He moved forward a few steps and I could no longer see his face.

I belly-crawled towards the rear of the car where it sat higher and I could see more. The man was within a few feet of the vehicle. I worried he planned to steal it. Had Eli taken the keys out of the ignition?

He came to a stop on the driver's side. I crooked my neck to see his feet. When his shoes paced towards the back, I debated my next step. Stand up and point Betsy at him and yell at him to halt? But he had weapons too, and I didn't know how quick of a draw he was.

But luck and a large stick were with me. The one laying in the dirt beside me. Cracked, but good enough. As the man walked along the tail end of the Camaro, I stuck the branch out about ankle height. He was too busy looking in the car to pay attention and fell flat on his face. Before he figured out what was going on, I stood and ground my foot into the middle of his back, lording over him like a conqueror planting a flag.

"Don't move," I said, deepening my voice to sound threatening. "I've got a gun. And the sheriff is on his way."

I wasn't lying. An engine revved as a car climbed the hill. Who else could it be?

By the time Deputy Chicos handcuffed the guy and dragged him to his feet, the rest of the cavalry arrived. Eli first, because he'd been tracking the man through the woods. Shortly after, Freddie showed up. In an unofficial-official capacity, because outside of city limits, he had no authority except for what the interlocal agreement between the county and city allowed. Then Drew and all four of his men appeared, and another deputy.

It seemed like overkill. The guy didn't resist. He hadn't fought me, either. Just laid there. He wasn't talking, not even providing his name. A pat-down found more ammo and several dangerous-looking knives, but no wallet.

As they loaded him into Deputy Chicos' patrol car, he turned to look at me. Eli and I stood on the far side of the parking area, watching the proceedings. A frown took over his face and he spat on the ground. "Bitch," he snarled before Chicos shoved him into the back seat.

❀ ❀ ❀

"His name is Evan Bluffs," Deputy Nelson told us. We were at the Sheriff's Department giving our statements. They'd allowed Freddie to observe the questioning of the subject, but we couldn't. "He's well-known to the department, at least the more experienced crew. He's a bottom-feeder, lives off odd jobs, the government, and drug deals, although we haven't been able to prove that part. I've only had one run-in with him, and that was for vandalism at a county park. He carved a crude message into a support beam of a pavilion."

"Shooting at us is a huge leap from simple mischief," I said. "And what was with the name calling?"

"That bush he wore is known as a ghillie suit. It's used by the military and been adapted by hunters. He claims he was just practicing his survival skills and didn't shoot at anything but trees. Since he missed everything, we can't prove otherwise. We didn't even find any dead birds so charging him with poaching is out of the picture."

"What can you hold him for?" Eli asked.

"Because he refused to provide his name, we'll charge him with resisting arrest. Illegal discharge of a firearm. Endangering public safety. Those won't go very far. He's got pushing the limits of the law down to an art form."

"What's up with him calling me a bad name?" I couldn't bring myself to say the word.

"Chicos can ask in the interview. I can't imagine the public defender will stop him from answering. If you want to hang around for a few more minutes, I'll check how things are going."

I did. Want to wait. And so did Eli, judging from the nod he gave me. So, we sat in Nelson's cubicle, pretending to sip the atrocious coffee and browse the wanted posters, while he went off to see how the interview was proceeding. We waited long enough that Eli left to find a soft drink machine, so we'd have something decent to drink.

We'd almost finished our sodas when Nelson came back with Freddie. Both men wore frowns. Eli squeezed my hand.

"Well?" I asked as Nelson sat at his desk and Freddie grabbed a spare chair from the next cubicle.

"You won't like it. Bluffs demanded that we charge you with assault. Claimed he'd done nothing wrong. Chicos told him he was lucky he wasn't dead, that you had every chance and legal right to shoot him in self-defense. The public defender agreed, but he didn't want to accept it.

"But you don't have to worry. We won't charge you."

That was some consolation, anyway. Still, I sensed there was more to the story.

"What else?" Eli asked.

Freddie blew out a deep breath. "He said it was because Harmony is Chief Sorenson's pet and law enforcement protects you. Not in those words."

I was a glutton for punishment. "What words did he use?"

"He called you the chief's sidepiece. His bitch. Whore. And other such descriptions."

I flinched. Words are only words, but these cut deep. Eli rubbed the top of my hand to comfort me.

Nelson handed me a tissue I hadn't realized I needed. "You're in good company, Miss Duprie. He calls all women those names, including the department's chaplain and our other female employees."

I dabbed at my eyes. "How did he know me?" And how many other people believed the same thing? I wouldn't get the answer here, so I tucked it into a corner of my mind to worry about later. "Is he involved in harassing me?"

Freddie shook his head. "He didn't realize who you were until your name was mentioned during the questioning. When he heard it, he sat up straighter, blinked his eyes, tensed his muscles. Purely a reflex action. That's when he spouted off the filth. And he provided an alibi. If it checks out, it will place him out of town for the past couple of weeks."

Another dead end.

"But," Nelson said, "He hinted he knew something about the other incidents and would tell us for a deal. Lesser charges, that sort of thing. Then his attorney shut him up, but we'll keep pushing."

It didn't feel like a ray of hope, more like the culprit grasping at straws to make things better for himself.

"The process could take several days," Nelson continued. "And there isn't a guaranteed outcome. Don't hold your breath while you wait for an update. Go home, get back to work, hang out with your friends, live your life."

My life had been on hold for too long. I needed to reclaim it.

Chapter 30

"How do you spell Johnny Saunders' name?" I asked as I turned on my laptop that evening. I figured as long as we wouldn't be going out, I'd resume my research.

"It's J-O-N S-O-N-D-E-R-S," Drew spelled out, never moving his eyes from the display of the security cameras on the big screen. Eli had set it up so all four videos were running in real-time. "Why?"

"He's a potential lead. It's far too much of a coincidence that Bluffs started playing his military game just as Eli and I showed up. And I don't believe in coincidence." Although Drew and his men had given Jonny a hard time, they hadn't run him off, figuring it would do more good to keep an eye on him. "You told your guys where we were going, I'm assuming."

"Yes."

"And did you inform Chief Sorenson?"

"Of course. I left a message for him, anyway."

Eli poked at the fire he'd started in the fireplace

and chuckled. "I win." A spray of sparks rose and drifted up the chimney.

"You win what?" I asked.

A wide grin lit his face. "Drew thought after our adventure today, you'd be too tired to do anything but watch TV or read. He wouldn't take my word for it, that you'd be more determined than ever to find the culprit. So, we made a bet. He's on the hook to cook breakfast tomorrow."

I had my doubts. Drew didn't strike me as a guy who knew much about cooking. But Eli seemed pleased with himself, so I kept my mouth shut and opened my browser.

"You know, we checked Sonders out," Drew said. "No wants, no warrants, no record."

"Yeah, but did you find out where he was born? What clubs he joined in high school? Where he works? I'm trying to develop a profile. Find out his motives for butting into your operation."

"You think he has something to do with the incidents?"

"I'm undecided. I didn't get a good look at him. He's the right build, but that isn't enough to count. I presume you got his date of birth?"

Drew took his notebook out of his pocket, flipped a few pages, and tossed it to me. I caught it cleanly. And went to work.

Jonny's social media seemed straightforward. Pictures of him and his friends, his dog, his mother. An occasional rant about a bad date.

But there was no mention of his job. Or anything else beyond the perfect picture he presented of his life. And the entries were rare. Perhaps it was a public account, and he had a second one hidden. No amount of digging and scrolling gave me a clue to another profile.

I moved on to a different site. No luck there, either. Then a third. And a fourth. Where I hit pay dirt.

Sonders' primary account was scout-clean. But his likes led me to a second profile, with an altered version of his name. JP Sonders instead of Jonny. But the face in the picture was the same. I wondered what the 'P' stood for.

On the surface, the second account was where Jonny? JP? posted his political views. Which didn't bother me, because I'd read it was a way to keep potential employers satisfied—having two accounts. But the JP one was filled with 'Blue Line' posts and listings of cops killed on duty. I didn't know what to make of it.

"Bedtime," Eli whispered in my ear.

I looked up to see Drew had fallen asleep on the sofa. "But look what I found," I whispered back.

"It'll be there tomorrow." Eli closed the lid of my laptop and raised his eyebrow. "Time for bed."

I got the hint.

❀ ❀ ❀

The morning started with breakfast, courtesy of Drew. Although he cheated and got breakfast burritos from the best—and only—Mexican restaurant in town, La Cantina.

Eli, as was his habit, read emails as he ate, though it was still an hour until the official workday began. I'd learned not to make conversation with him while he checked for any emergencies that might have arisen overnight. As a result, by the time Darla started her day, he was ahead of the game.

He shoo'd Drew outside so he could talk to Darla through a video call. I waved to her before moving out of camera range. That way I wasn't a distraction as she read him his messages and caught him up on what was happening in the office. I took notes to give to Eli once the call finished.

While he reached out to key employees, I busied myself by checking various websites for articles concerning general computer security news. I longed to return to my research on Jonny, but it was a workday and I owed Eli my best effort.

When he took a short break, I decided I deserved one, too. Armed with the knowledge of Jonny's alias, I hit up the biggest social website. And hit pay dirt.

I scrolled through the same posts supporting the police as he'd posted on the other site. And there were lots of them. I practically worked for the cops, and the level of fanaticism he displayed creeped *me* out. Which eliminated him as a suspect. Anyone that pro-law enforcement couldn't be involved in any shady dealings, right?

But small details were what I'd built my reputation on, so I kept digging. There had to be personal information in there, somewhere. If he had it locked down so only his friends could view it, I'd be out of luck.

"What are you working on, Buttercup?" Eli asked.

Like a kid caught swiping a piece of penny candy, I turned my screen so he couldn't see it. "Sorry, I didn't hear you come back."

"Finding anything interesting?"

Not really. "There's an article in the Business Journal you should read, but it isn't urgent. Or I can send you a summary. The link is in your email."

He settled into his desk chair and woke up his laptop. "I'd appreciate an analysis. But that's not what you had up on your screen."

"I picked up where I left off last night. Jonny Sonders isn't what I expected, but I feel like I'm missing something."

"Want to tell me about it? Maybe it will help you organize your thoughts." He glanced at his watch. "We have five minutes before my meeting."

He was better than a spreadsheet or a whiteboard. "He's running two accounts. One for show with only a few posts here and there. The second is more interesting. All kinds of posts supporting the police. Links to articles that take the cop's side in the unfortunate nationwide instances we've had of cops shooting supposedly innocent people. Very one-sided, almost unhealthy in his focus." I was no psychiatrist but wasn't above making an armchair diagnosis.

"What if his family is in law enforcement?"

I hadn't thought of that. "Could be. But the few pictures he's got posted of friends don't include anyone in a uniform."

"They might have asked him not to post any to protect their privacy."

Someone I knew was like that. Eli didn't exist on the internet except on the company's website. "That would explain a lot. But it's odd that he doesn't list his job or any hobbies. Not even his motorcycle. Most guys brag about their bike's performance."

"Unless he just bought or borrowed it."

I made the leap. "To fit in with Drew's men? It's the wrong kind of motorcycle for that."

"Sometimes you have to take what you can get. Now, back to work. I've got a call with our contact for the Maine project."

"Sure thing, boss." In unison, we winked at each other. It was good working for the man I loved. But before the meeting started, I sent Drew a text asking him for the plate of Jonny's motorcycle. Jonny was hiding something, and I needed to use every tool I had to find out what.

❄ ❄ ❄

We sat on the front porch to eat supper and enjoy what remained of a gorgeous spring day. Just the three of us—Eli, Drew and me. I wondered if Drew felt like a third wheel along on a date, because Eli and I had stopped making any attempt to hide the depth of our feelings. At least two of his men were hanging around and we'd asked Drew if they wanted to join us, but he turned down the offer.

Jonny was out there, too, and the invitation hadn't included him, but he was heavy on my mind. His bike was registered in his name, and his driving record was clean. I needed to move to another possibility. But I was running out of ideas.

"What are you thinking about?" Eli asked as he refilled my iced tea.

"The usual." I crossed my arms. "The meaning of life, how we're going to take over the world tonight, and wondering if Freddie has any new leads in the burglaries."

"Did you want to call him?"

"Freddie? No. I've been enough of a distraction already. If I don't have any news that will help him, I should leave him alone."

We sat and watched the sunset. As it touched the horizon, Drew suddenly said, "Holy shit."

"It is beautiful, isn't it?" I asked.

"Yeah, but that's not what I'm talking about. It's what you said."

"I'm confused. Why should I bother Freddie?"

"Not that. You mentioned a distraction. What else is going on that someone might want the police not to notice?"

In Oak Grove? "You've seen it, nothing big happens here."

"What's the selling point? What brings people here?"

"If you figure that out, the Chamber of Commerce would love you." The Chamber had hired a consulting firm a few years back to study the issue and gotten their money refunded when they didn't receive a satisfactory answer.

"There's got to be something."

I tried to think like a criminal and decide what a big score would be and came up blank.

Eli stared at his phone. "What's the Bird Counting Festival?"

"The annual event Oak Grove shares with two other towns every spring. People come from all over to count birds, like the name says."

"That's it?"

I shrugged. "There's a street fair and vendors and the normal assortment of nonsense. I mostly stay home and hibernate. Why?"

"It's this weekend."

"If your guys are staying in a motel, Drew, they'll probably get kicked out. Everything around here gets reserved months in advance for the event."

Drew nodded. "I'll pass along the word. Do any celebrities show up?"

Eli swiped at the screen of his phone. "Nobody I recognize. Your men can hang out here if they need too. Harmony and I will go stay at her place, give them more room."

I hated the idea of anyone besides me and Eli sleeping in his bed.

"You've got two spare beds upstairs," Drew said. "Since they're sleeping in shifts, they'll be good."

If they didn't mind sharing, I wouldn't object.

"I'll share our new theory with the Chief in the morning," Drew continued. "Get his input."

I wasn't convinced they were barking up the right tree. I still had my doubts about Jonny. As usual, Eli read my thoughts. "I don't want Sonders in the house."

"We haven't let him come any closer than the sidewalk out front. We'll keep it that way," Drew agreed.

I could live with that—for now.

Chapter 31

Eli and I headed to bed earlier than usual after the busy day. Or, should I say, we retired to our bedchamber. I wasn't ready for sleep and, taking my cue from him, the laptop came with me.

We propped our backs against the heavy wooden headboard and held hands while we waited for the laptops to come to life. If we pretended to be asleep, Drew would relax for a few minutes before making his bed on the couch.

"What are you working on?" I asked.

"I want to read the article you sent me this morning. I glanced through it and spotted a few things deserving of a second look. How about you?"

"Jonny Sonders. Something about him bugs me."

"You mean how he joined a bodyguard operation with no references?"

"I blame that on Drew's inexperience. But there's more. On the surface, he's just the boy next door, but it's like a cover story. Who is he?"

"Half an hour. We'll work on our projects for half an hour and then call it a day. Agreed?"

It was a solution we'd worked out to keep either or both of us from staying up all night. "Set your alarm. And I'll set mine for five minutes later."

He leaned over and our lips met in a bare touch. "I love you."

"Love you, too. Now, the sooner we start, the sooner we can move on to other things."

Until I got Jonny out of my system, I wouldn't be able to concentrate on those 'other things.' I patted his hand and returned to where I'd left off.

I finally found where Jonny lived from a people search website. Not in Oak Grove, but in a smaller outlying township, Clayville. One of those places that if you blink as you go through it, you miss it. I'd gone there once because I'd heard it hosted a decent second-hand store, but I wasn't impressed. Didn't end up buying a single thing, despite my compassion for the little old man running the shop.

Anyway, I didn't have to worry about Jonny trying to push his way in on us, playing the sympathy card that he needed a place to stay. He could just go home.

I was still convinced he was hiding something. I hadn't found it by the time Eli's alarm sounded. And still hadn't figured it out when my alarm went off. Eli, true to our agreement, shut his laptop, fluffed his pillow, and turned off the light on his side of the bed. I wanted to keep digging, but a promise is a promise.

❅ ❅ ❅

It was bound to happen. Especially with people coming into town to watch birds. Spring came back with a torrential thunderstorm, chasing away the nice streak of weather we'd been enjoying.

Two of the Bobs were upstairs sleeping, one was over at my place, and the other sat on the front porch wrapped in blankets. He was trying to stay warm and look menacing at the same time. And failing. The pink and green striped blanket didn't give off a hazardous vibe. They still hadn't shared their names, so I kept calling them Bob in my head and not calling them anything when I talked to them.

Jonny disappeared after being told he wasn't welcome on Eli's property. He'd waited until it started raining to ask. I got a perverse satisfaction from knowing he'd be soaked before getting to his destination.

Drew had borrowed Eli's rental car to go to the station and talk to the Chief about his newest theory. I still found it unlikely that someone would target the festival, but the decision belonged to the experts.

In the meantime, Eli worked on redesigning his program for police departments to make it function for three different agencies to use at the same time. His method was to figure out the basic setup and then give an outline to his programmers to fill in the holes. I couldn't help, so I returned to my research on the companies he hoped to partner with.

Work is work, but occasionally he'd reach over

and hold my hand as he considered what appeared on his monitor. I'd peck at my keyboard one-handed until he resumed typing. I didn't think he even realized he was doing it. But I liked it.

Suddenly, after staring at the screen for an exceptionally long time, he put his laptop on the coffee table. "I need to go for a walk and clear my head. Want to go with me?"

I knew he lived in his own world when he was programming and here was more proof of it. "Have you looked outside? They don't make raincoats heavy enough to protect us from this downpour."

He wandered over and stared out the window. "You're right. How about we go for a drive? I don't care where."

"The Bobs can't go with us." They'd wrangled two of the bikes up on the porch and under the roof. We covered the other two with an assortment of tarps left over from the house restoration, pulled from the basement.

"We won't leave town or stop anywhere, and we'll stay on the main roads. What's the worst that could happen?"

I drove. I didn't expect Eli to enjoy the scenery, so I stuck to the main streets. We'd told the Bobs on duty what was happening and texted Drew. I think they were happy to get a break. We left the alarm system off, so they'd be able to move in and out of the house freely.

Eli brought along an old-fashioned paper notepad, and on our third trip down 1st Street, he started scribbling in it. But there were only so many times I could stand traveling the same route, so I veered onto a side street. Still part of downtown, but with older businesses. It didn't take me long to get bored with that one, too.

I switched to running a grid pattern, gradually moving away from the city center, the occasional one-way street the only impediment to my method. Eli didn't notice, obsessed with his work. He'd make a note, scratch it out, tear off the piece of paper, and start over. I finally understood why he'd wanted the whiteboard.

At a stop sign, waiting for cross traffic to clear, I spotted him across the street. At least, what I thought was him. Jonny. After all, I hadn't had a good look at him other than in pictures. He was hanging out in front of a long-ago closed hardware store, smoking. Not wanting to be overly obvious, I made a right-hand turn to avoid driving past him.

But two lefts put me at the other end of the block, and his back to me. He wore a pair of black jeans and a black hoodie, and it stirred up a memory. It stuck in the back of my brain, out of reach. I glanced over at Eli. He was no longer writing but staring at a blank piece of paper.

"Eli," I said softly. "Eli."

"What?" he asked, jerking his head up.

"Sorry to interrupt, but I need you to take pictures for me."

"This isn't a very scenic spot."

I didn't have time for sarcasm. "The guy on the sidewalk. Dressed in black. With his back to us. Get as good of a shot as you can."

"Why?" But Eli had his phone out, snapping pictures. A car pulled up behind me, and I had to proceed through the stop sign.

"I got him, but why?"

"We'll go down the other side of the street. I need pictures of his face." I made the two needed lefts again. "We only have one chance before he gets suspicious, so make it count."

"Whatever you say. You can explain it to me later."

As we cruised past the intersection, another man joined maybe-Jonny. I had the right-of-way and didn't have the excuse to stop and watch them. Besides, the Camaro was too obvious. I had to take whatever Eli managed to get.

"I'll tell you in a minute." We headed to a nearby convenience store to park and see what Eli had captured.

❄ ❄ ❄

"I know I'm paranoid," I told Freddie. "But I have every right to be."

Luckily, he'd been available when I called. Or almost available. He was returning from an investigation and got back to the station a few minutes before Eli and I got there.

"So, you're grasping at straws." Freddie took Eli's phone.

Maybe. Probably. Definitely. "You decide when you see the pictures."

Freddie cocked his head and pushed the button to light up the screen. He blinked several times and scrolled to a new picture.

"They aren't very good," Eli apologized. "I took them from an awkward angle."

With a nod, Freddie studied the next picture. And the next. As he got to each new photo, the frown on his face deepened. "What am I looking at, Harmony?"

"I think that's Jonny Sonders, a guy who's been hanging out with Drew's men."

"And?"

"The ones where his back is turned—do they remind you of anything?"

"Not in particular. Why?"

I grimaced. "It's there in the back of my brain, but I can't put my finger on it. I've seen him somewhere else. I hoped it would click for you."

"Sorry, I can't help. Although the older guy with him? Him, I know. You should too." He handed the phone to me.

"Really? I've been concentrating so hard on Jonny I haven't paid attention to the other man."

The pictures were on the edge of being blurry, but that wasn't surprising because the car had been moving when Eli took them. But the man's face was clear enough that I should have been able to identify him. But I couldn't.

"Who is he?"

"The camo paint he had on yesterday did a good job of disguising his face. That's Evan Bluffs."

"I don't get it. Why would a guy who is such a big supporter of law enforcement be hanging out with a criminal?" I asked as we waited for Freddie's return. He'd gone to talk to Chief Sorenson.

"Why do you hang out with Jake?" Eli asked.

"He's a friend!"

"He's also a convicted felon."

Point taken. Jonny might be trying to save Evan in the same way I was trying to save Jake.

Or not. I couldn't talk myself into believing it.

It didn't take long for Freddie to come back, trailing Chief Sorenson. And Drew. I was surprised Drew was still there. Maybe he and the chief had been discussing old times. Or plotting strategies for dealing with the weekend crowds. I straightened as he came in, the normal reaction to his presence. He took Freddie's chair, and Drew and Freddie stood behind Eli and me.

He gave us no greeting except for a nod. "You stumble into all the wrong places at all the right times, don't you, Miss Duprie? May I see the pictures?"

I wondered why he was being so formal. I thought we'd moved beyond that.

Eli handed over the phone. The Chief's face never changed from his stoic expression as he reviewed the photos. Then it was Drew's turn. He wasn't so reticent.

"That's Jonny. No doubt. And I wouldn't know Bluffs unless someone pointed him out. But who's the guy with his back to you?"

That was an odd reaction.

The Chief held up his hand. "Wait. Before anyone answers that question, tell me why you ask, Dawson."

"Because," Drew said, "Studying the body shape and structure, I'd say it looks like the guy who graffitied Harmony's rental."

That was the memory I couldn't recapture. "Holy crap," I said. "He's right. Is that video handy?"

"Who is it?" Drew asked again.

"That's Jonny."

Chapter 32

Eli hadn't seen the video of the night when the previous rental car was vandalized. As the moment played out on the screen in the conference room, his lips formed a taut, thin line and he squeezed my hand. When the playback finished, the place stayed silent.

Chief Sorenson left during the display and returned carrying a manila file folder. He leaned forward in his chair. "Dawson, you're the only one who's had any interaction with Sonders. What's your gut say?"

"Instinct says it's him. But if you asked me to testify in a court of law, I couldn't honestly identify him. We never see his face." Drew rubbed his hand across his hair. "I can't believe I let this guy get close to Harmony. I thought it was a good community policing effort."

"Under normal circumstances, it would be. These aren't normal circumstances."

What was Sorenson talking about?

"What I'm going to tell you can't leave this room. Agreed?" he asked, looking around the table.

That sounded bad, but I nodded my head. So did everyone else.

"When you were talking about Jonny Sonders, the name seemed familiar, so I did some digging. The originals of this paperwork," Sorenson tapped the file, "are with the city's HR department. I kept a copy."

Against city regulations. I learned the proper procedure during my time filling in for Janine as Chief Librarian.

"Sonders professed a desire to enter police work after graduating high school. His interest sprang from a tour he did his senior year. Or so the story goes. He attended two different civilian academies after he graduated."

That seemed perfectly normal.

"He applied for an open position we had a while back and cleared preliminary background checks. He barely earned the grade needed on the initial law enforcement exam, but he passed.

"However, based on the interactions I had with him, I requested he take the psychological test before adding him to the candidate's list for the Academy."

Sorenson had my rapt attention.

"He failed. Miserably."

A puzzle piece snapped into place. "That explains it," I said, the words running from my mouth. "His social media. I knew I missed something. All those posts about law enforcement and not a single word about Oak Grove's finest, good, bad, or ugly. Just a black hole."

"You think he's attacking Harmony in revenge?" Eli asked.

"Or he's trying to prove he's better than the current officers," Drew suggested. "And Harmony is a soft target."

I straightened my backbone. This meant war. "How would he know about me?"

Freddie shrugged. "If he spent any time here, he might have overheard staff discussing you. Or he was here when you brought in a report. Maybe he heard about your relationship with me, as outdated as that gossip is."

I hadn't tried to hide my work for Sorenson. I'd have to rethink that.

"Do you think he's tied to the robberies, too?" Eli asked.

Civilian mistake. Technically, they were burglaries, but now wasn't the time to correct Eli. No one else did, either.

"I requested information from the Cranberry franchise of Harlington, the company that sells the security systems. They refused to give me anything without a warrant. The owner was willing to say the number of burglaries they've seen recently is within the expected parameters and they have reimbursed the customers per their contracts."

"Any chance Jonny worked for them?" I realized I was bouncing my foot and hoped no one else noticed.

"I'll ask, but I doubt they'll tell me."

Sorenson opened Jonny's file and flipped through

the contents. "At the time of his application, he was employed by a janitorial firm out of Franklin Park."

That didn't help at all.

"What's the name of the company?" Freddie asked. "I'll see if I can get a list of their customers."

I pulled out my phone. They might post testimonials on their website.

"Franklin Cleaning Services," Sorenson read from the file.

Original. Not. I worried I'd get too many hits to make a search efficient, but it was worth a try.

The first query was worthless. I lost track of the conversation as I tried a different combination of words for my second search. The results narrowed when I added in the city and state. I didn't locate a proper website but found a page on a social media site. That lessened the chances of getting what I wanted, but I followed the lead, anyway.

"Bingo!" I said out loud.

"What, Miss Duprie?" Sorenson said. He sounded perturbed.

"Sorry for interrupting. But Cranberry Security Systems is a customer of Franklin Cleaning Services." I raised my head and grinned. "There's our connection."

The pieces fit in together nicely. There was one problem. It was all circumstantial. No proof. And how did Bluffs fit into the equation?

Okay, that was two things. Make it three, because where did the Japanese inros belong in the puzzle?

"We don't have enough evidence for a warrant," Freddie repeated. "Not that will cross jurisdictional boundaries. The Sheriff's department will have to partner in this if Sonders still lives at the same address."

"It's his mother's, by the way," Sorenson said, rifling through Sonders' file.

It didn't surprise me. Working for a janitorial company couldn't pay much. "That leaves the question of what he was doing talking to Bluffs. And what was Bluffs doing out of custody so fast?"

Freddie shrugged. "Without being able to read the mind of the judge who presided over the preliminary hearing, it's hard to say. The public defender may have convinced him that Bluffs is a harmless old man playing out childhood fantasies."

With real guns.

"What's the next step?" Eli asked, squeezing my hand.

"For the two of you?" Chief Sorenson pointed at me and Eli. "Go home and let us do our jobs."

❃ ❃ ❃

"*They aren't going to be able to do anything*," I texted Eli.

We sat side by side on the couch, but texting was the only way to talk to each other without being overheard. Drew was in the kitchen, doing who-knew-what. One of the Bob's was on the front porch, one patrolled the grounds now that it had stopped raining, and I'd lost track of the other two.

"I know. How is your research on Sonders going?" Eli didn't even glance my way as he typed away on the phone's keyboard.

"I'm trying to identify the location of these pictures he posted with his friends. If I can figure it out, it'll tell us where he hangs out."

"Do you recognize the interior of every restaurant and bar in town?" He followed it with a smiley face.

I knew lots of them, anyway. *"He left tracking on for most of his pictures. That makes it easy."*

"What are your plans once you've tracked that down?"

"Under consideration." He wouldn't like what I had in mind. Time to change the subject. *"Have you resolved the problem you were fighting this afternoon?"*

"Yes. I took another look at it, and the answer is clear. Sometimes I have to step away from the issue to find a solution."

Maybe that's what I needed to do. Take a fresh look at the question. *After* I figured out which bars were in the pictures.

As we cuddled in bed much later, I tried to figure out what to do with Eli. I could disguise myself, but how to make him appear different? There'd be no way to get away with dying his hair. A hat would have to do. A bulky jacket would help cover his broad chest, but it was the wrong season for that. And none of his shoes had big heels. He was already tall enough. But he'd never let me go on this mission by himself.

I'd figured out the bar where Jonny hung out. Charlie's wasn't the greatest bar in town, but not the worst either. I'd visited it once, not as myself. I'd have to create a different personality for a second trip. Older. That'd be safe. And I could make Eli older too, with the right makeup. No glasses for me, some of my out-of-date ones for him. And talcum powder to make our hair gray.

The tricky part would be getting past Drew and the Bobs. With all of them in and around the house, even the plan of slipping out through the basement door wouldn't work. I'd noticed they were getting better at paying attention to what was going on. No, I'd have to bring Drew into the plan. But how to convince him to help?

"What are you plotting over there?" Eli pulled me closer, and his lips caressed my neck.

In a flash of weakness, I confessed. "How to turn you into an older, but still distinguished gentleman."

His lips withdrew from my skin and he propped himself up on his elbows. "Is this a new fantasy? You can't wait until we grow old together?"

My heart fluttered. His words left me speechless. At that moment, I considered packing up and moving to Florida with him.

Instead, I threw my arms around his neck and tugged. He landed halfway on top of me. It was a good start.

One bathroom wasn't big enough for six adults in the same house. Thank heavens two of the Bobs were sleeping, and we had a half bath on the first floor. I took the shortest of showers, and Eli was getting dressed when I returned to the bedroom.

As I chose my clothes, I stealthily watched in admiration as he fastened his belt, his chest still bare. At least, I thought I was being sneaky. But he noticed and grinned.

"Like what you see, Buttercup?"

"Absolutely." Emboldened, I raked my eyes up and down the length of his body.

His grin reached from ear to ear. "Take a good look now because it will have to last you. I've got a meeting in twenty minutes." He held up a hand. "Yes, it's Saturday, but I had a call from Fairwood. He wants to discuss details for the cooperative group suggested by his lawyer. He agreed that you should join the conversation."

I revamped my plans for my wardrobe. "I need ten minutes to get dressed."

He pulled on a tailored button-up shirt in my favorite shade of light blue. I wondered if an oversized shirt and suit coat would help with the old man outfit. "I set up in the office. That way we don't have to worry about privacy."

"Make coffee, please," I said. "I'll be down in a few minutes."

I chose a blouse that almost matched the color of his shirt. A deliberate ploy to show the two of us as a united front.

"I apologize," I said after the meeting. As much as Fairwood impressed me, I suspected he hid a secret. I'd have to do more research on him and his company. "I forgot to turn my phone off."

Eli chuckled. "No worries. Fairwood's went off twice. Was it anyone important?"

"Gary from the pawnshop. He just said he wanted to talk to me. Which is weird. Usually, if he stumbles across a book he thinks I'll be interested in, he'll give me the title and other details. I'll clarify a few notes from the meeting, then call him."

Eli was already deep into typing an email to Kris. "Uh-huh."

I'd lost him. Probably for the next fifteen or twenty minutes. That was okay, it would take me that long to rank my notes in the order that I wanted to tackle them later.

Chapter 33

We made an odd procession, pulling up in front of Gary's. First Drew on his bike, then Eli and I in the Camaro, followed by one of the Bobs. Another Bob had peeled off and gone down the alley behind the pawnshop. I'd agreed to the arrangement with the stipulation that everyone but Eli had to stay outside. Gary didn't need the extra bodies in his shop taking up room from paying customers.

Gary looked up and nodded when we strolled in. While he finished dealing with a couple purchasing a ring, I browsed the small assortment of books and Eli perused the display case holding guns. He'd talked about buying one to leave at the house instead of transporting his to and from Florida. It made sense, although I didn't approve of storing it in an empty house. Not even locked up in a weapons vault.

"Would you guys like to join me in my office for a cup of coffee?" Gary asked once the couple was out the door.

I was one of the few people Gary allowed in the

back and took it as a sign of honor that he included Eli in the invite. "Sure. Coffee is fine."

As straightforward as they make them, Gary didn't have time to mince words. "The cops were around a couple of weeks ago asking about a stolen item. An inro, to be specific. Gossip has it you might be tangled up in it."

I'd told Gary about the break-in, but not the inro left behind. I wondered who his source was.

Gary continued. "I had a call from a friend who runs a shop up in Erie. He knows my interest in all things Japanese. A customer came to his shop to pawn an item he supposedly inherited from his mother and my friend had a few questions about it."

He turned the screen of his computer so Eli and I could see it. "Does this look familiar?"

I flipped through the gallery on my phone until I came to a matching picture. Well, almost. The inro on Gary's screen had one less of the skinny boxes than the one stolen from the Cookes. But that would have been an easy way to disguise it.

"Can you enlarge the fastener?" I asked.

"The netsuke? Sure enough." He fiddled with his mouse. I did the same with the picture on my phone. We compared the two pictures. "They match."

I agreed.

"I'll tell my friend to contact his local precinct. And I'll get in touch with Detective Thomason." Gary shook his head. "It's a bad deal all the way around. My friend will be out the money he gave for it and insurance won't cover the loss."

"I hope he didn't pay too much for it."

"Naw. He got it for a bargain. The guy who brought it in didn't have a clue what it was worth and didn't want to stick around for an expert opinion. That should have been my friend's first red flag."

"Did he get a name from the customer?"

"If he followed procedure. He can retrieve an image from the security cameras, too. The police will want both."

"Any chance you could share the info with me?" I wanted the information yesterday. Waiting would make me crazy.

Gary grinned. "You want me to give you the info before the cops?"

No. Yes. I sighed. "I suppose I should wait."

He flipped the screen to face him and typed. "You owe me. My friend didn't give me a name, but here's a snap of the guy."

I leaned forward, half-expecting to see Jonny. I was wrong. It wasn't Jonny. The man in the blurry picture was older. Like Evan Bluffs old.

Eli whistled. "When did this happen?"

"You recognize the guy?" Gary asked.

"We've run into him recently. And not in a good way."

Gary's eyes widened. "What are the chances? The sale happened four days ago. My friend got swamped and didn't get with me until today."

The burglary didn't square with Deputy Nelson's assessment of Bluffs. It was way over the line of legality, not just skirting it. Unless he was selling the inro for someone else? "We've got to contact Freddie," I said.

Gary blew out a deep breath. "We pawnbrokers hate this stuff. We try to stay legal, and then this happens. Destroys our reputations."

And cost them money, too. "Is there anything I can do to help?"

"Beyond contacting Thomason for me?" Gary shook his head. "I'll be expecting his call. Or visit."

❋ ❋ ❋

I called Freddie from the parking lot of the Dairy Barn where we went for a late lunch. I didn't feel the information was urgent, so I left it on his office phone's voice mail. Knowing him, he'd check it once or twice over the weekend, but he deserved some time off.

It was well past the noon rush, and only a few teenage couples were scattered through the restaurant. Anyone who was looking for something to do was at the street fair for the bird watching event. As we'd discussed, Drew and the Bobs split between two tables and Eli and I grabbed a booth as far away from them as possible.

"You aren't convinced Bluffs stole the inro," Eli said as we sipped on our drinks and waited for our food.

"Was my body language that much of a giveaway?" I frowned. "I can't reconcile a guy who was out playing in the woods with someone who has the skill to disable an electronic alarm. Besides, if his alibi holds up, he was out of town."

"Then how did he get his hands on it?"

"You already know what I think."

"Can Freddie prove it?"

I waited while the waitress set down our food. Her nametag read 'Ruby.' Eli was having a double cheeseburger while I stuck with a small Philly cheesesteak sandwich. It always amazed me how much he could eat and never gain weight. Of course, we'd both been working off calories with our nighttime activities. It helped to make up for the time spent in front of our computers.

"If Freddie can't, no one can," I said once Ruby returned to the kitchen, although part of me worried. Whoever was responsible was doing a good job of not leaving behind any evidence. But Freddie might be able to pressure Bluffs into ratting out his source.

"Although I'm sure you plan to give him any assistance you can."

I wouldn't say it out loud, but I had helped him get his last promotion. "He and Chief Sorenson keep hinting that they are working on something they can't share. Maybe this will be the piece they need to put it all together."

Conversation lagged as we concentrated on our meals. The Dairy Barn wasn't a five-star restaurant, but its food was way ahead of the typical chain restaurant. I stared out the window at the dark clouds rolling in, wondering if we were due for another rainstorm. We'd lose our bodyguards if they couldn't ride safely. Not that they'd done much, but I suspected their mere presence helped. I was getting soft—they didn't bother me anymore.

An old pickup rolled into the parking lot and stopped in a space as far away from the front door as possible. I'd seen new cars parked there to keep from getting scratched, but it appeared to have plenty of dings in its faded blue paint. Maybe the owner worried it would fall apart if it got hit one more time.

The driver didn't get out and I stopped paying attention because Eli put down his burger and reached over for my hand. And then Drew got up and came over to our table.

"I'm sending the guys to the house," he said, "before the storm rolls in. I'll stick with you."

"We're almost done here." Eli shoved his plate to the side. "My eyes were bigger than my stomach."

"I hate to rush you, but I'm feeling antsy." Drew rubbed the back of his neck. "Like something is about to happen. Can't tell you what."

I knew a thing or two about that tingly sensation but wasn't experiencing it at the moment. Still, I'd trust Drew's instinct. "Go. We'll be right behind you. Looks like a good afternoon to take a nap or read a book."

As soon as Drew left the table, Eli's grin spilled across his face. "A nap, eh? Is that what you had in mind?"

It had been, but wasn't any longer. I kept my expression blank—I hoped—and stood. "Guess you'll have to wait to find out."

The first drops of rain hit the pavement as we walked to the door. Drew saluted us and rolled away.

Eli held out his hand. "My turn to drive."

Darn, he hadn't forgotten. As I dug into my purse for the keys, he grabbed my arm and pulled me back inside. I nearly dropped them.

"What the hell?"

"Pretend you're reading a sign on the door. But take a gander at the guy by the truck in the parking lot. Who does it look like?" Eli asked.

I did even better. I found the little mirror I carried but rarely used. With my back to the door, I held up the mirror, adjusted it, and used it to peek over my shoulder. "No way. That's Bluffs."

"And he's not even pretending he's coming in."

A peal of thunder announced the true beginning of the storm. Moments later, a torrent of water descended from the sky. Bluffs hurriedly hopped into his truck. I wasn't sure, but it looked as if there was someone seated on the passenger side.

"What's he up to?" I asked, stepping to the side of the door where I couldn't be seen from the outside.

"Can I help you, folks?" Ruby called from the back.

"We're just waiting for the rain to slow down," Eli said loudly.

She came around the counter, carrying a package of napkins to refill the napkin holders on the tables. "It may be a bit. There's a big green blob on the weather radar."

Not what we needed to hear. "Thanks. If it's okay with you, we'll sit here until it lightens up or we get bored."

She grinned. "Your call. If you need anything, holler."

Her route started on the other side of the restaurant, leaving Eli and I some privacy. "I'm getting real tired of this," I said, "being followed. I wish there was a way to flip this."

"You're thinking we should make him the prey instead of us?"

"Precisely. Only I don't know if it's him or them. I thought I spotted a second person in the truck."

"What did you have in mind?"

Nothing. Everything I came up with was so far out of the realm of reality it was useless. "I'm fresh out of suggestions," I admitted.

The rain eased up enough for me to get a better view. But the windshield was fogged up, so I still couldn't see how many people were in it.

"I'd put a bug in the truck, but I forgot to pack one," Eli joked.

It wasn't that much of a joke. He'd planted one in my apartment once upon a time.

"Or we could sneak up behind them and listen to the conversation," I suggested.

"You don't mind getting a little wet?"

More like a lot of wet, but all for a good cause. "How do we get in place without them noticing?"

"Go out the back door," Ruby said. I hadn't even noticed she'd moved to a table near us. "I'll take you through the kitchen." She grinned. "I know who you are. And what's been going on. Anything I can do to help, count me in."

I decided now was not the time to ask how much she knew. Ye Olde Gossipe network in action.

"If you wait a minute or two, we're expecting a

crowd of bird folks to show up. The rain shut down the street fair for now," she continued.

She was as good of a person to ask as any. "Do you recognize the truck out there?"

"Bluffs? Yeah, he used to come in all the time. The boss banned him after we figured out he was stealing silverware and the tips other people left. Legally, we can't keep him out of the parking lot without a lot of paperwork the boss didn't want to mess with. It makes me nervous knowing he's sitting out there."

Chapter 34

It made me nervous, too. Not because Bluffs sat in the parking lot, waiting for whatever, probably us, but because I didn't know his motivation. I'd come out on top in our first encounter. Was he looking for a rematch? He didn't stand a chance with Eli by my side.

Eli and I slipped out the back door as a wave of customers hit the front door. The perfect cover. We ducked behind the dumpsters and followed the fence to the property next door, a chiropractic office that was closed on Saturdays.

We kept to the alley to get to the other side of the building, strolled down the sidewalk and joined a group of people heading for the Dairy Barn. They seemed excited about the bird watching walk scheduled for later, despite the rain. When they cut through the parking lot towards the restaurant, Eli and I hung back by a car parked along the street. The oak tree we stood under provided some protection from the rain. We still got soaked.

We used the distraction caused by several vehicles pulling into the parking lot to creep alongside the truck, Eli on the driver's side, me on the passenger's side. And there was a passenger. One I couldn't identify from the back of his head.

The trick was getting into a spot where we could listen to them without them being able to spot us. At the same time, we couldn't look suspicious enough that someone would call the cops. I had the easier job because pieces of the side-view mirror had fallen out, and the truck hid me from the gazes of customers in the restaurant.

Eli didn't have the same advantages. We might have pulled it off under the cover of darkness, but during the day it was an impossible task. Besides, the rain had gotten heavier. He jerked his head, and I abandoned my post to follow him down the street. I hadn't heard them talking, anyway.

We took shelter a block away, under the awning protecting the entrance to a laundromat. "Well, that was a bust." Like a wet dog, I wanted to shake all the water off my fur. Or, at least, get my bedraggled hair out of my face. "What now?"

He was already on the phone with Drew. "Yeah, bring the car and blankets. And have the heat going. No, it isn't cold. Do it anyway. I'll explain when you get here."

He was silent for a moment. "315 Juniper. It's a laundromat. We'll be inside. Just honk when you pull in."

He put away his phone and glanced my way.

"You're shivering. With the machines running, it should be warmer in there than out here."

Drew showed up quicker than I expected. Or maybe I didn't pay attention to time because I was busy enjoying the feel of Eli's arms wrapped around me, trying to warm me. Once I was in the back seat of Eli's rental, bundled up in blankets, I was ready to resume cuddling. But he and Drew had other plans.

"Did you bring the camera?" Eli asked Drew, opening the front door on the passenger side.

"On the floorboard."

"Good. When you pull out, head north a block and a half, then turn right into the alley." Eli reached down and pulled a black case into his lap as Drew climbed into the driver's seat.

"What are we doing?" I asked, leaning forward into the gap between the two front seats.

"If nothing else, getting pictures of who was with Bluffs. I have my suspicions, but suspicions don't count." Eli brushed a lock of wet hair out of my face. "I spotted the perfect location to get pictures without them knowing. I texted Drew while we were in the laundromat."

"It feels like we're just spinning our wheels."

"If we get lucky, they'll get frustrated waiting for us to come out of the restaurant and try something. And we'll catch them on camera."

The only place I'd been getting lucky lately was the bedroom. But I didn't have the energy to argue.

The seconds ticked by, then the minutes. It was a standoff. Other than Eli taking a series of photos after we first parked, nothing happened. While we were gone, they'd backed the truck up to the Camero. The truck's rear window was fogged up, so there was nothing to see.

I was bored. And still wet under the blanket. And ready to go home. "How long are we going to stay here?"

"I didn't think they'd sit there this long," Eli admitted.

"Which makes it more interesting," Drew said, a note of excitement in his voice. "Under other circumstances, I'd suspect a drug deal. But usually, the suspects in one of those are more prompt."

"It won't be long until someone calls the cops on us." I pushed the blanket off my shoulders, hoping the warm air would dry out my shirt.

"We'll give it a few more minutes. Now that the sun has come back out, most of the tourists will return to the street fair. That will give Bluffs the chance he's waiting for."

Drew's patience outweighed mine, but he was the expert. I settled back in my seat to wait. I was half-asleep when Eli hissed.

"Finally!"

I blinked my eyes to adjust my focus as he snapped picture after picture. My view, blocked by a telephone pole, didn't reveal anything of interest. "What's going on?"

"They're out of the truck," Drew said. "And headed toward the Camaro."

"Who are they?"

"Bluffs. And Sonders."

"Together? Again? That's no coincidence."

"Nope. And neither is that oversized screwdriver he's carrying. At least, that's what I think it is."

"Do I call 911 now? Or do I need to wait until he breaks in?"

"Wait. That way we can have absolute proof."

I supposed the cost of replacing a broken window was worth it.

Eli opened his door slowly and swung his legs out, still snapping pictures.

"I'll sneak around in behind them," Drew said. "Harmony, you stay here. Eli will give you a signal when it's time to call 911."

Staying in the car wasn't an option. I tucked Betsy into my almost-dry waistband and waited to get out until Drew made it too far down the alley to yell at me. With the pole out of my way, I could see the action. Or non-action. Bluffs and Jonny were standing with their backs to the restaurant, talking, apparently waiting for some customers to leave. Either that or they'd changed their minds. It didn't matter, because it gave Drew more time to move into place.

I found a spot where I could see without being seen and not be in Eli's way. As long as I held my phone, I might as well use it for something. While Eli continued to take stills, I started filming.

Then it happened. I almost missed it. Jonny pushed the screwdriver against the car window. It shattered. He reached in, unlocked the door, and opened it.

I didn't find out what the next part of the plan was, because Eli tossed the camera onto the car's seat and pulled his gun from his shoulder harness. Drew sprinted towards them from the street. In the excitement, I forgot my assignment. The call to 911. Instead, I traded my phone for Betsy and followed Eli.

He hurtled past the end of the fence hiding the dumpster. My sleeve snagged on the edge of a board as I cut the corner too sharp. I tugged and it came loose. But that put Eli ahead of me. This was *my* moment. *My* resolution. I should be in front.

A car pulling into a parking space slowed him down. That put me in front. And gave me a good look at the state of affairs.

A tow strap dangled from Bluffs' hands. Jonny held the industrial-sized screwdriver in one hand like a knife. In the other, a book I'd left in the Camero. A page from it fluttered to the ground.

I skidded to a stop a few feet away and raised Betsy. My grip on her was perfect, and I aimed at Jonny's center mass. He was the threat. From the corner of my eye, I spotted Eli taking a similar position.

"Drop it!" I screamed.

"Police!" Drew yelled. "Put your hands where I can see them!" Old habit, I guess, because he wasn't a cop. Not anymore.

Bluffs dropped his head and raised his hands. The tow strap clattered on the pavement. Jonny tensed, ready to run. With Eli on one side of the car, me on the other, Drew at the rear, and a police car pulling into the parking lot, he had nowhere to go.

The plastic handle of the screwdriver shattered as it struck the blacktop.

It was over. At least that's what I thought.

I was wrong.

As fast as a gold-medal sprinter, Jonny dashed for the alley. Nothing stood in his way. Except me. I had two options. Aim for center mass or step aside. I chose neither.

I lowered Betsy and braced for impact. Planted my feet solidly and squared my shoulders. Angled to the right so my strong side pushed forward. Bent slightly at the waist. Took a deep breath. I'd never played football, but this was my chance to be the star blocker.

The yelling and shouting blurred in the background and faded. Only Jonny and I existed in our shrinking world. Five feet. Four feet. Three feet.

One foot. Jonny chickened out and swerved. He decided too late. Our eyes locked. He knew that I knew. He was bigger, heavier, and had momentum working for him. I had the rage of weeks of pent-up anger going for me.

I imagined a soft ball attached by velcro in the small of his back. The memory of Sarah's tears fueled my fire. I clenched my hands together and swung.

And missed my target. But the butt of Betsy's handle struck the middle of Jonny's back. Right on his spine. He stumbled. Fell. And didn't resist when two hard bodies piled on top of him. Eli and Drew.

❋ ❋ ❋

"He almost got away with it." Freddie shook his head. "Until he became overconfident in his skills and picked on the wrong person."

Meaning me.

At least I'd changed my clothes before meeting with Freddie in his office. I was warm, dry, and a bit smug. Well, a lot smug. I'd caught the bad guy. With help, but I'd done it.

"Does he hate the Oak Grove Police that much?" Eli asked.

Freddie shuffled uneasily in his chair. With the four of us—Eli, Drew, me, and himself—it felt cramped. He needed a bigger office. "Sonders isn't talking. Not until he gets a lawyer. But there's speculation that it was more directed at Chief Sorenson because of his refusal to hire him. Now that we have good cause, it'll be easy to get warrants to track down the other potential leads. Like the places he cleaned. And whether he rented a car from the local agency."

I knew two of the town's public defenders. I hoped he wouldn't be assigned either of them. He deserved the one I'd never met and didn't like by reputation alone.

Freddie's lips twitched. "Bluffs, on the other hand, is telling the deputies everything, despite repeated

Miranda warnings. Sonders was lying to him the whole time. At least, that's what the sheriff thinks."

To avoid any conflict of interest, they'd turned the case over to the Sheriff's Department. Freddie was disappointed, but his personal ties put him out of the running to lead the investigation. It moved all of Oak Grove's force into nothing more than a support role.

I picked at a hangnail. "I don't understand what the two of them have to do with each other. What's the connection?" And why hadn't I spotted it during my research?

"It's sad. Bluffs refers to Sonders as his kid. But on his application, Sonders listed his father as deceased. So, we don't know if Sonders manipulated Bluffs into thinking they're related or if they really are.

"Either way, Sonders bragged about his exploits and grievances, and Bluffs listened. Now he's telling the deputies everything, hoping to get the charges against him lowered or eliminated."

"They won't let him out soon, right?" Eli laid a protective hand on my shoulder.

"Not a chance. No matter how much data he gives us. The DA has reassured Chief Sorenson that he'll serve time, and they'll request no bail at his initial hearing."

"What about other accomplices?"

"None that we know about. The deputies will keep pushing, but it makes sense that it was a one-person job. Mostly. That's why no one caught a break and got information from our regular sources."

My life could go back to normal. No more Drew and no more Bobs. But no more Eli. My heart broke a little. "Do you need us for anything else?" I asked. "I'd like to head home." My home. And get Dolores out of storage. And hope for one more day with Eli before he returned to Florida.

❋ ❋ ❋

Eli and I cuddled in bed. My bed. In my apartment. Drew and the Bobs were no longer guarding the castle. Oh, they were there, but watching a game and drinking the beer Eli provided, a celebration. Chief Sorenson had lined Drew up with an existing bodyguard agency to learn the ropes. Paying for the party was the least we could do as a thank you. There'd be more once I figured out how much Chief Sorenson had paid them, but it was a start.

"What are your plans for tomorrow?" Eli asked, nuzzling my neck.

And there they were. The words that shattered my heart. "That depends on what time your flight is," I said, keeping my voice at an even keel to hide my disappointment. I was playing the little spoon, so I didn't have to worry about him reading my expression.

"I haven't bought a ticket yet."

"Is something wrong?" I flipped over to face him.

He tugged me closer and our lips met. Just a tender kiss with promise. "Nothing. But this experience made me appreciate over and over again how much you do for me. I'd like to stay a few extra days and work from the house without the added pressure of things going wrong. If that's okay with you." He sounded anxious.

What did he think, that I would turn him down? "But tomorrow is my day off."

"Mine too."

"That works out nicely."

He rolled on top of me. "I thought so."

I adopted my best Southern accent. "Whatever will we do with a whole day to ourselves?"

The answering kiss demanded more. Much more.

The End
(for now)

Thank you for reading *The Samurai's Inro*, the 5th book in the Harmony Duprie Mysteries. I hope you enjoyed it. Next up, take a sneak peek at *The Ranger's Dogtags*, coming soon.

The Ranger's Dogtags

P. J. MacLayne

Chapter One

Four alarms blared as one. I rolled over to grab my phone from my bedside table and silence them before the phone exploded. Or my ears did. They weren't normal alarms. It wasn't time to get up. They were part of the security system at Eli's house. But what could have happened to set all four off at once? Temptation urged me to dash out to the garage in my pajamas, jump in my car, and speed over there to find out. Instead, I did the right thing and called 911.

As I pulled on a pair of jeans, my phone rang, a normal ring. I grabbed it, expecting Eli, my boss-slash-lover. Instead, it was Lando, a co-worker and friend.

"You aren't at the house, are you?" he asked without a hello.

"No, I'm heading there now. What happened?"

"I don't know. I've lost the camera feed and can't reach the computers. The last thing recorded was a huge flash of light."

"The strobe lights?" I used my shoulder to hold the phone in place as I unlocked the garage.

"No. It came from behind the security cameras."

The wail of sirens in the distance sent a shudder down my spine. "I'll call you back when I get to the house."

"Have you heard from Eli? I can't reach him." Lando's anxiety bled through the words.

"We talked earlier. He was set to spend several hours catching up on developments in one of the programming languages he uses. I can't believe the alerts going off didn't get through to him." Something was wrong—terribly wrong—but neither of us was willing to admit it.

"Hold on," Lando said. "I've got another call coming in."

I used the opportunity to put the call on the car's speaker and back out of the garage. I broke every traffic law on the books in my quest to reach the old Victorian house Eli owned. Not that it mattered. I was the only one on the streets at three in the morning.

I slowed as a police car screamed by, then blew through a stop sign. Ten blocks to go. Dolores, my Jaguar, growled when I smashed the gas pedal to the floor, sensing my need for speed.

Five more blocks. Ahead, no red glow colored the night sky. I pretended to stop at the intersection of Elm and Fifth. Then Lando returned to the call. About time. I thought it had dropped.

"That was Scotty. He can't reach Eli either."

Scotty was another of Eli's long-term employees. I sometimes thought of them—Eli, Lando, and Scotty—as the three Musketeers. Four blocks to go. I cursed as I pulled to the side of the narrow street to allow a fire truck to roar past. I didn't question where they were going. They needed to get there before I did.

Two blocks. "How about the tracking app?" I asked. Several years ago, Eli had created a GPS tracker but never released it to the public. Only Eli, Lando, and I had it installed on our phones.

One block. Red, blue, amber and white lights flashed, piercing the canopy of the oak trees lining the street. I swallowed hard, choking down the bile in my throat.

My question was met with a long silence. "I'm blocked," Lando admitted. "We were messing and made a dare a few days ago. Eli blocked me, and if I can hack into it in less than five days, I get a bonus. He's going to win this time."

Or lose, depending upon how I looked at it. I wrangled Dolores into an empty spot between two police vehicles half a block from the house.

"Let me try." I switched to the app and chose Eli's contact. As hard as I stared at the screen, the dot beside his name remained a solid red instead of changing to green. Either his phone was off or he'd blocked me, too. I refused to believe the other option. That something had happened to Eli and it destroyed his phone.

I turned off Dolores' engine and climbed out after waiting for another police vehicle to zip past. They'd called for reinforcements. This had to be worse than terrible.

Smoke obscured my first view of the house. Smoke, but no flames. None that revealed themselves through the multitude of flashing lights. I pushed my way through the small crowd of neighbors gathered to watch the show until I reached the police barrier. With one hand, I shaded my eyes to seek a familiar face among the police and firemen swarming the scene.

Officer Bo Holt, the town's rookie, found me first. "Harmony. Thank God you're here and not in the house. We were worried." He raised a hand to forestall an anticipated flood of questions. "Let me call this in."

I ignored the police mumbo-jumbo that poured from his lips and strained to make sense of what was happening. Three fire trucks lined up in the circle drive, but only one maintained a steady stream of water on the roof.

Lando's voice broke through my stupor. "Harmony. Harmony. What's happening?"

"The house is on fire. But it isn't. I don't understand. I'll call you back when I figure it out. I have to talk to other people right now." I pressed the screen, ending the call without giving him a chance to protest.

I wasn't lying. Chief Hinds, Oak Grove's fire chief, and Chief Sorenson, the police chief, headed my direction. The two of them together at the scene of a minor house fire rang its own alarm bells. Worst case scenarios played out in my head.

Someone shoved a foam cup into my hands as I sat at the wobbly card table serving as a command center. I sipped it, not tasting anything but warmth, my eyes on my text messages. Lando was on his way to check Eli's house. Scotty was heading to the office. From here, I couldn't do anything. I needed to get back to Dolores and start the long trip to Florida to join in the search.

Claire—Chief Hinds—opened the questioning. I wondered which one was playing the good cop and who was the bad? "What can you tell us about the fire?"

Nothing. "First, you tell me. Did anyone die?"

"What makes you say that?" Claire exchanged a glance with Chief Sorenson. Her gray hair shimmered like a holo in the glow of the headlights.

"The two of you together at the scene of a simple house fire?"

"Nothing is ever simple when it comes to you, is it, Miss Duprie?" Chief Sorenson asked.

This was the beginning of an argument I couldn't win. I was too tired and worried to play games. I didn't even straighten my back, my normal reaction to his commanding presence. "Do I need to call my lawyer?"

Sorenson shook his head. Somehow, I found the fact that he wore a short-sleeve shirt and khakis instead of his uniform comforting. "Not unless you want to convince me you set fire to the house you renovated. If that were the truth, I'd be asking for a mental health evaluation, not arresting you. Perhaps we should ask a different question. How did you know about the fire from your apartment across town?"

"Easy." I held up my phone. "Eli's security app entered panic mode. I didn't even know it existed until it woke me."

Claire leaned across the table. "Interesting. Can you recreate it?"

"If I dug around, I might find it, but you'll hate me for the headache you get."

A corner of her mouth twitched. "I'll take your word for it."

"That's not why you pulled me aside."

"No. We are concerned for your safety."

So, she was the good cop. When would Sorenson jump in with his piece?

I took my time reading a message from Lando with no real update before answering. "Let me ask again. How can a simple house fire be a threat?" I repeated my other burning question. "What else requires the presence of top law enforcement and fire officials? Meaning you two. It would make anyone assume the worst. So, who died?" I studied their faces, but their stoic expressions revealed nothing.

"We'll need to do a secondary sweep of the house after the hot spots cool," Claire said. "But the initial assessment indicates no one was inside."

Good to know. "But," I prompted.

She fidgeted with the ring on her right hand. "Based on eyeball reports from my senior officers, the fire may have been caused by an incendiary device. This was no accident. If it hadn't been for the sprinkler system, there's a good chance the house would have been destroyed."

It was too much to take in. I stared at the ground. Then the sky. Then the house. When my phone vibrated, I stared at it before checking the two messages that came in. One from Lando. One from Scotty. Nothing from Eli.

Scotty's was short and complete on the preview screen. "*No one here.*"

I switched to Lando's. I didn't have time to read it because someone jiggled the table. When I looked up, both Claire and Chief Sorenson were staring at me,

"Something interesting to share?" Sorenson asked, arching an eyebrow.

Like a kid caught reading a comic book, I put my hand over my phone's screen. I debated my answer. Sorenson had enough of his own problems, and there wasn't anything he could do about mine. But he'd pressure me until I caved. Still, I could hold off for a bit. Long enough to read Lando's message.

"*Eli isn't home. Checked the house. It looks fine. No sign of a disturbance. His car isn't in the garage.*"

"Miss Duprie?" Sorenson repeated, his voice harder.

I placed the phone on the table. Then set my hands on my lap to hide them. I clenched and unclenched my fists. Clenched them again, so tightly my fingernails dug into my palms. I forced the words from my constricted throat.

"Eli is missing."

More words spilled out, and I was unable to stop them. "He should have responded to the alarm. There's been nothing. He's not at home or at the office. And when I call him, it goes straight to voice mail like his phone is turned off. He never turns his phone off." Unless he was with me. In bed.

"Besides, it's Tuesday." Technically Wednesday now, but they'd know what I meant. "It's his night to kick back and review changes to his coding languages. I talked to him before I went to bed and everything was fine."

Tears ran down my cheeks. I didn't hide them. "And there's nothing I can do. He's there and I'm here."

Out of nowhere, an old-fashioned cotton handkerchief appeared in Sorenson's grasp. He thrust it towards me. I took it.

"You throw in the suspicion that the fire was deliberate and everything is worse," I sniffed. Ten times worse. Or more.

Chief Sorenson allowed his mask to slip. Wrinkles formed on his forehead, and he frowned. "Maybe his battery died. Or he's out of range of a tower and doesn't realize it. And he's just getting snacks."

For over an hour? Besides, Eli had been on his third beer when we talked. He didn't drink and drive.

But it was nice of Sorenson to comfort me. I wiped my eyes, blew my nose, took a shuddering breath, and put my mask into place.

"I'll assign an officer to patrol here tonight," Sorenson told Claire, "While your crew finishes the cleanup." He turned to me. "I'll assign another to keep an eye on your place as a precaution. I don't expect anything else will happen, and by morning, you'll have heard from Hennessey. We'll find out that this was all coincidence."

Except I didn't believe in coincidence.

Other Books in the
Harmony Duprie Mysteries Series

THE MARQUESA'S NECKLACE

Harmony Duprie enjoyed her life in the quiet little town of Oak Grove—until her arrest for drug trafficking. Now she has to figure out who is behind the sinister incidents plaguing her, and why.

HER LADYSHIP'S RING

Harmony Duprie is back, and so is trouble in Oak Grove.

Her ex-boyfriend Jake is out of prison and a suspect in a murder. Can Harmony clear Jake's name and solve the mystery of her own heart?

THE BARON'S CUFFLINKS

What starts as Girl's Night Out ends in murder, and Harmony Duprie is a suspect.

She's innocent, of course, but with no alibi, the sheriff's department won't remove her from the list of suspects. But caution isn't Harmony's middle name and she plunges head first into danger to defend her honor.

316

The Contessa's Brooch

A firebug is stalking Oak Grove and internet researcher Harmony Duprie is on the case. It starts as a simple data analysis project for Police Chief Sorenson, but things get personal when the house she renovated is targeted.

The arsonist is in it for the glory, posting videos of his exploits on social media. Can Eli, Lando and Scotty, Harmony's favorite computer hackers, help her track down the pyromaniac before someone gets hurt? Or, worse yet, killed?

P.J. MacLayne
can be reached at

NEWSLETTER

eepurl.com/cL73Cz

WEBSITE

PJMacLayne.com

FACEBOOK

facebook.com/pjmaclayne

TWITTER

twitter.com/pjmaclayne

BOOKBUB

bookbub.com/profile/p-j-maclayne